A Streetcar Named Murder

Also available by T. G. Herren, writing as Greg Herren

The Chanse MacLeod Mysteries

Murder in the Arts District
Murder in the Irish Channel
Murder in the Garden District
Murder in the Rue Ursulines
Murder in the Rue Chartres
Murder in the Rue St. Ann
Murder in the Rue Dauphine

The Scotty Bradley Mysteries

Royal Street Reveillon
Garden District Gothic
Baton Rouge Bingo
Who Dat Whodunnit
Vieux Carré Voodoo
Mardi Gras Mambo
Jackson Square Jazz
Bourbon Street Blues

#shedeservedit
Bury Me in Shadows
The Orion Mask
Dark Tide
Lake Thirteen
Timothy
Sara
Sleeping Angel
Sorceress
Shadows of the Night

A Streetcar Named Murder

A NEW ORLEANS MYSTERY

T. G. Herren

CROOKED LANE

NEW YORK

Copyright © 2022 by Greg Herren

Published in the United States by Crooked Lane Books, an imprint of The Quick Brown Fox & Company LLC.

Crooked Lane Books and its logo are trademarks of The Quick Brown Fox & Company LLC.

Library of Congress Catalog-in-Publication data available upon request.

ISBN (hardcover): 978-1-63910-132-0
ISBN (ebook): 978-1-63910-133-7

Cover design by Brandon Dorman

Printed in the United States.

www.crookedlanebooks.com

Crooked Lane Books
34 West 27th St., 10th Floor
New York, NY 10001

First Edition: December 2022

10 9 8 7 6 5 4 3 2 1

This is for Paul, with all my love,
and for everyone at

THE TENNESSEE WILLIAMS/
NEW ORLEANS LITERARY FESTIVAL

*Thank you—I wouldn't have a career
without you.*

Chapter One

The first rule of life in New Orleans is *Any time you leave your house not looking your best, you'll run into your nemesis.*

You'd think as many times as this has happened to me, I'd know better by now. I guess I'm just a slow learner. But in my own defense, I was just walking the couple of blocks to Big Fisherman Market on Magazine Street to get a pound of shrimp fresh from the Gulf, and I figured the odds were in my favor.

It was obviously not the day to buy a Powerball ticket.

I was tucking my wallet into my purse and reaching for the bag of peeled, deveined shrimp resting on the counter when a voice behind me said, dripping with sugar, "Valerie Cooper! Is that you?"

I froze. My heart sank. I knew that voice all too well. I'd become very familiar with it over years of countless, seemingly endless parents' association meetings and events. When my twin sons graduated last spring, I'd hoped I'd never hear it again.

I took a deep breath and choked back a moan. My chestnut-brown hair was pulled back into a ponytail. I hadn't even put on lip gloss. I glanced down at my worn, ratty old sweatpants. The ancient, paint-stained Jazz Fest T-shirt I was wearing didn't help either.

I steeled myself, plastering a phony smile on my face.

I turned around to face Nemesis.

Okay, *nemesis* is probably a bit harsh. Collette Monaghan wasn't *that* awful. I'd managed to keep Collette at arm's length through all the years of being active in the Loyola High School parents' group, the Cardirents. (Cute, right? Short for Cardinals' Parents. It started out as the Cardimoms until some moms guilted their husbands into joining. A unanimous vote changed the name to be more inclusive when my boys were freshmen.) I wanted to believe Collette Monaghan didn't *deliberately* try to make other women feel bad about themselves. Her rare compliments always seemed a bit backhanded.

Whenever she offered you a rose—check those thorns.

I'd gotten the impression she disliked me when we first met, but soon I realized I wasn't special. She treated everyone the same way—like we were lucky she talked to us at all—so there was no point in taking it personally. She liked to remind anyone listening that she was a member of the old-line aristocracy of New Orleans and managed to smugly work "I was a maid in Rex" into almost every conversation. Collette wasn't one to hide her light under a bushel. She'd married into one of Louisiana's political dynasties, and her husband was always running for some office or another. He was currently serving a second term on the city council, representing a mostly white Uptown district. He had almost been elected secretary of state in our last election, and rumors were circulating that he was going to try for lieutenant governor the next time around. I'd felt sorry for him . . . until I met him.

Let's just say they were perfectly matched and leave it at that.

That first year in the Cardirents had been tough. I found myself doing deep breathing exercises while counting to ten a lot more often than one would think necessary. There were times when Collette made me so angry that I had to walk away from her. I wound up bonding with some of the other moms, and we'd formed what we called the Collette Monaghan Support Group. We watched out for each other, rescued each other when she managed to corner one of us, and always volunteered to work on things together to spread her malice equally between us.

Come to think of it, I owed some of my fellow support group members a call. It had been a hot minute.

I'd decided that the best way to deal with Collette was to interact with her only when it was unavoidable and let her passive-aggressive digs roll off me.

Her issues were my problem only if I let them be.

Her son Rodger had been in the same class with my twin boys at L-High. She had five sons, ranging in age from teens to late twenties, of varying shapes and sizes. Her boys had all inherited her red hair and pale skin, and their resemblance to their mother was almost clone-like. Collette worked full-time as a realtor and never ventured out in public without looking photo-shoot ready. Collette had been president of the Cardirents the entire time I'd been an active member, and always ran unopposed. She liked being in charge and giving orders, but to give credit where it was due—she was ridiculously efficient and a tireless workhorse. She was always taking notes on the phone that rarely left her hand and never had to be reminded about anything. She was kind of intimidating that way. I scribbled my grocery lists on the backs of the envelopes bills came in, or on whatever scrap of paper was handy when I needed to make one.

It hadn't taken me long to understand that Collette's perennial reelections as president didn't mean she was popular. It was just easier for everyone to put her in charge to begin with. Collette could mobilize with the ruthless precision of a Prussian military officer. I kind of grudgingly admired the way she could get even people who disliked her intensely to work hard.

Stronger souls than I would start looking for the nearest available exit when they saw her coming their way, purpose in her step as she reached into her Louis Vuitton purse for the notepad containing her ubiquitous lists. No excuse was strong enough to justify saying no to her, and she had this uncanny ability to make you feel like a complete failure as a parent if you did. And after her hooks were into you came the onslaught of texts and emails and calls checking in "just to see how things are coming along, hon!" She'd go behind your back to other volunteers, making sure you were doing things the way she wanted you to do them.

She was exhausting.

I'd hoped I'd seen the last of her when the twins graduated last spring.

I should have known better. New Orleans has always been an incredibly small town.

"Collette! What a lovely surprise. How are you, darlin'? It's been too long!" Inwardly I winced at how phony I sounded as I put my arms loosely around her in a feeble hug, pressing my cheek against hers as I air-kissed her cheeks.

I'd forgotten how beautiful Collette was. She didn't look old enough to have a son in law school and another in medical school. Her face didn't have that peculiarly rigid look Botox and fillers gave women. Her gleaming thick red hair with golden highlights cascaded in waves and curls from the center part down past her shoulders. Her makeup was skillful enough to not be obvious. She was blessed with gorgeous skin, the pale porcelain kind that burns easily. Her vibrant emerald-green eyes were enormous and expressive, the dark curled lashes too long to be natural. Her simple green cotton dress, which dropped to just above her knees, was cut low in front, emphasizing her deep cleavage and the golden cross with a single sparkling diamond hanging just above. Her leather sandals looked expensive, and diamonds flashed at her ears. Her slender fingers ended in a French manicure. She smelled faintly like lilacs. Her perfectly straight teeth were bleached an almost blinding white. She was maybe an inch or so taller than me but gifted with far more generous curves.

She clutched my free hand tightly. "Oh, Valerie, I was just thinking about you last night! It's just not the same at L-High these days without you at the Cardirents meetings. But with your twins off to—now, what school did they get into?" She tilted her head and looked up, like she would find the answer at the tops of her eye sockets. "LSU, right?"

I kept smiling. She knew perfectly well the twins were at LSU. She loved to take little jabs like that—one of the other moms called it "the death from a thousand cuts."

Collette could have taught the master class on that.

She barreled on, not giving me a chance to reply. "But, while *of course* we can't expect moms without kids at L-High to stay involved, it's still a shame. We really do miss you."

Translated: she wanted something from me and wouldn't let me out of her sight until she asked.

And I was too far from the exit to make a break for it.

"Oh, Collette, that's so sweet, thank you," I replied politely.

"What are you doing with yourself these days?" she went on. "Are you working?"

I could feel color creeping into my face. She had an uncanny ability to go for the jugular. "I—well, no, I was thinking . . ."

Her eyes glinted malevolently. "You know, you can't spend the rest of your life just being the widow Cooper."

Ouch. "Did you mean to say that out loud?" I replied before I could stop myself.

She had the good grace to look stricken as the blood rushed to her face. "Oh, darling, I'm so sorry. You must think I'm horrible. I am horrible. Can you ever forgive me?" She grabbed my free hand again and squeezed it, her obnoxiously large diamond engagement ring pressing against my skin. "I just get so worried about you, all alone in that big house, and with the boys gone . . ."

"I—"

She cut me off. "You know . . ." She opened her Louis Vuitton bag and rummaged through it, finally retrieving a little gold case for business cards with her initials monogrammed on the front in calligraphic script. She flipped it open expertly with her thumbnail. "Are you lonesome in that big old house with the boys gone? Or have you downsized already?"

"No." It had never crossed my mind.

Until now, anyway.

Her green eyes glittered as she pressed her card into my hand. "Well, you really should think about selling it. It's a seller's market right now in the city!" She lowered her voice and leaned in closer to me, like she was sharing a dark secret. "You wouldn't believe what people are getting for places not nearly as nice as yours!"

Wait—she thought my house was nice?

That wasn't the impression she'd given me the few times I'd hosted a Cardirents meeting.

I examined her card. It was thick cream vellum. Her name was printed in a flowing, elegant font above her various phone numbers and email addresses. Across the top, in gold, were the words *New Orleans Lifestyles: A Boutique Realty Agency.* The address was Magazine Street, further uptown.

"You know, with only two of my boys still at home, I know *exactly* how you feel—we have way too much house now too," Colleen went on. "And you know, it *really* is a seller's market, and that location . . ." Her eyes rolled up as she computed something in her brain, her head moving slightly back and forth. "I bet we could ask for one point two million and settle for three-quarters of a mil. At worst. Just say the word, Val, and I'll get things rolling." She pulled out her phone and scrolled through it. "I have some time tomorrow afternoon. What do you say I stop by around three? This lovely young family came into my office yesterday— the husband's a doctor, going to work at University Medical—and they have three young ones, and your place—"

"I'm not interested in selling, Collette."

"Are you sure?" She opened her eyes wide and tilted her head coquettishly. "I mean, it's so much house for one person, and it must be filled with memories." Her eyes glittered. "Sad ones, too."

"I—"

"Well, you don't have to decide now, of course! I'm sorry, you know me—always just trying to help!" She emitted her little high-pitched giggle. "You just keep my card and think it over!" She flashed a predatory smile. "Your house is so darling, I just know I could sell it in no time!" She snapped her fingers just as the chorus of Cyndi Lauper's "Girls Just Want to Have Fun" started blaring out of her phone. She scowled at the screen. She held up a finger. "I have to take this. One sec?" She pressed the screen and said, "This is Collette. What do you want now?" Her voice hardened, the friendly mask dropping as she turned away from me.

I held up the bag of shrimp apologetically, mouthed *Talk to you later*, and escaped out the front door.

The widow Cooper, I thought with a roll of my eyes as I started walking home. *Is that how people see me?*

Sure, it had been five years since Tony died. And the boys had left for Baton Rouge in mid-August, two months ago.

It is *a lot of house for just one person*, I realized.

She really was good at getting under my skin.

I had never once thought about selling the house. The very idea of putting it on the market for over a million seemed insane. I'd heard property values in the city had been going up since Hurricane Katrina. Vacant lots were disappearing beneath new apartment buildings, and many of the beautiful big old houses were being split up into expensive condos. The boom in short-term rentals was also driving up property values and rents. Everyone on our block had been grumbling resentfully since three houses on the other side of the street had been bought by absentee owners to use as short-term rentals. I'd also received a notice from the city a few weeks earlier that my house was going to be reassessed for property taxes in the new year—a sure sign property values were going up in the always cash-strapped city.

But the property boom was good for the family business. Cooper Construction was doing so well I felt guilty when my brothers-in-law sent me my quarterly profit-share check. But Tony *had* owned a share of the business. Tony had worked there summers in high school, but as soon as he was old enough, he'd pursued his childhood dream of being a fireman. I'd even worked there, in the business office, part-time after the kids started school. But when Tony was killed . . .

I sighed. I still missed him.

If only he'd gone into the construction business . . . no, best not go down that path. It wouldn't change anything and would only make me sad.

The widow Cooper. I shook my head. I still couldn't believe she'd said that. That was bad, even for Collette. She'd never been that nasty and hurtful before—at least not to my face.

I smiled to myself. *Did you mean to say that out loud?* had just come out of my mouth without thinking. Lorna would be proud of me.

But maybe Collette was right. Maybe the house *was* too big for just me. Just because she was the one who'd brought it up didn't mean it wasn't true.

But she was wrong about the memories. The history stored in the house never made me sad. I'd learned to live with that lonely ache in my heart. And my boys had grown up there.

Sure, sometimes being a homeowner in New Orleans could be a challenge. Between shifting foundations, Formosan termite swarms every spring, watching for black mold, and the occasional hurricane, sometimes it seemed like the city's nickname "The Big Easy" was meant to be ironic.

But I loved our big old house on Constance Street. Our neighborhood was wonderful. I loved being able to walk a few blocks to the Breaux Mart for groceries, and the Fresh Market was just a few blocks farther. Big Fisherman had the best, freshest seafood in the city. And being so close to funky Magazine Street, with its eclectic mix of restaurants, bars, shops, and salons, was cool. You could find almost anything on Magazine Street, including things you never knew you needed until you spied it in a shop.

The street was already decked out for Halloween, with ghosts and cobwebs and witches and spiders and pumpkins in all the windows. Halloween was one of my favorite times of year. The heat and humidity usually broke in late September, and the weather became spectacular, like Mother Nature was trying to make up for the brutality of the long summer season. I loved making costumes and dressing up . . . although for the first time in eighteen years I didn't need to make costumes for the boys.

It felt weird, but I needed to get used to it.

I crossed Magazine Street in the dying golden light of a beautiful October afternoon. The sky was a lovely cerulean backdrop, a few cotton candy clouds scattered across the canvas. I stepped aside to let a group of tourists pass on the sidewalk. I could smell grease and french fries from the Dat Dog across the street. I'd stop in there for a margarita if Lorna and Stacia weren't coming over for our weekly girls' night in.

I glanced at my watch. Four thirty. They weren't due until six. Plenty of time for me to get cleaned up and start dinner before Lorna arrived and opened the bottle of wine she'd brought over from next door.

I smiled. Lorna never brought only *one* bottle of wine. The woman traveled with a corkscrew "for wine emergencies."

I shifted my shoulder bag. It was a few blocks from Big Fisherman to my house. It was getting cooler and the shadows grew longer as the sun descended in the west.

It was, I reflected, a great little neighborhood. Collette probably *could* sell my house for that much money.

Had someone told me when we bought the big house twenty years ago that it would someday be worth over a million dollars . . . well, I'd still be laughing.

When we told Tony's parents where the house was, they'd both been concerned. "That neighborhood isn't safe, isn't it?" his mother asked, her face gone pale.

"The Irish Channel is no different than anywhere else in New Orleans," Tony replied. "And the house needs a little work is all."

The reason we got the place so cheap was because our side—the river side—of Magazine Street was considered dangerous and doomed around the turn of the century. A lot of houses were blighted. Crime was up—carjackings and purse snatchings and break-ins almost every day. The streets were littered with potholes. Old wiring in crumbling houses started fires. Most longtime residents had fled as the Channel slowly decayed and rotted. Some letters to the editor in the *Times-Picayune* recommended bulldozing the entire neighborhood.

But those old houses had good bones and just needed people—young couples like me and Tony—to see their value and renovate. The house had been in bad shape when we bought it. We'd sanded floors, ripped out and replaced drywall, hung new wallpaper, replaced fixtures, and had to rewire some of the rooms. Tony's summers working for Cooper Construction had come in handy, and I'd gotten pretty good with tools myself.

No one could have predicted the way the neighborhood would change after we moved in. Two just-married kids in their twenties with twins on the way could never afford a place in our neighborhood now.

We were lucky we'd bought when we did.

Remembering Collette's clients, I corrected myself. *A fireman and his unemployed pregnant wife couldn't afford the place now.*

It was hard to wrap my mind around the idea that my property's value could have shot up so high. The house hadn't been reassessed for taxes . . . since when? Probably after Hurricane Katrina. That assessment was much higher than what we'd paid, but the change hadn't been *that* dramatic. And it shouldn't have surprised me, because the house had been a wreck when we bought it.

Gentrification had also come for the Irish Channel since we'd bought the house. I couldn't begin to name all the businesses on our section of Magazine that had come and gone since we'd moved in. Our Breaux Mart used to be our A&P. The CVS at the Louisiana Avenue corner used to be the Blockbuster Video where we rented movies. The Rue de la Course where I used to get a midafternoon cappuccino on my way to pick up the boys from grammar school had turned over several times and was now the Balcony Bar. The funky thrift stores and antique shops where I used to love to browse looking for costume possibilities were long gone, replaced by boutiques and cafés and other businesses targeted toward a more upscale clientele.

I liked that the neighborhood kept changing, but sometimes I missed the old days.

I walked down Harmony another block to the corner of Constance, admiring the Halloween decorations. The Watsons' yard now looked like a cemetery, skeletons dancing between the Styrofoam gravestones. I turned downriver at the corner. My neighbor on the uptown side, Michael, was rooting around in the massive pothole in the middle of the street in front of the double shotgun where he lived with his partner, John. The house had been in the Domanico family since before the Second World War. John's mother, Rosalie, lived in the other half of the house and had babysat my twins a lot when they were young.

She'd also taught me how to make real Italian red gravy.

"Val!" Michael grinned me, climbing up out of the pothole. A handsome man in his late forties, he wasn't wearing a shirt, and the black hair in the center of his muscular chest was damp. He wasn't much taller than me and had dark eyes, thick eyebrows with a natural quizzical arch, and a great smile that deepened dimples in his cheeks. His beard and thick black hair were speckled with gray now. He worked in IT at Touro Infirmary. He'd turned my boys on to anime and comic books and had spent hours with them playing computer games.

I gestured to what everyone in the neighborhood called The Pothole That Won't Die. It had been there when we moved in and stubbornly resisted every effort at patching. Every few years or so, the city workers would come fill it in and pave it over. Within a few months, the pavement would start buckling and the hole would reappear and start growing again. City workers would eventually show up and put an orange cone in it to warn drivers—but the cone inevitably also started disappearing into the hole as the ground below the pavement kept sinking. Only the very tip of the cone's top was still visible now.

Michael loved decorating the cone for holidays. "Have you figured out the cone's Halloween costume yet?" I asked. Last year he'd made it look like a shark's fin, rigging up a sound system with an electric eye that played the *Jaws* theme when anyone got within three yards of it.

I'd been a bit relieved when Halloween passed. There's nothing worse than hearing that music when you're in the bathtub.

"I haven't decided yet." He frowned. "I'm trying to figure out how much gravel I'm going to need to make the cone visible again—not much sense in dressing it up if no one can see it. Maybe I can just rig a net of some kind to hold it up? I don't know. I don't think I want to buy gravel." He wiped his hands on his gray sweatpants. "By the way, a courier came by with a letter for you—I signed for it. Wait and I'll get it for you."

"A courier?" I replied, confused. "For me?"

"It'll just take a sec." I stood in front of his gate while he climbed the steps and went inside. While I waited for him, I took a long, hard look at my house, trying to see it from a buyer's perspective. The house, originally built in the 1870s in what was called the antebellum double style, had well over four thousand square feet in total. Both floors had sixteen-foot ceilings, huge windows, and hardwood floors. We'd torn up a lot of horrible carpet to expose those floors, which we'd sanded down and refinished. The house was raised off the ground to protect it from flooding, so there were six steps up to the front gallery, with the front door on the left end. The covered gallery on the second floor was accessible only through the master bedroom. Tony and I used to have breakfast out there on weekends he wasn't on duty, letting the twins sleep in. The roots of the massive live oak in front had buckled and cracked the sidewalk, and our front gate, painted black, wouldn't close as a result and caused the rest of the fence to lean at weird angles. But the tree shaded both galleries, and we'd hung ceiling fans on our private gallery to help keep it cool up there. Tony had bricked over our little front yard and installed a little black fountain. Tony and I had painted the house coral with black trim.

And it looked like it might need to be touched up.

Michael interrupted my reverie a few moments later by holding a large manila envelope out to me.

This can't be good, my mother's voice whispered in my head.

"Here you go," he said with a grin. "So fancy, getting documents couriered by lawyers now."

My name and address were printed on a label on the front of the envelope, and *LIPPERT ABBOTT & SLOANE, LLC* was stamped in the upper left corner, above an address uptown on Magazine Street, past Jefferson Avenue.

Lippert, Abbott & Sloane LLC was a law firm. I'd passed their offices on Magazine Street any number of times on my way to Whole Foods.

"Thanks, Michael," I said, pushing my own gate open until the bent sidewalk stopped it. "Tell John and Rosalie hello for me."

I closed the front door and flipped the deadbolt. Scooter, my orange tabby, weaved himself between my legs, making figure eights and purring loudly while I disarmed the alarm. I carried him back to the kitchen, then opened a can of food and emptied it into his bowl.

He immediately lost all interest in me, but I filled his water bowl anyway.

"You could at least pretend a bit more," I said. He'd been more the boys' cat than mine, always moving back and forth between their beds at night. He'd become more attached to me since they'd left, but I wasn't fooled—I knew where I rated. I carried the envelope to where my computer desk nestled in a cozy little area. This was where I paid the bills, clipped coupons, charged my phone—Tony called it the house's nerve center. Lining the wall above my desk were the shelves where I kept my cookbooks hidden behind a cabinet door. Grabbing the Venetian glass letter opener Lorna had brought back for me after her last trip to Italy, I slit open the end of the envelope. I slid out a single piece of paper with the firm's logo embossed in shiny black across the top.

It was dated today.

Mrs. Cooper:

We are writing to inform you of a bequest you have received from one of our late clients, Arthur Cooper. Mr. Cooper was a great-uncle of your late husband, and in his will, he left his entire estate, including the Rare Things Antiques and Estate Sales Company, LLC, to your husband or his heirs.

After a lengthy review process and working with the probate court, we have determined that this inheritance now comes to you and your sons. We shall submit Mr. Cooper's last will and testament for probate, and I will serve as executor of his estate, per Mr. Cooper's instructions.

If you could give us a call at your earliest convenience, we would like to speak to you about the bequest, as some conditions of the bequest might seem unusual.

Sincerely,
Lucas Abbott, Esquire

The signature was a scribble. A business card was attached to the back of the letter: Lucas Abbott, attorney-at-law and partner.

This was bizarre.

I hadn't known Tony had an uncle named Arthur.

I sank down into the desk chair.

Scooter jumped into my lap and started kneading me with his front paws.

I thought I'd known all the Coopers.

Try as I might, I couldn't remember Tony ever mentioning any great-uncle Arthur. The Coopers were a tight family, a big clan that loved getting together and laughing and having a good time.

Family was everything to the Coopers.

A long-lost uncle didn't fit into that picture, did he?

Tony's mother had died before we met, and his father suffered a fatal heart attack while the twins were still in diapers. Tony had been a late baby, born when his next youngest sibling was twelve. His two brothers and sister were still around. I glanced at the clock. Rafe and Louie were probably still at work, but Tony's sister Therese might already be home from work. She was the oldest, three years older than Rafe and almost fifteen years older than Tony. She lived on the north shore in Rouen, and we'd been close as sisters since the first time we met. I didn't see her as regularly as

I'd like, but we talked on the phone several times a week, and she always stopped by whenever she came to town.

I grabbed my cell phone, pulled up Therese's number, and pressed call.

She answered on the second ring. "Valerie! You must be psychic! I was just about to call you. I'm coming to town this weekend to make a Costco run"—Therese loved shopping at the Costco on Carrollton—"and thought maybe we could have lunch or something?"

"Just come by the house and I'll make something," I replied.

"I was hoping you'd say that! You're such a good cook."

Therese was a terrible cook. Tony used to joke that she could burn Jell-O. "You're so sweet," I replied. "Listen, Therese, I . . . I have a strange question to ask you."

"Shoot."

"Do you have a great-uncle Arthur?" I pinched the bridge of my nose between my fingers.

Silence.

Finally, Therese said, in a quiet voice, "Yes, yes, I—we do. Wow. I haven't heard that name in a long time. How on earth . . . I mean, why . . . how did you hear about Uncle Arthur?"

"It's the weirdest thing, Therese," I replied. "I just got a letter from his lawyers. Apparently he's passed away, and he's left me—well, Tony and his heirs—his estate." I racked my brain, trying to remember where I'd seen the name Rare Things Antiques and Estate Sales Company before. "I don't remember Tony ever mentioning him."

"He's—was—Poppo's older brother, so yes, our great-uncle," Therese said. Poppo was their Cooper grandfather—their grandmother had been called Mommo. Both Poppo and Mommo had died before I met Tony. "That's so weird. There was something that happened a long time ago—one of those *Never darken our door again* kind of things, I guess? Maybe? Something like that, I don't really remember. Nobody really talked about it. I think it came up once at Thanksgiving when I was a kid?" She clicked her tongue. "Mommo hushed everyone up, and that was the end of it. I asked Dad about it later, and he told me not to worry about it. I got the impression that there was a scandal of some kind, maybe? None of the older folks wanted to talk about it. Wow." She sighed. "Oh, drat, look at the time. I've got to run back to campus"—she worked in the administration office as vice chancellor at the University of Louisiana at Rouen—"so I'll call you Saturday when I'm on my way to town."

"See you then, Therese," I said.

I hesitated before dialing the number on the letterhead. A female voice answered. "Lippert, Abbott & Sloane. How may I direct your call?"

"Valerie Cooper calling for Lucas Abbott," I replied.

"Oh, Ms. Cooper!" Her voice warmed. "I'm so sorry, but Mr. Abbott has already left for the day, I'm afraid, but he told me that if you called to see if you were free tomorrow morning? He has an opening at ten. Does that work for you?"

I didn't have to check my calendar. With the boys gone, my time was my own now. "Yes, I can make that."

"Yes, ma'am." I could hear her typing. "So we'll see you tomorrow morning at ten! Have a good evening, Ms. Cooper!"

"You too."

I pressed the space bar on my computer, bringing the screen back to life. I typed in my password and pulled up my web browser, carefully typing in *rare things antiques and estate sales company*. I glanced at the clock. I needed to get in the shower.

It could wait until after the girls went home.

I headed upstairs to the master bedroom to get cleaned up.

Chapter Two

I still managed to get myself quite worked up by the time I'd finished showering.

Why had Tony never told me about his great-uncle? They had to have been close, because why else would Arthur Cooper have left him—well, *me*—a bequest?

What else had Tony kept from me? And why?

I'd believed we'd told each other everything.

We'd met on Fat Tuesday during my first year at the University of New Orleans. Some of my high school friends and I had gotten up early to march with the Krewe of St. Anne. It was the first time my parents had let me go down to the Quarter for Mardi Gras Day without them, and I'd barely been able to sleep the night before. I spent the night at my friend Ashleigh's house in the Marigny—her parents were in the krewe—and we got up around five to put on our costumes and march through the streets into the Quarter. The three of us were going as the witch sisters from *Hocus Pocus*. People kept passing me Jell-O shots once we started walking, and by the time we reached Esplanade Avenue, I was a bit tipsy. I was worried I'd get sick and ruin everything. I started pretending to down the shots people handed me, but when no one was looking, I'd discreetly toss them into gutters already clogged with garbage and beads and feathers and glitter.

Unfortunately, Kylie and Ashleigh weren't as smart. They kept getting more and more wasted. Ashleigh's parents materialized out of the crowd at Esplanade, assessed the situation, and hustled them back to the house. Her mom, dressed as Marie Antoinette, whispered to me, "Stick with the marchers, and we'll catch up to you after we get them settled, okay?" I nodded, just as Kylie turned a bit green and bent over at the waist.

I managed to jump out of the way as brightly hued vomit came spewing from her mouth. I saved myself from that splatter but also managed to jump right into a total stranger. "Easy there," a deep male voice said as two big strong hands grabbed me, keeping me from going sprawling in the street.

My face aflame, I started stammering out apologies as I looked up into the face of one of the handsomest zebras I'd ever seen. I got lost forever in his sapphire eyes. All he was wearing was a pair of sneakers and a tight bikini-like bathing suit. He was covered head to toe in zebra-striped body paint. Even the skimpy bathing suit and sneakers were painted to match the stripes on his skin. "I'm so sorry, miss." His chest was massive, as were his shoulders. He had an impossibly small waist for a man. His thick arms were corded with veined muscle. "I didn't mean to knock you down. Are you okay?"

Struck dumb by his beauty, I couldn't speak. He guided me out of the crowd of people around the corner to a house. "Have a seat," he ordered, and I sat down on the concrete front steps. He knelt in front of me. Under the paint, he was so handsome it almost hurt to look at him. Men this good-looking shouldn't exist, I thought.

We started talking once he was sure I was all right. I spent the rest of the day walking around with him, looking at costumes and dancing and catching beads, my little hand tucked in his big one.

And as the sun started to go down, we exchanged phone numbers as he flagged down a cab for me. I couldn't help but look back as the cab pulled away from the curb. He smiled and waved.

I was certain I'd never hear from him again, but he called the next morning to make sure I'd gotten home safely.

He also asked me out to dinner.

Within a year we were married.

Why didn't you tell me about your uncle Arthur? I thought as I pulled on my jeans. *What was the big secret?*

I'd thought I knew all the Cooper family secrets, and some were doozies. Tony loved nothing more than cuddling in bed and making me laugh with outrageous stories about his family. I knew about Uncle Steve's affair, Cousin Mary's DUI, and that Uncle Barry wasn't Cousin Beau's biological father. I knew his own parents had separated twice, and that Therese had run away to marry her childhood sweetheart when she was a teenager—but hadn't gone through with it.

I'd thought he'd told me *everything*.

So why was Uncle Arthur so different?

You're overreacting.

And why hadn't Arthur reached out to me and the boys when Tony died?

It had been five years, and not a word from the man? Definitely not cool.

I went downstairs. Lorna and Stacia weren't due for at least thirty minutes if they were on time, but they never were. I had time to do some snooping around online before starting dinner. Scooter hopped into my lap and started kneading my legs, purring. "I know, I miss the boys too." I scratched his head. He curled up into a ball and closed his eyes.

He really was the sweetest cat.

I touched the space bar and typed *rare things new orleans* in the search engine bar. I hit the enter key, and after a few moments the rainbow-colored wheel stopped spinning. The boys kept telling me I needed a new computer, but I thought mine still worked just fine.

We don't always need everything instantly.

The home page loaded. On a black background were a man and a woman dressed like eighteenth-century New Orleanians, complete with buckled shoes and towering wigs. Their hands stretched out to a button in the center reading ENTER. I clicked and found myself staring at a building on St. Charles Avenue that looked familiar. There were several buttons across the top—FURNISHINGS, ART, DÉCOR, KITCHEN—but I clicked on the ABOUT RARE THINGS button.

Rare Things Antiques, LLC, has been buying and selling antiques, relics and special collectibles for over sixty years. Located in a classic old New Orleans home on historic St. Charles Avenue near the Euterpe streetcar stop, Rare Things is just the place to find that gift for that impossible-to-buy-for friend! We also handle estate sales, can find just about anything you could be looking for, and can ship anywhere in the world!

There were buttons for CURRENT INVENTORY and CURRENT ESTATE SALES as well as a CONTACT US FOR HELP button.

I went back to the home page and started to click on the DÉCOR button.

How much, I wondered, *is Uncle Arthur's estate worth?*

Right now, I had Tony's meager pension. I'd leaned on Stacia's expertise as a lawyer heavily in those months after Tony died. He'd died intestate, and I never could have gotten through dealing with the probate court and Louisiana's bizarre inheritance laws without her help. I wasn't independently wealthy, by any means, and tried to live off the quarterly profit-share check from Cooper Construction.

Since he'd died intestate, the forced heirship laws (which I didn't quite understand; thank God for Stacia) meant everything the probate court determined to have been "community property" was mine—the house, for example, and the quarter interest in Cooper Construction.

The court had decided the city's payout and the insurance had to go into a separate living trust that would go to the boys when I died, appointing me as trustee. The boys could access the trust themselves when they turned twenty-five. I tried not to touch that money—since it was for the boys—but I'd used it to pay for their tuition and their dorm fees. I did worry that the money would run out before they graduated, but the boys also wanted to get their own apartment off campus next year. They'd spent last summer working at Cooper Construction and saving their money to help pay for that future apartment.

But if the new assessment tripled my property taxes . . . I *might* have to sell the house. Hadn't Collette said over a million? A new assessment could easily gobble up those quarterly checks from Cooper Construction, and that would be a problem.

I didn't want the boys to come out of college in debt. Any number of the Cardirents parents had bemoaned the expense of college and worried about their kids having to take out absurd loans to pay for it. Tyler wanted to study veterinary science, and for now, Taylor wanted to be an engineer, though he'd changed his mind about his major every few months for the last few years. That meant at least eight years for Ty, and no telling how long Tay might be in school.

I heard Collette's voice in my head again. *I could probably get at least 1.2 million for your house.*

I licked my lower lip.

Maybe . . . maybe I *should* think about selling.

It was a lot of room for one person, and I seemed to spend most of my time trying to keep it clean.

But if I sold this business, and the estate was worth a lot . . .

Or maybe you could run the business. That would get you out of this rut you've been in since the boys left for school. Give you something to do instead of watching old movies on TCM all day and cleaning.

Maybe this was a sign.

Maybe this Rare Things business was just the thing I needed.

And the business might be teetering on the verge of bankruptcy, I reminded myself as I got up. I needed to start dinner, and I could search for information on Arthur Cooper later.

But you know nothing about antiques.

On the other hand . . . I had worked in the office at Cooper Construction. I did know something about how to run a business.

I put Scooter back down on the floor. Lorna had requested I make my shrimp and grits. I turned the front burner to a medium flame and reached for my cast-iron skillet. I added four slices of bacon to my skillet. I got down my colander, dumped the shrimp into it, and ran cold water over them.

I retrieved two bunches of green onions and two shallots from the hanging baskets over the central island and a bag of corn kernels from the freezer.

I started dicing the shallots as the bacon began sizzling. I've always loved cooking; I find the repetition of dicing and slicing and stirring soothing. I used tongs to lift out the cooked bacon to dry on paper towels and added a cup of frozen corn kernels to the bacon grease. After a minute, I scooped the corn back out into the measuring cup and added a half stick of butter to the grease. Once it melted, I added the diced green onions and shallots into the skillet and started stirring with a plastic spatula. The smell of sautéing onions made my stomach grumble. I turned on the burner beneath my soup pot and poured a chicken stock/half-and-half mixture into it, adding the corn kernels and stirring them in. I lowered the flame under the skillet while I waited for the liquid to boil.

I heard someone coming up the back steps.

"Darling, you wouldn't believe the day I've had!" Lorna Walmsley and her husband had moved into the house next door when the twins were still in grammar school. As she'd told me when we'd met, "I'm a lot to handle, and most can't." Her mother was British, her father Italian; she'd grown up in London, had attended Cambridge, and was fiercely intelligent. She was fluent in English, Italian, French, and Spanish. She spoke in a low, sexy voice with a heavy British accent, and sometimes, when she was excited, she talked so fast it was hard for me to follow her.

She also wrote bestselling sexy romance novels under the name Felicity Deveraux.

Lorna gave me an air kiss as she removed a wine opener from her jeans pocket. "I lost an entire afternoon of work to my mother." She rolled her brown, almond-shaped eyes in exasperation. Her next book was due in less than a month. "And by the time the wretched woman finally got off the phone—such a *narcissist*; never lets me get in a word edgewise and just prattles on and on about nothing and then complains about the cost of the call so much you know she wants me to offer to write her another check, and *then* wanted to stay on the line *forever*? I practically had to hang up on her!" The words fired like bullets from a machine gun while she made quick work of the cork and filled two glasses. "Mmm, that smells divine." She gave me another air kiss and sat down on one of the barstools at the island. "And by the time I *finally* got her off the phone, I was so shook I couldn't possibly have written another word. That woman is *impossible*." She clicked her glass against mine. "Cheers." She took a big gulp from her glass and topped it off again. "She's found another man. You know, you'd think she'd learn by now, but she simply can't bear to be alone . . . my, that smells fantastic. I just had a smoothie for lunch and am starved . . . how was your day?"

"Yes, well, that's a story," I replied, stirring the shrimp again. "Can you keep whisking this for me?" I gestured toward the pot with the grits mixture in it.

"Of course, darling!" She slid off the stool, finishing off her second glass of wine with a gulp, and took the whisk.

I wiped my hands on a towel and walked over to my desk. "So, check this out." She took the letter from me with her free hand.

She gave me a quizzical look before her large eyes darted back and forth as she read it, her mouth making a larger and larger O as she went. Finished, she wrinkled her brow. "Rare Things? I think I've been in there—it's on St. Charles, isn't it?"

I nodded. "Yes. I've never been inside."

"You're an heiress!" Her infectious laugh filled the room. "But this is marvelous!" She gave the letter back to me. "Oh, speaking of—that reminds me—have you given a thought about our costumes for the Boudicca costume ball? The invitations were dropped off today, *personally*, by the membership chair." She rubbed her hands gleefully. "It's a cinch we're in."

I sighed. "Lorna, I told you I don't want to join a krewe."

Boudicca was the most recent women's krewe to have started parading during Carnival season. Iris was the oldest, of course, and its membership primarily drew from New Orleans's oldest families in high society, or those on the outer fringes of it. A second ladies' krewe, Muses, had formed in the last twenty years. Muses had rapidly grown to one of the biggest and most popular of the season. Muses rolled on the Thursday night before Fat Tuesday with an insane number of floats, marching groups, and bands. The decorated shoes they gave out—themed and covered in glitter—were some of the most coveted throws every season. (I'd never managed to get one. The boys, on the other hand, always managed to come away with several per year—and refused to let me put them away anywhere. So their shoes proudly decorated the bookshelves in their bedrooms, collecting dust and shedding glitter.) The scuttlebutt around town was that the waiting list for joining Muses was so long that some of those who'd been on it for years had gotten impatient and decided to just form their own krewe.

Hence, Boudicca was born.

Lorna had become interested in joining Boudicca during the previous Carnival. Boudicca had grown rapidly to over three thousand members in just five years, and their Mardi Gras parade had grown into one of the larger ones. They were trying to make their signature throw—wands, individually decorated, usually with sequins and glitter—as coveted as Zulu's coconuts, King Arthur's goblets, and Muses' shoes. Per *Arthur Hardy's Mardi Gras Guide*, required reading for locals every Carnival season, they'd already achieved "super-krewe" status, putting them in the same rarefied air as Endymion, Muses, Bacchus, and Orpheus.

Lorna had somehow managed to wrangle us free tickets for Boudicca's Halloween ball, hoping I'd join the krewe with her. It was also a kind of a meet-and-greet thing—sort of like a sorority rush party, only in costume.

Stacia had flatly refused to go, and nothing Lorna tried could change her mind. She'd grown up in a family that belonged to two krewes, and she'd been a maid in the court of one and queen of the other. "I've had enough of that debutante/leftover Confederate nonsense to last me a lifetime," she liked to say with a shudder. She thought it was all terribly backward and regressive. "Even if it is a women's krewe, that stuff just doesn't sit right with me."

Lorna had finally conceded defeat—"Well, if you hate it so much, you wouldn't be any fun at the ball anyway"—and changed her focus to trying to talk me into joining.

"I know I'm horrible and have been no help with our costumes, but this deadline is killing me." She rubbed her temples. "And my mother . . ." She shook her head. "But we have to come up with something. You're a *genius* with costumes." She batted her long lashes at me. "What do you think?"

"I haven't really thought much about it," I replied a little guilt-ily, adding heavy cream to the shrimp and giving everything a quick stir. I covered the skillet and turned the burner down to simmer while switching off the burner beneath the grits. I'd not put any effort into thinking about the costumes because I kept hoping I could get out of going. "Right now, I'm a little more con-cerned about Tony having a great-uncle I never knew about—one who lived here in the city too."

"Family, darling!" Lorna waved her right hand airily. "You know how families can be." Her perfectly arched eyebrows came together over the bridge of her nose. "You know, I've actually *researched* your new business, when I was writing *Masque for a Dreamer*—you know, the one about the antique masks?" She gulped down more wine. "The manager I spoke with—now what was his name?" She prided herself on her memory. She snapped her fingers. "Randall Charpentier!" She pronounced it the way a French speaker would—*shar-pen-she-ay*. "That's it! Absolutely charming old southern gentleman—you know the type, very gen-teel, in a seersucker suit. I never met any Arthur Cooper, though."

Felicity Deveraux's books were sold everywhere: in airports, in drugstores, and on endcaps in bookstores. Lorna produced at least one romance novel per year, if not two—and I'd read them all. Her heroines were feisty women who didn't tolerate fools gladly—rather like Lorna herself—and the books were often laugh-out-loud funny. But they were also full of heart, and her characters were women any reader could relate to—her strength, as she liked to say, was writing real people, no matter how fantastic or ridicu-lous the situations they found themselves in. Her husband piloted jets for Transco Airlines and so was gone a lot, leaving her with lots of free time for writing. "It's perfect," she'd told me once. He also tended to stay away when her deadlines loomed.

His name was Jack Farrow, so she called him Captain Jack Farrow.

I'll never forget the day she came over to introduce herself, carrying a bottle of Italian white wine with a shrimp on the label and hardcover copies of her first two books. I was having a day—Tony was on duty at the fire station, and the twins were being a handful—so when I answered the door, harried, harassed, and wondering if it was too late for me to get away with putting the twins up for adoption, I must have looked like I needed a straitjacket. She took one look at me and said, "I'm Lorna and I just moved in next door. These are some books I've written." She pressed two hardcovers into my hand. "We're going to have some wine, and YOU TWO BOYS NEED TO STRAIGHTEN UP RIGHT NOW! CAN'T YOU SEE YOU ARE DRIVING YOUR POOR MOTHER QUITE MAD?"

And wonder of wonders, Tyler and Taylor stopped running and yelling, their eyes wide open in stunned surprise.

"Off to your room with you now!" She shoved the wine into my free hand and clapped hers at the boys. "Your mummy and I need some quiet time to get to know each other. Go on with you now; it won't kill either of you to read a book, you know!"

I stared in astonishment as the cowed boys quietly went upstairs.

"Thank you?" was all I could manage to get out. "I'm Valerie."

"You just have to let them know you're the boss," she said with a disarming smile. "They're just little men, after all, and think they can walk all over women. You've got to tame the little beasts when they're young or they'll grow up to be monsters. Date rapists or something equally horrible." She shuddered. "Let's have some wine, shall we? Perhaps on that lovely back gallery I saw from my windows?"

And since then, she's become the sister I never had.

"Can you set the table on the back gallery?" I asked now. "I thought it would be nice to eat out there." I glanced at the clock. "What's keeping Stacia?" She was usually more punctual than Lorna. I picked up my phone to see if there was a message.

There wasn't.

"Probably lost track of time at the office, as usual." Lorna picked up her wineglass, grabbed some plates and silverware, and went out the back gallery door just as the front doorbell rang.

I wiped my hands on a towel as I walked through the house to the front door. "Sorry I'm late." Stacia gave me a hug and a kiss on the cheek. "I hope Lorna brought wine, because I didn't have time to stop for any. I lost track of time and dashed over as quick as I could. I haven't even been home yet." She turned and aimed her car clicker at the black BMW parked in front of her yellow camelback shotgun house. The lights clicked on and off, and there was a loud chirping sound.

"Have you ever known Lorna to go anywhere without at least two bottles?" I closed and locked the door behind her.

"I could use some." She tiredly pushed a lock of her silky dark hair off her forehead. Stacia was tall, nearly five ten in her bare feet, with a strong, sturdy frame. She'd moved in down the street about a year or so before Tony died. She'd just divorced her third husband and sworn off marriage. When I needed legal help, she'd stepped in, and we've been friends ever since.

I followed her into the kitchen, where she filled a wineglass and took a healthy gulp. "Some days I wonder what I was thinking when I went to law school." Stacia shook her head as Lorna walked back inside.

They exchanged hugs and greetings. "Has she told you about her mysterious inheritance?" Lorna refilled our glasses. "Who knew our Valerie was capable of such great secrets and surprises? She's practically Jane Eyre!"

"Hardly," I laughed, shaking my head. "Besides, it's not *my* secret. It was Tony's." I filled them both in on everything as I spooned grits into bowls. I added the shrimp and some of the sauce before using a wooden mallet to smash the bacon into crumbles, sprinkling the bits on top and tossing on some more diced green onions as garnish.

"That's so not like Tony." Lorna picked up her bowl and followed me out to the back gallery. "He never told you this uncle existed? And the uncle didn't get in touch after Tony died?" Her eyebrows arched upward again. "I wonder what the big scandal was?"

"Hopefully, Therese knows, and I can get it out of her Saturday." I sat down on one side of the small bamboo table and placed my bowl down on the plate. I unfolded the napkin and spread it over my lap.

"Darling—we can do research." Lorna nodded as she sat down on the other side from me. "You know how people in this town *love* to talk. I bet Randall Charpentier knows what happened." She shook her head. "You *know* I can get anything out of anyone." She batted her eyes like a femme fatale from an old silent movie. "All we have to do is find some people who knew Uncle Arthur."

34

"The name's familiar," Stacia mused. "So is Randall Charpentier. I'd swear I know them . . . but I am so brain-dead right now I can't think straight. But I know of Lucas Abbott and his firm. A sterling reputation." She took a bite of her food and moaned in ecstasy. "This is fantastic. Thank you for cooking this week. When are you meeting with Abbott? Do you want me to come with?" She frowned. "I'd have to reschedule a few things . . ."

"Tomorrow morning." Stacia wasn't wrong—this was one of the best batches of shrimp and grits I'd made. "But I think I can handle it without you." I grinned at her. "And I know not to sign anything without you looking it over first."

"Do you want me to come with you? I'll make sure they don't put one over on you!" Lorna is exceptionally good at dealing with problems—insurers, contractors, rude salespeople, airlines. She often jokes about turning her skill for problem-solving into a second career. She claims it's the accent: "Americans let anyone with a British accent walk all over them. And in a pinch, I can go all Mary Poppins on them, and they literally melt into a puddle at my feet."

"No, I think I'll be fine, but I appreciate the offer," I replied. "You've been in the store?"

"I want to say it's across the street from the Burger King, but it might be further downtown than that? Maybe another block?" Lorna waved her hand airily. "Anyway, the building on St. Charles is the headquarters for the business, and they have a warehouse way out in Jefferson Parish, near the airport, I think. They don't keep everything there in the store. I also think they have an online store?" She changed the subject again. "And don't forget, we really need to figure out our costumes for Boudicca. Do you have any ideas, Stacia?"

Stacia rolled her eyes. She was one of the few New Orleanians who didn't like to wear costumes. "Why not go as a British author and her personal assistant?" She winked at me.

Lorna stuck her tongue out at her. "Just because you're not going doesn't mean you can't help us figure out our costumes, Stacia."

I laughed. "Like you, I have an entire room of costumes to choose from." Everyone in New Orleans does. Come to think of it, I could probably clean out mine, now that the boys were in Baton Rouge. There wasn't any real need to keep their costumes from when they were smaller, was there?

A mental image of the two of them walking along the sidewalk, dressed as clowns, holding hands and big plastic pumpkins for candy clutched in their free hands, flashed through my mind. They'd been eight or nine then . . .

Maybe getting rid of their costumes could wait a while.

"I thought it might be more fun if we went as a set of something—like salt and pepper shakers. You know, something," Lorna went on.

"We don't have to decide right now." I was starting to feel the wine a bit. "Let me find out about this inheritance first. We can figure the costumes out this weekend, I promise."

"Fine." She pouted, adding, "You know, you were just saying the other day you needed to find something to keep you occupied now that the boys are up at LSU." Lorna refilled my glass. "This antique shop might be just the thing."

"Maybe." I was getting full but took one last spoonful anyway. "I don't know."

"You know, I met the nicest single guy the other day." Stacia gave me a sly look.

"Stacia!"

"It's been five years since Tony . . ." Lorna let her voice trail off. She didn't like to say it out loud. "Anyway, the boys are off at school now, Val. I worry about you spending all day alone in this house by yourself. And if you don't want to start dating again—which is fine, I totally get it—then maybe this business you've inherited is just the thing you need to snap you out of this funk you've been in."

"I've been in a funk?"

Stacia nodded. "Not depressed, but not cheerful?" She reached over and patted my hand, sending a glance over to Lorna. "Rudderless, maybe?"

It had been nearly two months since I'd helped the boys move into the New Acadian Hall dorm at LSU, and now my days felt as empty as the house. I'd cleaned it from top to bottom, reorganized closets and shelves and drawers, read lots of books, watched lots of old movies on TCM, and even looked at the University of New Orleans website to see about possibly finishing my own degree—which I'd interrupted by marrying Tony and having the twins.

I wouldn't call it empty-nest syndrome, but I needed something to do.

I had looked at help-wanted ads both in the *New Orleans Advocate* and online, but I wasn't really qualified to do much of anything. I knew Rafe and Louie would find something for me to do at the construction office if I asked, but I didn't want to bother them. I'd thought about doing volunteer work somewhere, even talked to the folks at the Latter Library about helping out there a few afternoons a week, but they didn't need anyone.

Maybe the girls were right and this had come along at the perfect time.

Who cared if I didn't know anything about antiques? I could learn, couldn't I?

I don't have to decide right now anyway, I thought, picking up the dirty bowls and carrying them into the kitchen, Lorna and Stacia on my heels with the wine and the glasses. Lorna tossed the empty bottle into the trash and opened a second bottle.

Rare Things *could* be bankrupt.

This inheritance might have no value. It might just mean more debt, worry, and headache.

But everything could wait until tomorrow.

For now, I was going to drink some wine and watch a rom-com with my best friends.

Chapter Three

The next morning I wasn't at my best. Okay, I was a little bit hungover. The face I saw staring back at me in the mirror would have turned Perseus to stone. My temples throbbed. Brushing my teeth had not helped, and I was still praying for the aspirin to relieve the pressure in my head.

I added some drops to my bloodshot eyes before leaving the house. I'd stayed up much later than I should have—and that second bottle of wine had been a terrible idea. I didn't know what time Lorna and Stacia had staggered home. When I'd managed to walk down the stairs this morning, clutching the banister for support the entire way—I was horrified to discover my kitchen was a disaster area. Leaving leftover food out to congeal in the pans wasn't how I'd been raised. I'd gulped down water, scraped the food into the garbage, filled the sink, and put everything in the hot soapy water to soak. (Not my cast-iron skillet, of course, but I could deal with that later.) The hot shower helped get me to enough of a human state to put on some makeup and clothes to face the mysterious Uncle Arthur's estate lawyer.

Lorna was usually up by eight every morning, working her espresso machine for the caffeine jolt she needed to launch into a day of writing, but there were no signs of life at her house when I backed my car out of the driveway.

I hoped she felt more human than I did.

I was early. I'm always early. To everything. It's a compulsion I can't seem to break. Mom says I was born a day early and have been early ever since. I'm always the first to arrive at parties—if the invitation says eight, I'm parked nearby in my car at seven forty-five, watching as the clock on my phone slowly changes while impatiently tapping my fingers on the steering wheel.

Ty and Tay didn't inherit the *compulsively on time* gene from me. And one of Tony's few faults was his flippant attitude about being late. Sometimes he wouldn't even start getting ready until we were due somewhere.

I didn't know what the proper clothing was for meeting with a lawyer about an unexpected inheritance, but I figured I couldn't go wrong with a well-worn, comfortable pair of jeans and a cable-knit white cotton sweater. Maybe a little too casual, but I didn't need to impress Mr. Abbott—he represented the estate and had a job to do.

It doesn't matter what I wear or what he thinks of me, I reminded myself to calm my nerves as I found a place to park. I could get some coffee and maybe a muffin to help settle my stomach before ten. There was a CC's Coffee Shop just down the block from the law office at the corner of Magazine and Jefferson.

The crowded coffee shop was in full Halloween mode. The windows were covered with ghoulish and creepy Halloween scenes. Orange and black crepe streamers hung from light fixtures. Spider webs stretched across the front door as I pushed it open. "Monster Mash" was playing through the speakers. I got in line behind a couple of girls about the twins' age, earbuds in as they scrolled through their phones. Enormous spiders hung from the ceilings, alongside witches on brooms and ghosts spinning slowly in the breeze stirred up by the ceiling fans.

The only empty tables were dirty—wrappers, cups, and crumbs waiting to be cleared by a young, harried-looking young woman going from table to table with a gray plastic tub. But I'd missed the morning rush, and there wasn't a line at the counter. The occupied tables were piled high with textbooks, and their occupants looked like college students, most of them typing away on their laptops, pausing occasionally to stare at the screen with a look of concentration before their fingers started flying again. I felt a pang, wondering if the twins were in class or at a coffee shop, studying like these kids.

I ordered a cappuccino and a blueberry muffin, then waited by the pickup counter. The barista gave me my order with a smile, and I slipped a couple of ones into the tip jar. I sat down at a table still damp from being wiped down. I pulled out my phone to check the time. I still had twenty minutes before my appointment, and it was at most a five-minute walk from here. I picked at the muffin.

My phone vibrated, and a text message appeared on the screen from Lorna: *Darling so hungover I literally just crawled out of bed but good luck with the lawyer and do stop by when you get home. No writing today—my head feels like I've had electroshock.*

I smiled, typed back, *Will do feel better*, and slid the phone back into my purse.

I pulled out the letter from the lawyers and read it over again.

I still couldn't wrap my admittedly fuzzy mind around this unexpected family mystery. Marrying into Tony's seemingly enormous family had required some adjusting. I was the only child of two only children, and my father's parents had died before I was born. I'd been a late child. My parents had been married for fifteen years and had giving up trying when I came along. My maternal grandmother was the only other family I had, and cancer took her shortly after the twins were born. When I was a child, sometimes I'd wished for a bigger family, or at least just a sister. I'd been born in New Orleans, which made me a native, but other natives didn't know what to make of me. My parents were Not From Here, an important distinction to New Orleans purists who liked to play a game I called NOLA-ier Than Thou. My mother was from rural Alabama and my dad from Atlanta. They'd met in college at Auburn and moved here from Atlanta when my father got a job with Entergy.

So I was considered a native, even if my parents were Not From Here.

The Coopers had been overwhelming at first. Tony was the baby, with two older brothers and a sister, and had so many aunts and uncles and great-aunts and great-uncles that I needed a spreadsheet to keep track of them all. I spent many holidays and family reunions pretending I knew how he was related to whomever I was talking to. Tony turned it into a game to help me remember—pointing out someone and asking me to identify them not only by name but by how they were related to him. I gradually got used to being part of a big, boisterous family. Sometimes it seemed like endless, relentless drama—I needed another spreadsheet to keep track of the falling-outs and fights and hard feelings sometimes—but that drama always managed to work itself out in the end, because family was important to all of them. Tony and I had raised the twins to feel that way too.

Sometimes it took years, but the Coopers always eventually kissed and made up.

The very idea that any fight within the Cooper family had been so bad that someone not only was ostracized but had *stayed* ostracized, for decades, was hard for me to imagine.

What could Uncle Arthur have done that was so terrible that he'd been cut off so completely that I'd never known he existed? If the rift went back as far as Therese claimed, how *had* Tony managed to develop a relationship with him?

And more importantly, why had Tony kept Uncle Arthur a secret from me? And the twins?

For that matter, why had *all* the Coopers kept Uncle Arthur a secret from me?

Why hadn't Uncle Arthur reached out to me after Tony died?

The Coopers liked saying, "Family is everything, and nothing else matters." They always closed ranks against outsiders, no matter what kind of fight or feud currently had everyone in the family worked up. And sure, there had been times when holidays or family get-togethers had been awkward, like Tony's cousin Jessica's wedding, where half the family wasn't speaking to the other half, but no one was ever not invited or excluded.

What had Arthur Cooper done to warrant this kind of exile from the rest of the family?

I finished the muffin in a couple of bites, washing it down with another big swig of the cappuccino. It wasn't as good as the ones Lorna made ("I make them like real Italians," she always said smugly, "and even the best American coffee shops can't make them as good as the worst Italian dive"), but it was doing a much better job of clearing the cobwebs from my brain than the two big mugs of coffee I'd had before leaving the house. The fog was lifting from my brain, and I felt better, more human. I pulled out my phone to check the time, thinking, *Okay, you're not embarrassingly early now*. I left a tip on the table and walked back out into the sunshine.

It was a lovely cool October morning, a nice breeze blowing in from the river. There was dew on the grass and no clouds overhead in the richly blue sky. The breeze felt a little damp, which meant there would be rain at some point during the day. I hadn't bothered to check the weather—if I don't get a severe-weather text warning from my favorite local channel, I tend to not worry about it. I keep an enormous umbrella in the car in case of an unexpected shower.

Most of the year the weather forecast is *hot, humid, chance of rain*. The rest of the year it can turn on a dime—seventy degrees and sunny in the morning, pouring rain and colder by afternoon, then back to warm by sunset again.

But for now, it was lovely, and I enjoyed the sun's warmth as I walked along the crooked, broken, and tilting sidewalk.

The law office was in a double-camelback shotgun house that had been converted from a home to a business, like so many others on Magazine Street. Painted a cheerful electric blue with bright-yellow shutters and trim, it had ornate brackets supporting the roof of the front gallery rather than columns. A large brass plate attached to the front door read LIPPERT ABBOTT *&* SLOANE, LLC. The small front yard was enclosed in a classic black wrought-iron fence.

I opened the gate and climbed the front steps. There were enormous rosebushes with a few blooms on them standing in the dirt in front of the wide front gallery, dewdrops on the fading petals sparkling in the sunlight. The gallery itself looked new, like it had recently been renovated. When you've renovated a house, you can always spot newer woodwork and detail. The front door was painted the same yellow as the shutters and trim, and an enormous plate of clouded glass took up most of its upper half above the brass plate.

I turned the doorknob and stepped inside, shivering from the sudden drop in temperature. Cold air was pumping through a vent near the front door. The wall separating the two front rooms of the double shotgun had been removed to create a big, open welcoming reception area. It was painted a deeper, more sedate blue than the outside, and the tan wingback chairs looked comfortable.

The woman sitting behind a glass-topped desk looked up from her computer screen and smiled at me. "May I help you?" She was wearing a lovely gray silk wrap dress, and her long ropy braids ended in blue beads. She was maybe in her midthirties. A wedding ring glinted on her left hand, and an elegant gold watch decorated her slender wrist. A large appointment book lay open beside her keyboard.

"Hi, yes, I have an appointment with Lucas Abbott for ten?" I sounded tentative, apologetic. I could hear Lorna's voice in my head: *Be more assertive! More confidence! You're here to claim an inheritance! If you start off intimidated, they'll walk all over you!*

"Ah, you must be Mrs. Cooper." The big smile appeared again, and her voice grew even warmer. She got up and offered me her slender hand. Her nails were painted dark red. "I'm Patrice."

"Call me Valerie." I shook her hand.

"Have a seat, and I'll let Mr. Abbott know you're here." Still smiling, she picked up the phone on her desk, punched a button, and said, "Mrs. Cooper's here." She set the phone back down in its holder. "He'll be right out. Please, make yourself comfortable. Can I get you anything while you wait? Coffee or tea, or water?"

"Oh, no thank you, I'm fine." I held up my CC's cup. "I probably shouldn't have had a cappuccino! Too much caffeine!" I winced inwardly. *Don't overexplain.* To hide the flush creeping into my face, I walked over to one of the paintings hanging between two of the enormous front windows instead of sitting down. It was remarkable—vivid colors and elegant brushstrokes bringing what appeared to be the Crescent City Connection bridge over the river to vivid life. The bridge connected the city to the West Bank, and the cars on the bridge had been painted with remarkable detail. The river itself seemed alive: tiny whitecaps here and there, swirling currents moving across the surface, with a freighter coming around the bend downriver from the Quarter and the West Bank ferry out in the middle.

"Quite good, isn't it?" a male voice said.

"Yes, it's exceptional," I replied, turning to look at the man now standing next to me. He looked to be in his late forties or early fifties, his brownish hair thinning in front but still thick and long in the back. The brown eyes behind his big round black-framed glasses were warm and intelligent, and his smile was kind. His brown suit looked fitted, and the white shirt beneath the vest looked crisply starched. His bright-yellow tie matched the time on the house outside. He was a little shorter than six feet tall, with broad shoulders and a thick waist. An LSU class ring flashed on his right hand. "I don't think I know the artist?"

"He's a local. Bill Landry. He has a gallery on St. Claude, past Elysian Fields in the Ninth Ward. He's an old college buddy—we were in the same fraternity. You should stop into his gallery sometime. Some of his paintings of the swamps will take your breath away." He took my hand in his warm, calloused one. "I'm Lucas Abbott, and it's a delight to meet you at last, Mrs. Cooper. Won't you come into my office?"

"The pleasure's mine," I said, following him through a door down the hallway to an enormous room that screamed *man's office* at me, from the dark wooden furniture to the framed front pages of the *Times-Picayune* commemorating the Saints' Super Bowl win and national championship victories by the LSU baseball and football teams. A dark-chestnut bookcase was packed full of law books. The hardwood floor was polished to a deep shine, and a board groaned when I stepped on it. The floor, like so many in New Orleans, wasn't perfectly level. I sat down in an enormous, comfortable white wingback chair facing the big desk and sank into its soft plushness. "I . . . well, Mr. Abbott, I have to say I'm at a loss here. Your letter yesterday really caught me by surprise. I didn't even know my husband had an uncle named Arthur."

Overexplaining again. Knock it off, I reminded myself. I've always overshared when I'm nervous.

"Lucas is fine, Mrs. Cooper," he said smoothly. "May I offer you coffee? Tea? Water?"

"No, thank you, and please call me Valerie."

"I'm sure this must seem very strange to you." He kept smiling at me. "But . . ." His voice trailed off. He leaned forward and set his elbows on his desk, clasping his hands together. "Arthur Cooper . . . well, Arthur was a most unusual man. He didn't like

47

to talk much about personal things. He liked to keep his private life, well, rather private. But from things he let drop from time to time, I gathered there had been a big falling-out with the rest of his family when he was a young man, and he had . . . well, I'm afraid Arthur wasn't the type to forgive and forget."

"He carried a grudge?" I replied. "But . . . the rest of the family . . . it just doesn't make sense to me. I mean, my husband's family—*my* family—they fight and argue, but they always get over it. It just . . . I just can't see any Cooper carrying a grudge for so long against the rest of the family." I couldn't resist adding, "Outsiders, sure. But not family."

He shook his head. "Arthur had a long memory, I'm afraid. He never forgot a wrong—but he also never forgot a kindness." He cleared his throat. "Despite the falling-out, your husband reached out to him to try to . . . end the estrangement, is how Arthur put it. Arthur appreciated the gesture but made it clear to your husband, whom he always called Anthony—he was also a very formal man—that he was not open to having any kind of relationship with anyone else in the family. I believe they met for dinner or lunch every few weeks, but Arthur never relented. Anthony—Tony—always hoped Arthur would change his mind, but he never did."

"But why . . . why did I never meet him?"

"Arthur was content to let Anthony—Tony—be a part of his life, but he was afraid if he started letting other Coopers in, it would lead to more trouble, and he wasn't interested in that." He leaned back in the chair. "When Tony died, Arthur basically shut himself off from the rest of the world. I'm not certain he ever left his home again. He certainly stopped coming here to take care of his business; I had to go to him. I worried about him, Mrs.—*Valerie*, but of course, any time I tried to get him to reach out to you or the rest of the family, well, he would just give me an icy look and change the subject."

"So you don't even know what caused the rift?" I replied, my disappointment clear in my voice.

"No, I'm afraid I don't know. As I said, Arthur didn't like to talk about anything personal. He told me all I needed to know was that it was a fact, he had no interest in reestablishing ties with his family, and it wasn't any of my concern." He made a *What are you doing to do?* gesture with his hands. "It didn't make sense to me either. I knew Arthur for a very long time—he was one of our first clients when we first opened the firm. We drew up his will, and as I mentioned, I'm the executor. The will has been filed for probate." He steepled his fingers. "Unless there's a challenge to it, I expect the transfers of property and so forth to go through very shortly. Do you have an attorney?"

I nodded. "Yes, Stacia Baldwin."

He smiled. "I've met her a few times. She has an excellent reputation. There's some paperwork I'll need you to sign and have notarized; I am sure you will want her to review everything first."

"Of course." I smiled back at him. "Stacia would kill me if I signed anything I didn't let her look over." I shook my head. "I just hate the thought that my sons never got the chance to meet their great-uncle . . . I guess he was their great-great-uncle. If he liked Tony . . ." I left the sentence hanging, hoping it might encourage him to fill in some more blanks.

It wasn't likely he'd indulge in gossip about a client—even a dead one—but it was worth a shot.

"As I said, Mrs.—*Valerie*, Arthur was rather unusual." He retrieved a file from the rack on his desk. "And I wish I had more answers for you." His eyes were sad. "Arthur was a very lonely man."

"He never married?"

"I believe he was married once and his wife died, but again, he refused to talk about anything personal. But he never remarried. Whether he was involved with anyone, that I cannot say for certain one way or the other. Have you talked to your husband's family about him? They're much more likely to know."

"That's the thing," I replied. "I did briefly chat with Tony's sister yesterday—all she knew was something had happened a long time ago but didn't know any details. And all the people from Arthur's generation are gone now."

"Well, that's unfortunate. It seems like Arthur took the answers to the grave with him." He opened a file folder. "Well, shall we get down to the business?"

It all seemed straightforward, even to a nonlawyer like me. Arthur Cooper hadn't been a billionaire or anything, but he'd left behind a decent-sized estate. The bulk of his money, property, and investments had been left in trust for Anthony Cooper's heirs "until they reach the age of twenty-five years."

Lucas and I were to serve as trustees.

"Anthony Cooper's heirs?" I raised my eyebrows. "That's an odd choice of wording. Am I being naïve, Lucas? When did you draw up this will exactly?"

"Arthur specifically requested that wording." Lucas replied smoothly. "He drew up this will about a year ago." He hesitated. "We usually use that language when . . . it's encompassing, so if more heirs are born before the will can be corrected, it makes the probate easier."

I frowned. "But . . . I don't understand. When he made this will, Tony was already dead, and there's just the boys. Why not just use our names?"

Lucas cleared his throat. "Is it possible that Tony might have another child?"

I started to say no but stopped myself. It *was* possible. Tony had been six years older, twenty-five to my nineteen when we met. We'd gotten married a little over a year later. He always said he'd never been serious about anyone before me, but that didn't mean . . .

"I guess it's possible," I said slowly, an insidious voice whispering inside my head, *You didn't know about his rich great-uncle either, did you?* "I mean, I can ask the family . . ." My voice trailed off. "But when Tony died, the court . . ." I swallowed. My memory of those months after Tony had been killed were hazy. "I'm pretty sure the court was satisfied there was just me and the boys? When they set up the living trust for my boys?"

"That will help us get the will through probate faster." Lucas nodded, and when he spoke, his voice was soft and kind. "I will say I thought it was odd that Arthur insisted we phrase it that way, but he was a very strange and private man. I'm sure he had his reasons. Stacia Baldwin has all your paperwork for the living trust and from the probate court?"

I nodded.

"And you've drawn up your own will?"

I blushed. Stacia brought it up every so often, and I knew she was right. I didn't want the boys to have to deal with judges and courts when they were grieving, the way I'd had to, but . . .

"No, I haven't. Not yet. I keep meaning to." The boys were my only children, and Louisiana's forced heirship laws meant I couldn't disinherit them "except for cause" anyway, so I'd never seen making a will as a priority. The living trust would pass to them when I died, and the rest? Like I said, they were my only children, and a will would have to go through probate court anyway, so I'd never seen the point.

Note to self: have Stacia draw up the will immediately.

"You need a will, Mrs. Cooper, especially now," he replied. When I nodded, he continued, "It just will make everything easier down the road for your sons."

"Does this trust Arthur Cooper set up include the antique shop you mentioned in your letter?"

"No, that was separate from the trust for the heirs—which includes you, you know; you were one of Tony's heirs."

"Yes, of course." My head was swimming. I couldn't process any of this.

"He left his share of the antique shop to you personally. Arthur owned seventy-five percent of Rare Things Antiques and Estate Sales, LLC, with the other twenty-five percent belonging to his business partner, Randall Charpentier. Arthur was a silent partner in the business," Lucas explained. "At some point, Randall was in financial trouble and Arthur bought the business, with the understanding that Randall would gradually buy Arthur back out, but he's only managed to buy back twenty-five percent. Now, I've talked to Randall, and he's interested in buying your share of the business back—but he's cash strapped for the moment. I'm sure something can be worked out eventually between the two of you. He's done a terrific job building up the business."

Lorna had been right about the warehouse out near the airport and the shop on St. Charles Avenue in the Lower Garden District. I'd inherited the building on St. Charles, which Arthur had leased to the business—some tax write-off thing I didn't quite grasp. The warehouse in Kenner belonged to the business, which meant I now owned 75 percent of that building as well. Arthur had also owned a house on Harmony Street, not that far from our—my—house in the Irish Channel.

That house was part of the trust for "the heirs."

"The house . . ." Lucas hesitated. "The house on Harmony Street has been valued at around one point five million—"

I gasped, and he smiled at me.

"We are in the process of having the contents of the house inventoried and valued—estate taxes, you know—and I'm afraid Arthur was a bit of a hoarder." He coughed. "So it's not going as quickly as we might like. I'm also afraid that none of the heirs can access the house"—he gave me the address, which sounded like it was between Prytania and Coliseum Streets—"until the inventory and the valuation is finished."

So now I owned a piece of yet another house worth over a million dollars.

"I don't foresee any more delays in getting the will through the probate court," Lucas said as he escorted me to the front door. "I'm sure we can convince the court we've located all of Tony's heirs—after all, the probate court already did this once already. Everything should be settled sometime in November—maybe before Halloween. You never can predict how quickly a court will move. And the inventory . . ." He held his hands out with a slight shrug.

"Thank you," I said as he opened the front door for me. "It's a lot to take in."

"Feel free to have your lawyer contact me, and you can also get in touch with me at any time you like, if you have questions." He smiled. "It was a pleasure meeting you, Mrs. Cooper."

I shoved the envelope with my copy of Arthur's will and the documents I needed to sign into my purse. "I will."

As the door shut behind me, I realized I no longer had to worry about the boys' college expenses or them going into debt. Their mysterious great-uncle had provided very well for them indeed.

I'd never have to sell the house because of a property tax increase either.

My head was swimming from all the numbers and facts and figures and other information Lucas had thrown at me—and I still didn't understand why Tony had never mentioned Arthur once.

I was his *wife*.

The widow Cooper, Collette's voice taunted inside my head.

Even if Arthur hadn't wanted me to know about him, Tony still should have told me.

Lorna and Stacia weren't going to believe any of this.

I did kind of feel like Jane Eyre.

But with my luck, there was probably a madwoman in the attic of the house on Harmony Street.

Chapter Four

*H*ow, I wondered, shaking my head as I walked down the steps from the law office, *am I going to explain this to the boys?*

It was kind of dizzying, really. In twenty-four hours I'd gone from being worried about needing to sell my house to being sort-of-an-heiress.

I froze as I reached for the gate.

Right across the street was a storefront window. Written across the window in stylized gold script were the words *New Orleans Lifestyles: A Boutique Realty.*

I hadn't thought about Collette in months—and now here she was, popping up every day.

Well, Collette, I thought as I walked through the gate, *I don't need you to sell my house after all.*

I decided I'd throw her card away when I got home.

And knew it wasn't nice that the thought of tossing her card in the trash made me smile.

The widow Cooper.

At least I knew I'd been right about her all along.

The breeze was cooler and damper as I walked back to where I'd parked the car on Octavia Street. It was going to rain probably sooner than later. There were dark clouds in the sky over the West Bank on the other side of the river. I fished out my phone from my purse and checked for a severe-weather alert. There wasn't one, so I sent Lorna a quick text. *You aren't going to believe this—come by when you're finished working.*

She was apparently not working today—the hangover, no doubt—because the answer came back before I could put the phone away: *Can't wait! Will come by the minute I hear your car pull up.*

Lucas Abbott had said Arthur appeared to be in perfect health the last time he had seen him, which had been the week before he'd died. Lucas had stopped by the Uptown house to have him sign some paperwork—"he'd been as feisty and full of vinegar as ever" were Lucas's exact words. Arthur's housekeeper, Manuela, found him when she arrived for work one morning. He'd fallen down the stairs of his home and broken his neck. Manuela's phone number was included in the manila envelope filled with papers I needed to sign. Arthur had been in his eighties, but it bothered me he'd died alone and the family still didn't know.

Lucas had insisted Arthur's will had spelled out exactly what he'd wanted—no service, no party, and no second line; he'd just wanted to be cremated and have his ashes scattered in the river. Lucas himself had done the honors, going down to the Fly, the area outside the levee near Audubon Park, to shake them out of the urn into the muddy water.

"No fuss," Lucas had told me when I said I wished the boys and I could have been there. "And trust me, Ms. Coo . . . Valerie, you didn't know him. Believe me when I say that had I not followed his wishes, he'd have haunted me for the rest of my life. And if anyone could manage that, Arthur Cooper was that man."

He wasn't kidding either.

We don't joke about ghosts in New Orleans.

New Orleans is one of the most haunted places in the world.

I drummed my fingers on the steering wheel as the heavy rain pelted my car. I needed to let the rest of the family know.

But how would I tell them?

What would I say?

What *could* I say?

Hey, a great-uncle you may or may not remember died recently? I laughed to myself. Yeah, that would go over well. I was tempted to drive by the Cooper Construction office and talk to Rafe and Louie right now.

No, bad idea. I knew from the latest email about the business that they were putting up an apartment building on an empty lot in the Central Business District and had two renovation jobs. They were too busy to answer questions for me about the family now.

Besides, Therese was coming by for lunch Saturday. I could put off making any decisions about what and how to tell the family until I hashed it all out with her over lunch.

I'd make mac and cheese. She loved my mac and cheese.

And the boys could wait until our weekly phone call Sunday afternoon.

Yes, it was better to not rush and tell them anything before I'd processed it all myself. It was a lot to take in, really. I wouldn't tell the boys about the will's weird language, either—but that was something I could discuss with Therese.

And Lorna would be happy to help me figure out how to tell them. She enjoyed nothing more than sorting out other people's lives. I'd drop these papers off at Stacia's office for her to look over, and . . .

As I watched my windshield blur under the onslaught of the downpour, the occasional slow-moving car passing by, I took a deep breath.

You should go check out Rare Things—and you can drive by the house on Harmony. Just because you can't go inside doesn't mean you can't drive by and take a look, I thought. *You own 75 percent of that business now, and you also own the building. You've never even set foot in there. And there's no need to say anything—it's a business. You could just pop in and pretend to be a customer, get an idea of what they do, how the place is run.*

Why not? What else did I have to do today?

Well, the dishes from last night, but it wouldn't hurt to do them later.

I started the car and drove up Octavia to St. Charles slowly, the windshield wipers barely keeping pace with the heavy rain. The gutters were filling with water, and I could hear the spray being thrown up by my tires. It was raining so hard I decided to put off driving past the house. It could wait until the weather was better.

I usually avoid driving on St. Charles whenever possible. St. Charles is one of the more famous and beautiful streets of the city—which is the problem.

The streetcar has become a major tourist attraction. It isn't hard to understand—almost the entire stretch of the street from Jackson Avenue to Riverbend is stunningly beautiful, with massive live oak trees festooned with last season's beads (the street is also a major parade route during Carnival) making a canopy over the street. The streetcar lines run along the neutral ground in the center that divides traffic. Lined with beautiful old mansions, it's breathtaking during holiday seasons, when the houses are covered in decorations and holiday-themed scenes are depicted in stunning detail in the front yards. There's nothing lovelier than slowly riding uptown on the streetcar, taking in the gorgeous sights of one of the most beautiful streets in the country.

But that picturesque appeal also makes it a nightmare for drivers. Every year, more and more tourists come to New Orleans. Since the lovely old streetcars are often packed full with tourists crammed in like sardines in a can, others choose to sight-see by driving up and down St. Charles. The problem is they drive well below the speed limit as they ooh and aah at the glorious mansions from yesteryear.

Which makes driving on the Avenue a royal pain if you're in a hurry—which I was not.

Lorna had been wrong about the shop's location, but not by much. Rare Things wasn't across the street from the Burger King after all, but close. The shop was on the next block on the lake side of the Avenue. There was a spot in front of the Tacos & Beer restaurant. I used my debit card to pay the meter as a streetcar heading for the Quarter passed by.

I haven't been down to the Quarter in months, I thought. *Maybe Lorna and Stacia and I should go to Galatoire's for our next girls' night.*

I clicked the car doors locked. The air was fresh and cool after the rain, and puddles of clear water pooled in the low places in the cracked and broken pavement. I climbed over the roots of the massive live oak at the corner and looked over at the other side of the street.

There were three houses lined up across the street. They were similar in style and had probably been identical when originally built sometime in the nineteenth century. In the years since, they'd evolved and developed their own personalities. The one directly across the street from me was three stories tall and divided in two. The left side was a tattoo parlor, its window filled with neon signs in multiple colors. The other side was a small office for a property management business. The brick-red-painted building to the immediate right was a bar and grill, its sign obscured by the massive trees in its front yard. The final building was the one I was looking for, painted a white slightly tinted by grime. It was also three stories tall, with a dormer window breaking the roofline. There was a roofed balcony above a first-floor gallery that at some point had been enclosed with glass to make a show window. Above the steps leading up on the right side of the enclosed gallery hung an ornate sign reading *RARE THINGS* in a beautiful, flowing script. A red neon sign in the window of the front door flashed *OPEN* at me. I crossed the street to the neutral ground and walked along the streetcar tracks to get a better look. To the right of Rare Things, obscured from view by a tree, was a white graveled parking lot, separated by a brick fence from another lot.

There were two wingback chairs in the shop window, with mannequins sitting in them, a lovely table with a tea service resting on its top. The mannequins appeared to be wearing clothing from the 1920s.

That was a flapper dress if I'd ever seen one.

If my place in the Irish Channel could sell for over a million, I realized with a start, *how much is this property on St. Charles Avenue right on the parade route worth?*

Collette would know, wouldn't she?

Like I would ever ask Collette. I could look on websites—Lorna was addicted to Zillow—to get an idea.

If I wanted to sell the property, I'd find a different realtor. Maybe the one at the corner. Anything and anyone would be better than Collette.

Now, now, don't be so hasty. You know she's good at her job, and she's the kind who would take care of everything.

But I'd still have to deal with her, and would any amount of money be worth THAT?

I heard the words *the widow Cooper* in my head again, remembered the malicious gleam in her eyes as she said it. *I'll burn the house down before I let her sell it,* I thought while I waited for some cars to go by so I could cross the street. I could smell the grease from the bar and grill, and my stomach reminded me all I'd eaten was that blueberry muffin. *Maybe,* I thought to myself as I walked past, *I'll treat myself to a bar burger and a beer after I check the place out.*

Why not? It wasn't like I had any plans for the rest of the day.

I opened the gate and walked up the stairs. I hesitated just a moment. A bell rang as I opened the front door and stepped inside.

I was overwhelmed by the smell of lemon and pine. The store was an enormous space, with a highly polished hardwood floor. Walls had been removed to create the open layout, and I could almost imagine how the house had originally been constructed.

The remaining walls were painted a soothing shade of beige, and the shutters were closed on all the windows along the sides of the house.

And there was furniture everywhere I looked, sometimes crammed together with no space to walk between the pieces. All available flat surfaces—side tables, coffee tables, dining room tables—were covered with statues and bric-a-brac. The beige walls were almost completely covered with framed paintings, photographs, posters, or gilt-framed mirrors. Gorgeous chandeliers hung from the eighteen-foot-high ceilings, and everything had a tasteful-looking price tag tied onto it with red string.

"Hi there! How may I help you today? Is there anything you're looking for in particular?"

I would have testified under oath in court that the room had been empty, but unless she had materialized from another dimension, I'd been mistaken. Her smile was wide and lit up her face; her round dark eyes were friendly. She was a few inches taller than me, with long braids running down her back and round glasses perched on a pert nose. She was wearing black slacks, a silk salmon blouse, and a black blazer. She had what used to be called an hourglass figure. I couldn't tell how old she was from her gorgeous unlined skin.

"Oh, I'm not looking for anything. I—"

"Are here about the job?" She grabbed my free hand with both of hers. "Oh, thank *God* you're here. I'd just about given up on anyone applying! We pay by the hour, depending on your experience, of course, and we do offer health benefits. I know it may not look like it now"—she glanced around, gesturing with her eyes—"but we've been shorthanded ever since Brandy ran off to get married, and it's fall and that's our busiest selling season with Christmas right around the corner, and the online orders are backing up and there's so many other things to be inventoried . . . did you bring a résumé? You don't need a résumé, of course; we can always have you just fill out an application, and—"

"No, no, I'm not here about a job, I'm sorry!" I broke into her train of words when she paused for breath. I was beginning to feel foolish—maybe stopping in unannounced hadn't been the best idea.

"Oh, I'm sorry. Are you just browsing?" She put a hand up to her face and looked mortified. "I'm so sorry, you must think I'm . . ." She paused, took a deep breath, and said, in a very friendly, professional voice. "What can I help you find?"

"Well . . . I'm not here about the job—although I might be—and I'm not shopping." It was my turn to take a deep breath. "My name is Valerie Cooper, and—"

"*Cooper*?" She gasped and grabbed my hand again. "Valerie Cooper? Don't tell me you're Arthur's long-lost family?" She burst out laughing. "You must be Tony's wife." She peered at me. She squeezed my hand. "I was so sorry about Tony. I would have reached out—should have, really—but . . ." She swallowed carefully. "How are the boys?"

"You . . . know about the boys?" My head was swimming.

She examined my face closely. "I get the feeling you're finding out a lot of things you didn't know before?" She shook her head. "I always told Arthur he was an old fool." She gestured toward a pale-cream wingback chair. "Have a seat. Can I get you something to drink? I'll put up the *Be right back* sign, and we can chat a little bit. We have coffee or tea or water."

"Um, coffee would be nice." I sank down into the chair. There was a coffee table next to it, covered with what looked like vintage Mardi Gras ball gowns.

"Coming right up." She walked to the front door, turned off the OPEN sign, and tucked a cardboard sign into a corner of the door's window frame before closing the venetian blinds. She walked back past me and through a door behind the enormous table with the cash register sitting on it. Within a few moments, she was back carrying two Disney villainess cups filled with coffee. She handed Ursula the Sea Witch to me and turned another wingback chair to face me before sitting down herself.

"I hope you don't mind dark roast; it's all anyone drinks around here." She smiled at me again. "I'm Dionne Williams, but everyone calls me Dee. I've worked here for almost twenty years." She winked at me. "I don't know where all the bodies are buried, but I bet I could find most of them if need be."

I took a sip. The coffee was very good. "So, you knew Tony?"

"Not well. I only saw him whenever Arthur brought him around—which wasn't often—and truth be told, the first time I saw him, I thought he was an escort." She laughed at the look on my face. "Arthur . . . was interesting to say the least, you know, and then one day he showed up with this gorgeous, hot young man who looked like sex in blue jeans, and I thought to myself, *Ah, so that's how it is with Arthur.*" She coughed. "And then Arthur introduced him as his nephew." She made air quotes as she said *his nephew.* "I felt stupid when it turned out to be true."

"Did . . . Arthur bring him by a lot?"

"Maybe a couple of times a year? Arthur and Randall used to have a standing monthly lunch date, where they'd talk about the business and drink too many martinis, and a couple of times per year Arthur would bring Tony along." She smiled at me. "I'm so sorry for your loss." She reached over and patted my hand. "And now Arthur too."

I smiled sadly. "Yes, he was. He was . . . I know how this sounds, but it's true . . . he was my soul mate." *A soulmate who never told you about his great-uncle.*

"Arthur was never the same after Tony died," she went on. "You could see him start to decline once . . . once it happened. This last year before he died, he barely came by at all." She shook her head. "He was too old to be living alone. I told him he needed to sell that big old house and move into a condo, but he wasn't having it." She clucked her tongue. "That staircase was too steep for him. He'd just snap at me to mind my own business and tell me he wasn't feeble, but . . ."

"I didn't know Arthur," I replied, realizing how insane this all must sound to a stranger. It sounded insane to *me*. "Tony never told me. I never even knew Arthur existed until yesterday, when I got the letter from the lawyers about the will."

She pursed her lips. "Hmm. Typical Arthur. I knew he was mad at the rest of the family—he told me Tony wasn't anything like the rest of the Coopers—but why wouldn't he want to meet you? Or the boys?" She shook her head, the braids swinging. "He was the stubbornest old man. He could be impossible sometimes."

"And basically, all I've been able to find out—since yesterday—was there was some kind of family quarrel and Arthur cut himself off from the rest of the family." I looked down into my coffee cup. "I haven't even told the boys yet."

"You poor thing," she said sympathetically. "Arthur was . . . well, he was a very nice man, but he was weird, don't get me wrong. Weird but not in a bad way. He was always good to me—and to everyone who works here—but he was so intensely private." She leaned forward and whispered, "I always wondered why."

"And now I guess I'm going to own seventy-five percent of this business. And this building." I shook my head. It was a lot, really—was it only twenty-four hours ago that I had been cleaning out the guest room closet and wondering what I was going to do for the rest of my life? "I just don't understand any of it. And I don't know anything about antiques or estate sales."

"Do you want to learn?" She raised her eyebrows. "Are you working right now?"

I shook my head. "No. I haven't worked since—well, since I had the boys. I mean, I've had part-time jobs here and there, all of them equally awful, and done some volunteering, but now with the boys off at school and Tony gone—"

"Sounds like opportunity has just dropped into your lap." Dee smiled at me. "We really could use help here. I wasn't kidding about being desperate to hire someone. You wouldn't happen to know how to sew, do you?"

"Well, I can run a sewing machine," I laughed. "I have twin sons. It was either learn how to mend and patch or go broke. I also know how to refinish furniture—most of the stuff in my house we bought secondhand and Tony and I refinished it all."

"Heaven must have sent you." She glanced at the pile of ball gowns. "You wouldn't believe the way people treat vintage clothes. There are tears in some of those that need to be repaired—I was going to take them to a tailor. But if you can do simple repairs, that would be a godsend." She waved her hand. "We'll pay you twenty dollars an hour, and let me find that paperwork you need to fill out to get started . . ."

She kept talking, but my mind was racing.

I owned this building, I owned seventy-five percent of this business—or would, once I'd had Stacia look over those legal documents and signed them and the will was finished probating—and I didn't have anything better to do. I'd known halfheartedly since the boys left that I'd probably need to take a job, just to fill my days and keep my mind from turning to mush. And how many times could I clean out the closets or scrub floors or reorganize the kitchen?

And what better way to learn about the business than working there?

"Do you really think I could learn the business?" I heard myself interrupting Dee.

She clasped her hands together. "No one expects you to be an expert anyway." She smiled, raising an eyebrow. "Just get a copy of *Antiquing for Dummies*; that's a great way to start. Most of what you'll be doing won't involve sales or buying—we just need a kind of assistant so I can focus on selling and Randall on buying. And of course, we have an online store, and like I said, those orders are backing up. That was part of Brandy's job." She frowned.

"Are you sure Randall won't mind you hiring me like this?" I frowned. "Where *is* Randall, anyway?"

"He's out in Redemption Parish, looking over a potential estate sale. He probably won't be in today at all, or maybe even tomorrow, depends on how it goes up there." She sighed. "He wants me to hire someone, and fast. And he can hardly object to the new owner working here. I guess you're really the boss, aren't you?" She laughed. "Are you sure you don't mind doing this kind of work? Can you start like now? There's even more of those gowns needing work upstairs."

I drank the rest of the coffee and smiled. "Let's get to work."

Somehow, it felt right.

Chapter Five

It was after six o'clock by the time I pulled into my driveway. My back was a bit sore and my fingers still a bit cramped from spending most of the afternoon hunched over the sewing machine on the second floor of Rare Things. Some gowns hadn't been salvageable, but I'd impressed Dee with the ones I'd worked on.

"This is amazing." She'd scrutinized a red sequined gown that had needed its hem repaired as well as a tear just below the neckline. "I can't even see where it was torn! I was this close to throwing this one away!" She'd impulsively hugged me. "It's going to be so great having you here, Val!"

Antiquing for Dummies, I reminded myself as I waited for the electric gate to my driveway to open. The motion sensor turned on the driveway light once the gate started moving. I was tired and a little bleary-eyed. Dee had stayed downstairs to deal with walk-in customers while I worked on the gowns upstairs. The upstairs, like the first floor, had had most of the walls breaking it up into rooms removed, leaving an enormous space, but some of the rooms had been left intact. One served as Randall's office, and another was filled with boxes and smelled like damp. The open space was also crammed with furniture and bric-a-brac, with crates for pictures leaning against one wall and piles of unopened boxes scattered around. Some of the furniture, like the gowns, needed repair; there was one gorgeous old scroll-top desk that would probably be worth a lot once the scratches and scars on its surface were sanded down and refinished. There was also a back gallery, with a staircase leading down to the parking lot. Dee said it was used primarily for deliveries. Everything always went upstairs first, to be inventoried and evaluated. If furniture needed repair, it went back down the back stairs.

"We use professionals," Dee explained when she showed me the staircase. "We don't expect you to learn how to refinish or repair furniture, so don't worry about that. And anything small—like books and lamps and things—that are easily packed and shipped? That's what we sell online. We also do a lot of business with interior design firms here in the city." She smiled. "Decorators also hire us to find things for them. We stay busy around here."

As I'd worked on the gowns, I'd heard the bell ring a lot more often than I would have expected. Business at Rare Things was clearly booming.

"Come on, come on," I muttered impatiently. The gate seemed to take forever to roll aside. I just wanted to get inside, take off my shoes, and open a bottle of wine.

But as the electronic gate shut behind my car, Lorna popped through the gate in the fence between our backyards. She was holding two wineglasses and had a bottle of her favorite Italian Chardonnay tucked under her arm. She looked a little crazed in the glare of my headlights, locks of her wavy hair escaping from the bun on the crown of her head. It looked like she'd spilled something down the front of her white Jazz Fest sweatshirt. Her black yoga pants showed off her shapely legs, and I knew that look on her heart-shaped face.

"Darling!" She drew the word out to about five syllables as I got out of the car, remembering I'd forgotten to drop the envelope of papers off for Stacia to look over. "Where have you been? I've been worried sick! I was expecting you back here no later than noon! Are you all right?"

"I'm sorry, I should have texted you," I said as she placed the glasses on the hood of my car. A corkscrew materialized out of thin air, and she removed the cork and poured. "But thanks. I could use some wine." I picked up a glass and took a big drink. It was perfect, but my stomach was also growling. I'd grabbed an order of onion rings from the bar next door to the shop during a break, but that had been hours ago. And my kitchen . . . it was still a mess. "Long story."

"I've been absolutely dying to hear it all day! What did you find out?"

"First of all, I'm starving. I've hardly eaten all day. Have you had dinner? Do you have plans?"

She shook her head. "I had some soup for lunch." She sighed. "*My mother* called again this morning, and I didn't think to check the caller ID before I answered—that's how hungover I was. And she got my nerves so frazzled all I could do was open a can, and then I was so worried about you . . . let's order a pizza, shall we?" She walked around to the back gallery of the house, her phone already out. She had Reginelli's, our favorite delivery pizza, on speed dial. As she ordered, I unlocked the back door and grimly

71

surveyed the mess I'd left for later, hoping elves might magically show up and take care of it in my absence.

Darned elves. You can *never* depend on them.

I put the envelope with the papers on my desk and turned on the hot water spigot, taking another drink from my wine. Lorna closed the door to the gallery behind her. "Pizza on its way." She glanced at the mess on my island and made a *yikes* face. "Oh, what a dreadful friend I am—I should have helped clean this up last night."

"I don't think any of us were in any condition to wash anything last night." I closed the drain and started placing things into the filling sink.

One nice thing about working at Rare Things all afternoon— I'd completely forgotten the hangover.

"So where have you been all day?" Lorna asked, scraping plates into the trash and stacking them next to the sink. "I really was worried. My mother—" She waved her hand. "And the hangover didn't help much. I don't how she manages to get to me after all these years, but she can do it like no one else can. And then I panic about everything, and it spirals, and thank goodness you're home and okay." She laughed mirthlessly. "How did it go with the lawyers? I swear, Mother had me so worked up I was afraid they'd had you hauled off by the police or something equally crazy." She pointed at her temple. "The curse of a creative imagination and letting it run wild."

"It was . . . interesting." I nodded toward my desk. "Yes, I have some papers and things for Stacia to look over before I sign them." I began filling her in on the details of the inheritance, her eyes growing wider with every sentence, while I wiped the now-clear counter down and let the dishes soak in the hot soapy water for a few minutes.

The grits tended to achieve the consistency of hardened glue when left out.

"But darling, that's marvelous. I *am* going to start calling you Jane Eyre." She refilled both our glasses as I started washing the cups and glasses and placing them in the dishwasher. "Weren't you just worrying about how to pay for everything with the boys up at LSU the other day? And what to do with yourself? This couldn't have happened at a better time for you, could it?"

People who didn't know Lorna were often dismissive of her because she was so pretty and had that gorgeous figure. And she certainly could play the role of ditzy, empty-headed beauty when it worked to her advantage. But the truth was, she was quite intelligent, with a steel-trap mind that rarely, if ever, forgot anything.

"And this trust—and the business—should take care of all your money worries," Lorna went on. She was also very good with managing money. She handled all the finances for herself and Captain Jack Farrow. She loved nothing more than a good sale and had taught me to appreciate bargains, to clip coupons, and how to pinch a penny. Those skills had come in more than handy after Tony died and I had to not only keep us afloat but pay the boys' not inconsiderable tuition at Loyola High. I could have moved them to a less expensive school or even public school, but I'd thought adjusting to losing their father was enough for them to handle without adding a change in schools to their emotional load. "Are you thinking about selling the business?"

"I don't know." I shook my head as I moved on to washing the plates. I always washed my dishes before putting them in the dishwasher, which amused Lorna to no end. It was a habit I'd gotten from my mother. I liked to joke that my mom would have thought Joan Crawford was a slob. Mom's house had always been so neat and tidy that I was always stressed whenever she used to stop by. She never said anything, but I could almost hear her judging thoughts as she looked at dust accumulations and cobwebs and the boys' scattered things with a slightly raised eyebrow.

With them retired to the Gulf Coast, I now had enough warning about pending visits to have a cleaning service come in.

And I suspected that the cleaning team still didn't meet her stringent standards.

"But at least now I don't need to be so worried about the new tax assessment on the house."

Both her eyebrows went up. "You were worried about the property tax assessment?" She rolled her round eyes. "How much higher could it go?"

"Oh, that's right, I didn't tell you about what happened yesterday! In all the excitement about the inheritance, it completely slipped my mind." I proceeded to tell her about running into Collette Monaghan at Big Fisherman and her estimate of what my house was worth. "So, of course, that got me started worrying about that new assessment notice I got from the city and trying to figure out how to pay taxes if they valued the house at what she thought I could get for it . . . ugh."

"Collette Monaghan?" Lorna frowned, her right eyebrow going up.

"I'm sure I've complained about her to you before," I laughed. "She was one of the moms at L-High, and"—I changed my voice to what I hoped was a dramatic tone—"she was *difficult*, if you know what I mean."

Before she could answer, the doorbell rang. "Oh, thank God, the pizza." Lorna dashed out of the kitchen, leaving me to continue washing dishes and loading the dishwasher. I could hear muffled voices from the front of the house while I drained the sink, put a pod in the dishwasher's soap dispenser, and hit the start button. I got down some clean plates for the pizza and some paper napkins. We both loved Reginelli's pizza—it was our go-to when neither of us felt like cooking anything. I used to get one for us and one for the boys and send them upstairs to watch a movie or play a video game while Lorna and I entertained ourselves.

My stomach growled when she walked in carrying the box and set it down on the island. She scooped out two pieces for each of us, expertly sliding them onto the plates. I suspected at some point in her past, before she became Felicity Deveraux, International Bestselling Novelist, she'd been a waitress. "Let's eat out on the gallery, shall we?" Without waiting for me to respond, she headed out there, somehow managing to carry her glass, her plate, and the bottle.

I followed and collapsed into one of the gallery chairs. I took a bite of my pizza and moaned in delight. "Oh, this is perfect. Thank you for ordering and paying."

"I've been wanting pizza ever since I opened my eyes this morning—between prayers for death, of course." She giggled. "But Collette Monaghan—you know she came by my house yesterday?" She held up her hand to cut me off before I could reply. "She's the membership chair for the Krewe of Boudicca. I told you the invitations were dropped off personally, remember?"

"How strange," I replied. "That's probably what made her think about selling my house, but she didn't mention Boudicca at all when I saw her at Big Fisherman." I took another bite, then remembered. "Oh, she might have. She got a call on her cell in the middle of our conversation, and I used that as an excuse to get away." I made a face. "She called me the widow Cooper."

"*What*?" Lorna's eyes narrowed. Collette was lucky she wasn't in earshot. "She's one of *those* women, then?"

"She was asking me what I was doing now that the boys were off at school and I wasn't volunteering at L-High anymore. 'You can't just go on being the widow Cooper,' was what she said."

Lorna called her a not-very-nice name. "If she ever says that in front of me—"

I laughed. "She's not really that bad, I suppose. She gets a lot done for the Cardirents, and we probably would have been lost without her. I don't think she knows how she comes across?"

"You really are too generous when it comes to giving people the benefit of the doubt," Lorna replied darkly. "You know, she did ask a lot of questions about you, now that I think about it. I thought she was trying to scope you out as a potential member, since I'd applied for membership in the krewe and you were just my plus-one." Lorna looked dubious. She took another bite of pizza with a frown. "She asked more questions about you than she did about me, like she was fishing for information . . . if I hadn't been so mentally distracted by my mother . . . I wasn't really paying as much attention as I should have been."

"Well, it's weird she didn't mention knowing me," I replied.

She put down her pizza and leapt to her feet. "I'll go get the invitations right now." She rushed down the back steps and back through her gate again. The gate didn't catch and swung back open. I had time to finish my second slice of pizza.

I resisted the urge to take another piece. I could have it for breakfast in the morning.

I leaned back and looked out at the night sky. It was clear, but the temperature was dropping—a few more degrees and it wouldn't be comfortable out here anymore. On the other hand, there were blankets tucked away in the trunk in the corner . . .

Lorna came rushing back through the gate and handed me an envelope with a smirk on her face. "You know, the more I think about it, the more I don't like those questions she was asking about you."

The envelope was thick paper, and Lorna's name and address were written in calligraphic script on the front. I frowned, reached inside the envelope to pull out a single sheet of thick cardboard, and read:

The Mystic Krewe of Boudicca
Cordially invites you and a guest
To attend our fifth annual
Halloween Masked Ball
And membership party!
October 27th, from 7-midnight
At the Civic Auditorium
Parking provided
Looking forward to seeing you there!
Collette Monaghan
Membership Chair

It didn't surprise me that Collette was membership chair of a women's Mardi Gras krewe. The surprise was that I hadn't already known—it was the kind of thing Collette would have enjoyed boasting about to anyone who would listen.

Maybe she'd never mentioned it to me because she thought I wasn't Krewe of Boudicca material.

Which, come to think of it, was more likely.

I was surprised Collette didn't belong to either Iris or Muses. She'd always bragged about her society connections—how many times had I heard about her glory days as a maid in the court of Rex?—but I didn't know what was required to join a krewe. My parents had never bothered, and none of the Coopers belonged to one.

As for me, I was fine with just going to the parades and catching throws.

I turned the invitation over. "Do I want to know how you managed to get us invitations so we didn't have to buy tickets?"

Lorna smiled at me and gave me a sly wink. "Only the hoi polloi pays," she replied smugly, nodding at the invitations.

"If Collette is membership chair, I won't be joining. Besides, the expense—"

"Your inheritance has taken care of any money problems you might have," she replied airily. "And besides, I'm sure I can get the membership fees discounted or waived."

She was good at getting bargains and discounts, I had to admit.

"I mean, I used the Felicity Deveraux shtick to get the invite," she went on smugly. "And I played the Muses card—that they were after me to join, as a local international bestselling romance novelist—and so of course Collette was all about giving me and my best friend an actual invitation so we wouldn't have to pay." She waved a dismissive hand for the unfortunate rabble who had to buy tickets. "We still need to come up with costumes."

We finished off the wine while debating what costumes we should wear, and I refused her offer to leave the entire pizza before sending her home. I covered the slice I'd have for breakfast in tinfoil and put it in the fridge.

Before heading up to bed myself, I got down the old photo albums from their place on the top shelf of the built-in bookcases in the television room. I'm not too proud to admit I spent a few moments wallowing in self-pity and misery while finishing off the open bottle of Chardonnay chilling in the refrigerator. I missed Tony, I missed the boys, and I missed my old life. Lorna had been keeping a watchful eye on me ever since the twins left for Baton Rouge. "You've been putting off your grief by focusing on the boys" was her expert psychoanalysis, and much as I hated to admit it . . . she was probably right.

Again.

Anyone who saw me sitting on the carpet in my television room with photo albums scattered on the floor around me while I drank wine and sobbed would have probably called the men in white jackets to come take me away.

But . . . it felt good, you know? Cleansing, in a way, and when I rinsed out my glass and threw away the empty bottle before going up to bed, I felt like something had shifted in me.

Tomorrow, I thought as I slipped under the covers, *is the first day of my new life. No more widow Cooper.*

And when my eyes opened at six in the morning, the time I'd been getting up since the boys were small and just starting kindergarten, I firmly closed them and slept for another two hours. At eight when I got out of bed, I felt terrific—both excited and thrilled.

I had somewhere to be and something to do that didn't involve the twins.

It felt good.

I took my time with breakfast and the newspaper. I dropped off the papers for Stacia to look over at her office, and at promptly ten AM I walked through the front door of Rare Things in a Saints sweatshirt and a nice pair of jeans, ready to go to work.

But Dee wasn't waiting for me in the store this time.

"May I help you?" the man at the register desk intoned, looking at me over the frames of his wire-rimmed glasses. The disdain in his voice was matched by his facial expression as his eyes moved up and down, taking my measure and clearly finding it wanting.

I own 75 percent of this business—or will soon, I reminded myself, smiling back at his sour face. "You must be Randall Charpentier!" I crossed the room and held out my right hand for him to take. "I'm Valerie Cooper."

If I thought identifying myself would warm him up, I was mistaken. If anything, the temperature in the room dropped another ten degrees.

He looked at my hand before finally accepting that I wasn't going to drop it. He took mine and gave it a cursory shake. His hand was warm and dry.

He was a very handsome older man, somewhere north of sixty, if I had to hazard a guess, and his thick curly hair, now completely white, was immaculately styled. He was wearing a three-piece navy-blue suit with a crisp white shirt beneath. His tie was navy blue with yellow streaks and held in place by a gold bar with a small blue sapphire set in it. "Dee told me you'd come by yesterday and helped out some," he replied, his tone still frosty. "I looked over what you did, and it wasn't bad work."

"I guess I don't have to worry about getting a big ego from your compliments, but glad I could be of help," I replied, not letting him get under my skin. "I know I don't know much about antiques, but—"

"Yes, well." He waved his hand airily. "You can learn, one supposes." He fixed his pale stare on me. He expelled a breath, and I could see his entire body relax. "Actually, Dee said you were a big help to her yesterday. Thank you." He shook his head, the majestic white curls bouncing a bit. "My apologies, Mrs. Cooper—"

"Valerie."

"Valerie." He smiled, but it didn't quite reach his eyes this time either. "This situation is hardly one of your making, but . . ." He tapped his long fingers on the counter. "It was rather a shock to find out that Arthur hadn't . . . you see . . ." He closed his eyes for a long moment before opening them again. "Arthur had promised me that he would leave the business to *me* in his will. So, when I found out the terms of his will . . . you must understand my disappointment."

"Just spit it out," Dee said as she descended the staircase. She was carrying a box. "If you don't say it, I will. And I won't be as polite."

I looked at her, then back at Randall. "Polite?"

"Randall is too ashamed to tell you that he had some personal financial issues about twenty years ago." Dee set the box on the counter next to the cash register, retrieving a box cutter from underneath. "Arthur loaned him money, and Randall gave him ownership of the business with the understanding Randall would gradually pay him off and get ownership of the business back."

"I would have put it a little more delicately, but factually correct." Randall flushed. "He offered to simply make a loan, but I . . ." He lowered his eyes. "I—"

"You wanted to save your pride," I said sympathetically. "And he promised to leave it to you in his will. I can't imagine why he changed his mind." I looked around the store. "And to leave it to me, of all people."

"You can imagine my shock when I took my copy of his will to his lawyers after he died for them to probate," Randall said, "and Lucas told me there was a more recent one." He shook his head. "I was such a fool. I thought Arthur was someone I could trust. I should have known better. We'd been friends for nearly forty years . . ." He shook his head. "I guess you never truly know someone."

"And Arthur also owned this building?"

Dee cut the box open and started removing packaging. "Arthur owned the building before buying the business. The shop used to be on Magazine Street, past State Street. Part of the deal Randall made included moving Rare Things into this building so he wouldn't have to pay rent anymore. Arthur also invested more money into the business."

"How did you meet Arthur?"

"We met when he engaged me to sell some pieces for him, and we became friendly over the years. He collected things—with no rhyme or reason to it, really—and he often engaged us to find things for him as well," Randall said. He cocked his head to one side. "You didn't know Arthur, did you?" A hint of a smile played at the corner of his lips. "He was most peculiar in some ways. I know he resisted meeting you and your children, but your husband was a very charming and handsome young man."

"Do you have any idea why he wanted nothing to do with the rest of the family?"

He shook his head. "Arthur never talked about the past. When he showed up here with your husband, it was quite a shock. I had no idea he had any family." He looked at Dee, who was removing something encased in bubble wrap from the box. "Is that the so-called Lafitte dagger?"

Dee carefully removed the bubble wrap, exposing a dagger with what looked like rubies encrusted in its hilt. "Supposedly. Nasty-looking thing, isn't it?"

"It's beautiful," I said. "Lafitte? As in Jean Lafitte, the pirate?"

"That's what the seller claims." Randall took the dagger from Dee carefully. "It's just a story. And in this business, if you can't prove the provenance, it's worthless. But it is a beautiful piece, isn't it?" He frowned. "I told the owner that it's not nearly as valuable as he thinks. People won't spend money on a legend—especially not what he wants for it—without any proof." He slid the dagger back into the box. "Anyway, I hope you'll forgive me for my initial rudeness, Valerie." He sighed. "We'll just have to make the best of this arrangement, won't we?" He gestured for me to follow him. "We got some books in I want you to photograph and write descriptions for so we can put them up for auction online."

"I put some more clothes up there to see if you can repair them," Dee called after us as I followed him up the stairs.

I also thought I heard her say, "She's a godsend, Randall, so be nice to her."

Chapter Six

The adjustment to having a job wasn't as hard as I'd worried it might be.

Rare Things didn't open until ten, so I didn't need to be there until around nine thirty. Years of getting up around six every morning since the twins had started school made it easier; for me, sleeping in meant not getting up before seven. Every morning I had time to touch up the house and do some laundry while drinking my coffee. I had something light for breakfast—cereal, or fresh fruit and plain yogurt—and was out the door at nine fifteen on the dot, ready for another day's work. The shop closed at six, so I was usually home by six thirty. After a light dinner I'd curl up with my e-book reader and dive back into *Antiquing for Dummies* for a few hours before bed.

Wash, rinse, repeat.

Randall was out of town the rest of the week too. This wasn't a buying trip, though. Another revenue stream for Rare Things involved renting out furniture for use on film and television production sets at, in Dee's words, "a price so ridiculous it would be cheaper for them to just buy it outright." This client was a production company shooting a film at one of the more famous plantations along the River Road between New Orleans and Baton Rouge. Dee didn't know the name of the movie or who was in it or who was making it. Filming around New Orleans had become so commonplace no one gave it a second thought. I was disappointed. I'd hoped to be able to see what else I could find out from Randall about Arthur and Tony.

On the other hand, I didn't have a lot of free time at Rare Things anyway. Dee was a tough supervisor who took my "Treat me like you would any employee and forget I'm an owner" statement seriously. Every morning, there was a list of tasks for me to do on the scarred worktable upstairs. I patched dresses, skirts, and jackets and readied them for the dry cleaner. I learned how to polish silver. As I scrubbed away, I began to realize why silver wasn't as popular as it used to be. It took me a while to get a handle on the online auctions and sales—the boys always laughed at my inability to learn new skills on electronic devices—but before long, I was an old pro at closing out sales and sending invoices. I learned how to use the postage machine as well as how to properly package items being shipped the Rare Things way to avoid damage. It seemed like there were always boxes of new things coming in needing cataloging, sorting, and pricing. Everything going up for sale online also needed to be thoroughly photographed and a detailed description written. Dee wasn't kidding when she said things had backed up since the last employee had quit. Every time I filled the bins for the delivery guys to pick up, another series of auctions had ended and it was time to start the process all over again.

I was exhausted every night by the time I got home. Some nights I was so tired that the words in *Antiquing for Dummies* swam before my eyes, and I wound up streaming an old movie.

Stacia emailed me on Thursday. She'd checked out all the documents for Lucas Abbott and the probate court, and they were ready for me to sign. She told me she'd slipped the envelope through my mail slot and they were waiting for me at home.

On my way home from work, I swung past Arthur's house on Harmony Street, just to get a look at it. It was enormous, an Italianate side-hall double-gallery style, painted a dark blue with coral shutters. The front yard behind the black wrought-iron fence looked neat and trim—I guessed Lucas and the estate were still paying for the maintenance before the probate closed. I was sorry the shutters were closed, since I wasn't above looking in the windows. It was a beautiful house and probably very valuable. I wasn't sure if Harmony Street was still considered the Garden District; regardless, it was a much nicer address than ours on Constance.

Friday morning, I detoured uptown on my way to work. I stopped into Lucas Abbott's office, signed the documents, and had them notarized. I still hadn't figured out how to fill in the twins about everything. I thought about just calling or shooting them an email . . . but that didn't feel right. I felt like I had to do it in person. I was sure they would have even more questions than I did about Arthur and why we'd never met our benefactor.

When I got to Rare Things and went upstairs, there was no list of tasks for me. Surprised, I checked the online auction sites—nothing was due to end until two that afternoon, and the online store had only a couple of purchases from overnight.

Looked like it would be an easy day.

I went back downstairs to get some coffee. Dee was standing at the register counter with the Lafitte dagger in her hand, a scowl on her face. "Not much for me to do today," I said, joining her after pouring myself a cup of coffee in the little galley kitchen.

"No," she replied, without taking her eyes off the dagger.

"Everything okay?"

She sighed and placed the dagger back down on the counter. "Randall wants you—whenever you have time—to see if you can trace the provenance of this." She gestured to where it sat on the counter. "It's a waste of time, frankly. Randall knows damned well that dagger didn't ever belong to Jean Lafitte."

"It had to come from somewhere," I said, picking it up with my free hand. I put my coffee cup down on the counter and touched the tip with my index finger. It was sharp, and the edges looked like they could slice paper.

She shook her head. "You're going to be amazed at the stories people will tell you trying to get us to buy something from them." She pointed at the dagger. "Jean Lafitte never owned anything jewel encrusted in his life. He was a pirate, sure, but not from the age of Spanish treasure galleons sailing like sitting ducks across the Caribbean Sea. He was a rogue, but the ships he raided carried base cargo—coffee, bananas, molasses, that sort of thing. And of course, if we had *anything* he really owned—well, we'd probably either donate it to a museum or give it to Sotheby's to auction off. You'd be amazed at what collectors will pay for things."

Rare Things, she'd explained to me on my first full day, wasn't equipped to deal with most collectibles; specialty shops and websites handled those, "and we can't compete with them." There were military collectibles, autographs, toy soldiers, comic books—"it's impossible to be an expert on everything, so we have to refer people to the appropriate places. Sometimes we buy from the specialists if one of our clients is looking for a particular something."

"But it's possible, isn't it?" I held the dagger up to the light to see the red glow from the rubies. "And if it did belong to him—"

"Like I said, Sotheby's. We don't handle things this valuable." She took it from me and placed it back inside the mahogany carved box with the red velvet lining it had come in and closed it.

"If it's that valuable, shouldn't we keep it in the safe? I mean, the rubies alone . . ."

"They're paste, Valerie." She rolled her eyes. She handed me the box. "Just leave it on Randall's desk," she said, and smiled at me. "I also wanted to thank you—you're doing a great job."

"No better way to learn the business," I replied, carrying the dagger and coffee cup upstairs with me.

The compliment felt good. It had been a long time since anyone had made me feel—well, *appreciated*. I was glad I wasn't in the way. My endless questions would have worked Job's patience, and it seemed hopeless sometimes.

There was so just much to learn.

I put the boxed dagger on Randall's desk and went to work.

Around one o'clock in the afternoon, my computer froze. I groaned. I hadn't lost any work; I'd learned from the boys to save everything regularly, and this computer was even more ancient and troublesome than mine at home. But maybe the frozen computer was a sign that it was time to take a break. My stomach was growling, and since I had to wait for the computer to reboot anyway . . .

Dee and I had gotten into the habit of ordering something deep-fried for lunch from the bar next door—onion rings, french fries, fried pickles—and sharing them to lessen the damage to our figures and bad cholesterol levels. I looked forward to this time every day with Dee. She was a lot more open to answering questions while we indulged in the greasy finger food.

I also was going to have to break this habit soon. I'd gained a few extra pounds after the boys left for school and had let my haphazard exercise program lapse completely. Lorna said it was normal: "Darling, you're depressed! You're so depressed you don't even know you're depressed."

She'd been right again. Coming to work every day, having someplace to be, was making me feel more like myself than I had in a long time. I'd gone from my parents' house to marrying Tony to being a mom to being a widow. Was it any wonder I wasn't sure who I was or what I wanted from life?

And the more time I spent with Dee, the more I liked her. Her husband worked for the Saints in marketing ("If you ever want tickets, let me know; I can hook you up"), and she had two sons in school at St. Augustine's. She'd been working for Randall for about twenty years. She deflected any questions about Randall that didn't directly involve the business but was willing to tell what little she knew about Arthur. She also told me her theory of why he'd betrayed Randall by not leaving him the business after promising he would.

"About a month before Arthur died," she'd said Thursday afternoon, dipping a piece of fried zucchini into a little plastic cup of ranch dressing, "they had a hell of an argument. When Randall came back to the store, he was furious. I was worried he'd have a stroke, honestly. And before you ask—no, he never told me what they fought about." She winked at me. "I'll bet that's when he changed his will."

"The will was dated about a year before he died," I said. "So whatever they argued about, that's not why Arthur changed his will. He already had."

"Maybe that's when Randall found out," Dee said, "and that's what they argued about."

Arthur had died falling down the stairs. Maybe it hadn't been an accident?

But Randall had nothing to gain by killing Arthur.

It would have been in his best interest for Arthur to stay alive. At the time, Randall couldn't have known I'd take an interest in the business. It would have made more sense for him to think I'd sell.

For that matter, I could still sell it.

I slung my purse strap over my arm and picked up my phone. *Fried pickles today*, I thought as I walked to the staircase. *But next week I've got to start bringing healthy snacks.*

I was at the top of the stairs when I heard a woman's voice yelling at Dee.

"He would have told me if he was going out of town! Don't lie to me!"

That can't be good, I thought, hurrying down the steps in case Dee needed my help.

"You're such a liar! Just tell me where he is!"

It couldn't be a customer, I thought.

I was halfway down the steps when I stopped in stunned surprise.

Collette Monaghan was standing in front of Dee, her face bright pink, hands on her hips. Her face was twisted in rage.

I hadn't recognized her voice because I'd never heard her raise it before.

What on earth was Collette Monaghan doing here at Rare Things?

"As I said the first time"—Dee spoke slower than usual, clearly enunciating each syllable, her tone calm and reasonable—"Randall is on set for a movie being filmed in Redemption Parish. They are renting some of our inventory, and you know your dad doesn't trust film people."

I sucked in my breath. Dee had the situation in hand and didn't need me to rescue her.

But—Randall was Collette's *father*?

I was in business with Collette's father?

Selling Rare Things suddenly looked like a much more attractive option than keeping it.

"But—"

"And since he is on set, he probably can't have his phone on," Dee went on. "Why don't you just send him a text? I know he'll answer you as soon as he can."

"I should have known you'd be no help—as usual." Collette spat the words out as she turned and flounced to the front door. The bell rang as she opened it, and she turned back to take one last shot. "When this business is *mine*, the first thing I'm going to do is fire *you*."

The door slammed behind her so hard the house shook. I took a deep breath and walked down the rest of the stairs. Dee was still standing at the cash register, her arms folded, shaking her head slightly, her jaw clenched tightly.

"Well, that was something. I don't know what exactly, but something," I said.

She rolled her eyes. "Honey, I've been dealing with that . . . *woman* since I started working here. Nothing I haven't heard before and nothing I can't handle—and nothing I won't hear again." She sniffed. "Fire me. Good luck with that, girl." She winked at me. "And unless Randall buys you out, she's never owning this business."

"Collette Monaghan is Randall's daughter?" I said carefully.

She looked at me. "You know her?"

The widow Cooper. "Our sons were at Loyola High together. I know her from the parents' association."

"I'm sorry to hear that," she replied grimly. "That woman has brought Randall nothing but misery." She shook her head again. "If she ever owned this business, she wouldn't have to fire me, I can tell you that. I'd quit. I'm sorry if she's a friend of yours . . ."

"We aren't friends," I replied. "I mean, I know her and that's about it. I . . ." *The widow Cooper,* I heard her saying again in my head. "I don't like her at all."

"That woman doesn't have any friends." Dee sighed, resting her elbows on the counter. "Collette has run poor Randall ragged, made his life miserable." She clucked her tongue. "I don't like to gossip, but you're going to be around, so you might as well know the whole story. I don't suppose Randall told you why he only owns twenty-five percent of the business?"

"All I know is that he'd had some financial issues and Arthur stepped in to help him out."

She barked out a laugh. "*She's* the reason he had, and still has, financial problems." She expelled her breath. "I had hoped Randall would tell you himself"—she cocked an eyebrow at me, and I shook my head—"but she's a piece of work. Randall . . ." She sighed. "She thinks she's better than she is, if you know what I mean. A social climber. She wanted to go to the best, most expensive schools. She wanted to be a debutante. The Charpentiers used to have money back in the day, but it's long gone, by the way. But you know, they used to be in Comus and Rex. I think Randall's granddaddy may even have been Rex one year, but like I said, that money's long gone. Randall put everything he had into this business and did pretty well for himself, but that wasn't enough for Miss Collette, oh no. Randall paid for her wedding—she had to get married in St. Louis Cathedral, of course, and then the reception was in the ballroom at the Monteleone. Right around that same time he made some bad investments, bought some antiques he thought he could turn around for a good profit, but no one wanted them, and he lost his shirt. And he put down the down payment for that big house she's so proud of. If he hadn't been friends with Arthur, he would have lost everything. The agreement was that Randall would pay Arthur back and get the business back, but Collette is a nonstop cash drain." She sighed. "Arthur only had a twenty-five percent share in the business to begin with, and then got another twenty-five percent share, another and another—he didn't want to even take any of the profits from Rare Things either. He thought it would be best if Randall kept the money and used it to buy the business back, but Randall wouldn't hear of it." She frowned. "Maybe that's why Arthur changed his will and left everything to you. Maybe he thought if he left the business to Randall, Collette would just bleed him dry."

I didn't know what to say. I thought back to all those years at Cardirents meetings, Collette in her expensive clothes, with her jewelry and BMWs, bragging about sending her sons to Ivy League schools and the fabulous parties she went to and how she had been a maid of Rex when she was a teenager. "But don't the Monaghans have money?"

"Liam Monaghan keeps her on a tight leash, and don't think that the Monaghans can't go broke just because he sits on the city council." Dee lowered her voice and glanced at the front door again. "And if you ask me, I think a lot of her money goes up her nose." She held a finger up to her own nose, closed one nostril, and inhaled deeply. "She likes to come in here and lord it over me because I'm the help, you know, but if I didn't have so much respect for Randall and what he's put up with from her . . ." Her face twisted. "I'd snatch her bald-headed." She shook her head. "She's Randall's cross to bear." She looked over at me. "Arthur despised her."

"Smart man." Since Dee seemed willing to answer questions, I asked her, "Do you know where Arthur's money come from?"

"I don't know, to be honest with you. He didn't seem to ever have a job, you know, and he had that lovely house over on Harmony Street—I suppose you inherited that too?"

"It's included in the boys' trust. Lucas Abbott—Arthur's lawyer—said he'd get me a key once they've concluded the inventory for the probate court. Have you ever been inside?"

"No, I haven't." Dee frowned. "I know Mr. Cooper used to buy stuff from us, but he'd always hire someone to pick it up and deliver it to his place. He did have amazing taste." She sighed. "I always wanted to see the inside of that house. Arthur was such a lovely man. I'm so sorry you and your boys never got the chance to know him."

"So am I," I replied. "Fried pickles from next door?"

"Perfect."

After lunch, Dee sent me back upstairs to sort and photograph a set of Nancy Drew books so I could put the entire lot up for auction online. They were in almost mint condition, but I was surprised Randall wanted me to put all fifty-six books up with a starting bid of $150. "Should have kept my set," I thought as I took the pictures.

I was making some price tags for other odds and ends Dee had said Randall wanted to put in the showroom when Dee called up that it was time to close.

* * *

I slept late Saturday morning and was sitting at my computer answering emails with my coffee when the ringing of my phone made me jump. I glanced at the caller ID. Therese.

I'd forgotten she was coming for lunch.

"Therese!" I said, accepting the call.

"I'm on the causeway now," she said. "Should be there in a little over half an hour."

"Great! See you soon!"

I dashed to the refrigerator and glanced inside. I'd promised her mac and cheese, but I hadn't remembered to pick up what I needed. But there was sour cream, I had egg noodles in the cabinet and some ground sirloin in the freezer, and yes! There was still a carton of beef bone broth in the cabinet. It might be a little bit heavy for lunch, but Therese did like my Swedish meatballs. I tossed the sirloin into the microwave to thaw out and started dicing an onion.

By the time Therese rang the front doorbell, the noodles were draining through the strainer in my sink and the meatballs and sauce were bubbling on simmer to keep them warm. I hurried to the front door to let her in, getting an enormous hug as she stepped inside.

Therese, the eldest of the Cooper siblings, had kept herself trim with yoga and jogging. She'd had four sons of her own—the last had just graduated from the University of Louisiana at Rouen, where her husband, Bill Mueller, was chair of the English department. Therese herself was vice chancellor of the university, having started working there in the administration office part-time while attending classes and working her way up from there. They had a gorgeous home on the outskirts of Rouen, a small college town on the north shore, and hosted most family get-togethers at their home. It was a great place—enormous, really—on the edge of a forest, and the backyard was landscaped to blend into the woods.

"Do I smell Swedish meatballs?" She gave me another hug.

We made ourselves plates, and I poured glasses of iced tea, which we took out to the back gallery. "How are the boys doing?" she asked.

"Well, I guess." My smile was a little sad. "They called me every day when they first moved up there, but I guess now they're getting used to being on their own and don't call as regularly . . . making friends and things and having a social life."

"Just be glad they don't bring their laundry home every weekend." She snorted as she scooped up a spoonful of noodles, sauce, and meatballs.

"I wouldn't mind, to be honest," I replied.

"How are you keeping yourself busy?"

"Well, remember how I called you and asked about your uncle Arthur?"

She nodded and started chewing again.

"Well, it turns out there was quite an inheritance." I went on to explain about meeting with the lawyers, stopping by Rare Things, meeting Randall, and how I'd started working at the shop.

She dropped her spoon. "Uncle Arthur had that kind of money?"

"Come on, Therese. Spill. Tell me what you know about Uncle Arthur."

She ate another spoonful, sighing with delight. "I barely remember Uncle Arthur," she said. "He didn't live in our neighborhood." The Coopers had all grown up in the working-class Mid-City neighborhood, which had been destroyed in the flood after Katrina. "But he used to come around some when I was a little girl. I know he and Poppo had a falling-out, but Mom and Dad still cared about him, tried to have a relationship with him. He used to always bring me candy—peanut M&M's—and presents, dolls and books and things, and then one day he just stopped coming around. You know how kids are; I didn't really think about it all that much, and then when I was in high school, I saw his picture in the *Times-Picayune* on the society page and I asked Mom. She took the paper away from me and told me never to ask about Uncle Arthur again." She frowned. "And to be honest, I never thought about him again until you asked."

"Do you remember why he was in the paper?"

"It was some charity thing, I think? It was a long time ago. I don't remember." She shook her head. "But he knew Tony? I wonder how that happened."

"I was hoping you could tell me." I shrugged. "Maybe Rafe or Louie . . ."

"I don't think Rafe or Louie even know we had an uncle Arthur."

"But how did Tony find him? Or did he find Tony?"

She waved her hand. "New Orleans has always been a very small town, Val; you know that as well as I do. Maybe they ran into each other somewhere. Tony looked almost just like Poppo did when Poppo was young—you've seen the pictures. Maybe they ran into each other at the grocery store. You said he had a house on Harmony, right? So you probably saw him yourself a lot, at the A&P or the Walgreens or just around in the neighborhood, and just didn't know he was a relative." She finished her meatballs with a delighted sigh. "Tony wouldn't have known *him*, but he would have known Tony was a Cooper since he looked so much like Poppo when he was young." She sat back and smiled at me. "I wish we saw each other more regularly."

"Same." I smiled back at her.

She filled me in on all the latest developments with her own sons, regaled me with animated stories about the academic infighting at the university, and shared some other family gossip about Cooper relatives I didn't know very well. I told her about the antique shop and how much I was enjoying working there.

"I'm so glad." She reached over and touched my hand. "I was worried about you, with the boys gone." She smiled again. "You seem more . . . *you* than you have in a while."

The widow Cooper.

Collette really hadn't been that far off the mark, had she?

"Thanks," I replied, hesitating for just a moment before plunging on. "Can I ask you something else?" When she nodded, I closed my eyes. "Tony told me he'd never been serious about anyone before me, but . . . something Lucas Abbott said the other morning . . . I've tried not thinking about it, but . . . did . . . was there anything about Tony's life before he met me that I should know? A child?"

"A child?" She burst out laughing. "Come on, Val. You knew Tony. If he'd had a child, would he have turned his back on it? Never told you about it?" She exhaled. "Tony did see a lot of women before you came along—I mean, he was a magnet to women—but he was never serious about any of them. We used to tease him about it . . ." Her face darkened a bit. "I know sometime before he met you, he was seeing someone, but he never liked to talk about her. I kind of got the impression she was"—she made a circle next to her temple by rotating her index finger repeatedly—"kind of stalkerish?" She tapped her index finger to her temple. "I think she even came to the fire station once, made a scene."

Yikes. "Do you remember her name?"

"Oh no, it was too long ago. I don't think I ever did know, to tell you the truth." She laughed. "We never knew the names of Tony's women. That's why when he told us about you—and introduced you to us—we knew it was the real deal." She glanced at her watch, and her face blanched. "Oh my, look at the time! I've gotta run!" She got up. "Oh, this lunch was wonderful. But now I don't want to go."

I walked her to the front door, gave her a hug, and promised to come spend some unspecified weekend in the future on the north shore with her and Bill. They were only about thirty miles or so from Baton Rouge, so it would be easy for me to swing by to see the boys from there.

I went back to my computer to see what I could find online about Uncle Arthur.

It took a lot of scrolling, but I finally found his obituary in the *New Orleans Advocate*.

His very brief obituary didn't really say much. He'd died suddenly and was well known as a philanthropist—supporting a lot of local charities, including the opera, the ballet company, the school for the performing arts, and Boys Town.

But the last line of the obituary was the saddest thing: *He had no surviving family. In lieu of flowers, Mr. Cooper requested donations be made to Boys Town of New Orleans.*

That—*no surviving family*—broke my heart.

Chapter Seven

Shortly after Therese left, Lorna came by to work on our costumes. The Boudicca ball was now only a week away. Lorna was more concerned about the costumes than I was. She was trying to impress the krewe members, and I wasn't joining the krewe. But my strong sense of New Orleans pride in costuming was at stake. We take costuming very seriously here.

After debating and rejecting any number of ideas, we finally settled on Supreme Court of the Two Sisters, which we both thought was pretty genius. We'd worn robes before when we'd costumed as Judge Judy and Judge Marilyn from *The People's Court* for Fat Tuesday one year, so all we had to do was find the robes. We also decided on matching bright-pink fright wigs. I sewed lace on the collars to give us that Ruth Bader Ginsburg look and decided on black hose and black ballet flats to complete the look.

"Maybe we need to carry signs?" Lorna said as we looked at ourselves in the mirror late Saturday afternoon, in full costume. "Do you think people will actually get what we are?"

"If the lace collars and the wigs aren't enough, we've failed as costumers," I replied. Lorna remained dubious, so I made us lapel buttons that read SISTER.

I thought it was a cheat, but it wasn't a hill I was prepared to die on.

Stacia stopped by to drop off my will while we were working on the costumes and declined a glass of wine. "I've got a date, so I can't stay long," she said, pulling it out of her purse and handing it to me. "Look it over, and if you have any questions about the language or anything, give me a call." She hugged me at the front door. "And let me know when you want to come by the office to sign it."

"Will do." I dropped the will off on my desk and rejoined Lorna at the kitchen table.

When the boys called early Sunday afternoon for their "minimum one call per week" check-in, it took me a while to get in a word edgewise. Ty and Tay both seemed to be thriving at LSU, which was great, but . . . I kind of wished they missed their mom a bit more. Yes, I know how needy and tragic that sounds. They were making lots of friends and Tay was now interested in a girl in his economics class, but she was pledging a sorority and didn't have enough free time to suit him. Both were considering going through fraternity rush in the spring. I wasn't sure I was comfortable with them going Greek, but that fight could wait for another day. Finally, when they let me speak, I told them about the inheritance from their great-uncle Arthur.

They were both silent. I was FaceTiming them from my computer in the kitchen, so I could see both their faces on the split screen as they stared into their phones. They weren't completely identical—Ty had his father's nose and my gray eyes, while Tay had my nose and Tony's brown eyes—but I could see their father in their faces. They both had Tony's hair, the shape of his face, made the same facial expressions he used to. It caught me off guard sometimes.

Finally, Tay said, "So we have trust funds now?"

"Yes, you do. I don't know how much money there is, or how much your quarterly checks from the interest are going to be, but we don't have to worry about loans or anything for college anymore."

They both whooped, so I quickly added, "But that doesn't mean you can just blow the money. And you can't access the trust until you're twenty-five anyway. I expect you both to be responsible." And then, "Did either of you know about Uncle Arthur, by any chance?"

"It's weird Dad never told us," Ty replied. "I wonder why?"

We talked for a little while longer, and finally they had to go—both had tests Monday morning, or so they said—and I hung up myself just as someone began ringing my front bell. *Who could that be?* I wondered as I walked to the front of the house.

"Collette," I said, opening the front door and plastering a smile on my face. "What a pleasant surprise."

She was wearing a bright-yellow silk dress with a full skirt that billowed out from her hips and was cinched tightly at her small waist. Her reddish-gold hair spilled out from underneath a yellow silk sun hat. "I hadn't heard from you and was in the neighborhood"—she gestured aimlessly over in the direction of Lorna's house—"and so I thought I'd take a chance and stop in to see if you've thought about letting me sell your house?"

I wanted to slam the door in her face. I hadn't liked the way she'd talked to Dee at the store the other day, and *the widow Cooper* was still stuck in my head. But she *was* the membership chair of Boudicca, and I didn't want to do anything that might hinder Lorna's chances of getting invited to join.

I decided to be polite—but I wasn't inviting her in.

"I'm not selling the house," I replied, not opening the door any further. "I actually . . . well, it's the strangest thing. I recently— well, the boys and I—have come into an unexpected inheritance."

I wondered if Randall had told his daughter that Arthur had changed his will and Rare Things wasn't back in his hands after all.

"Isn't that lovely!" She clapped both hands to her face. "Oh, you must be so relieved." She reached out and touched my arm. "I know money can be an issue for a widow who doesn't work."

The widow Cooper.

"And who knew Tony's great-uncle owned an antiques business?" I knew I was being petty but couldn't resist. "Maybe you know it? Rare Things, over on St. Charles?"

"Rare . . . *Things?*" Her smile faltered only a slight bit.

"Uncle Arthur owned seventy-five percent of that business, including the property, and a warehouse out on Airline Highway too!" I gave her my best *Can you believe the luck?* grin.

"Um, wow, that's wonderful!" I could see the gears spinning in her head. "If you change your mind about selling the house—"

"You'll be the first person I call!" I started to close the door but added, "Looking forward to seeing you Saturday night."

She looked confused.

"The Boudicca ball, of course. Thank you so much for the invitations. I can't wait to see your costume!"

I started to close the door again, but she stopped me. "Would you mind terribly if I used your bathroom?" She gave me her winningest smile.

Ugh.

I opened the door. "Do you remember where it is?" I asked.

"Straight through this room here"—she gestured toward the television den—"and under the stairs, right?"

"Good memory."

"I'm a realtor. I always remember the interior of houses."

I sat down in one of the living room chairs and waited for her. I hoped letting her into the house hadn't been a mistake. *She's probably scoping out things to come up with an estimate*, I thought wryly. *Whatever, Collette. I'm not selling the house.*

I got up and started straightening up a bit. Some of the art on the walls wasn't even, and I really needed to dust the big serving plate on the big dining room table we'd filled with the coconuts we'd collected at the Zulu parade over the years. The front windows needed cleaning . . . what was taking her so long? I glanced down at my phone. It had been almost ten minutes! "Collette?" I called, walking through the dining room into the hallway with the stairs.

The bathroom door was open.

"Collette?"

"Oh, I'm sorry, I'm in here!" she called from the kitchen. She smiled sweetly as I walked through the door. She was running water in the sink and had taken a glass down. "I'm just so thirsty. I'll just have this glass of water and be on my way! Thank you!"

I didn't say anything, just stood there watching, and once the glass was emptied, I escorted her back to the front door. "Thank you—"

I shut the door hard in her face, taking several deep, calming breaths. *The nerve, making herself at home in my kitchen!* I didn't care if I did spoil Lorna's chances of joining Boudicca; she'd just have to understand. And she would understand. Lorna would have dragged her out by the hair.

Lorna was all about setting boundaries.

Outside I heard a car door slam and a car pull away from the curb. I opened the door again in time to see Michael opening my front gate. He was sweating, and the torn T-shirt he was wearing had paint spattered all over it, as did his gray sweatpants. "Michael! Is everything okay?"

He sighed. "I don't want to interfere in your life, Val, but I feel like—well, I feel like I'd be a bad person if I didn't say anything."

"About what?"

He took a deep breath. "Look, if you want to sell your house, I'm not going to try to talk you out of it—don't move, please—but if you are . . ." His voice trailed off.

"Sit." I gestured to one of the front gallery wicker chairs, and he plopped down. Scooter stuck his head out the door and looked at us both. With a sniff and a sneeze, he withdrew back inside. "Do you want something to drink?"

"No, and I won't take up much of your time." He scratched at the gray paint on his arm. "I was on my porch working on my Halloween costume when I noticed Collette Monaghan get out of her car and ring your bell." He scowled. "I didn't know you were friends?"

"Friends? Hardly. I know her from the parents' group at L-High. One of her sons was in the same class as the boys." I crossed my legs in the dying sunlight. "And yes, she does want to sell my house. I'm not selling, don't worry, but what she said she could get for it was kind of a shock and made me worried about the new tax assessment."

"You don't have to tell me. John and his mother are worried sick." He glanced back over at the double shotgun next door. "How much did she think she could get for your house?"

"Over a million, Michael." I laughed at the shocked look on his face. "It shocked me too, and that's when I started worrying about the new assessment."

"Over a million." He shook his head. "You know, John's parents only paid seven thousand dollars for our place. Granted, Johnson was president then, but still."

"Right? I can't wrap my mind around being house-rich. Anyway, I ran into her the other day, and she made the offer—to rep the house—but I got away without answering. She said she stopped by because she was in the neighborhood. I told her the answer was no, I'm not interested in selling. Maybe someday, but not now."

"Good, I'm glad to hear it. It would be weird not having you next door." He frowned. "And I'm glad you're not working with her."

"How do you know Collette?"

"I wish I didn't know her at all." He scowled again. "She's . . . not a good person."

"You don't have to tell me twice," I replied. I shook my head. "How do *you* know her?"

"You know John went to Loyola High," Michael replied. "And he's a member of the alumni club."

A bell rang in the back corner of my mind. "Liam Monaghan is president of that, isn't he?"

Michael nodded. "John doesn't give them money or anything, but every once in a great while, he likes to go to the meetings or reunions, you know? John and Liam were classmates—I think John was ahead of him in school by a year or two, I don't remember exactly. But after we got married, John took me to one of the reunions. Collette made a stink about us being there."

"*What*?"

"You know, the whole *Homosexuality is an abomination* and all that nonsense. She even got one of the priests to come over and lecture us about the wages of sin and so forth." He shook his head. "I thought John was going to punch someone—either the priest or her or Liam, I'm not sure which. Anyway, we left and decided we'd never go back. Not long after that—this was before John retired"—John had taught math at Newman High School, over on Jefferson Avenue—"someone called an anonymous complaint about him to the principal . . . being inappropriate with students." Michael's face darkened. "It had to be her. We couldn't prove it, but it took some time for it to get straightened out, and for a while it looked like John might get fired."

"I wouldn't put it past her," I replied.

"Well, I just wanted to warn you. I need to get back to my costume or I'll never get it finished." He stood up and gave me a kiss on the cheek. He rolled his eyes. "One of these days I'm going to learn my lesson about being so damned ambitious with costumes." When he got to the bottom of the steps, he turned back and grinned. "I'm really glad you're not moving."

Monday morning, I went into the shop at the usual time. A lot of auctions had ended over the weekend, so I spent the morning sending invoices and printing out address labels once the payments were made. The days seemed to fly by the more I worked in the store. I'd look up at the clock and realize the morning was past; then I'd do some more things, and before I knew it, the afternoon would be gone. Dee and I were still getting our deep-fried snacks for lunch; I kept promising myself I'd pack something healthy the next morning, but my evil subconscious mind always made me forget.

And when I had some free time—those rare times when I was caught up and needed to wait for more orders or for Dee to realize my hands were idle—I considered it good practice to try to find the provenance of the Lafitte dagger. Imagine if it turned out to be real! I entertained myself with fantasies: *LOCAL AMATEUR IDENTIFIES PRICELESS ARTIFACT!*

But the more I spent poking around online, the more I became certain Randall was right. This dagger with fake rubies in the handle had never graced a scabbard worn by the most famous Louisiana pirate. Someone had, at some point, attached this dagger to the legend to increase its worth to collectors. Dee pointed out more than once that collectors often lied about pieces to make other collectors envious.

I did find a record of another knife whose provenance couldn't be proven but also was claimed to have belonged to Jean Lafitte. It was just a basic, silver-handled knife but had sold at auction for over thirteen thousand dollars.

The first record of this dagger's existence I could find traced back to the Civil War; a rebellious New Orleans matron had placed a claim for some property with the federal government that she reported had been looted from her house by the notorious Benjamin "Spoons" Butler. One of the items on her list was a "steel dagger with a ruby-encrusted hilt that had belonged to Jean Lafitte." I made a note of the New Orleans matron's name—Claudette Volanges—to see if I could do some research on her. Maybe there was a family connection to the pirate?

But all that came up when I searched on *claudette volanges* was the same claim for postwar reparations.

And that was the only reference to this dagger I could find online. I would have to go to one of the historic collections to do any further research, and I wasn't sure I knew how to do that. I made a mental note to ask Lorna for advice.

I was about to go downstairs Thursday afternoon to see if Dee was up for onion rings when I heard someone on the outside stairs.

Dee had told me when showing me around that deliverymen occasionally used the back staircase for furniture or for packages needing to either come or go from the upstairs. The UPS guy, Fernando, came every day around four thirty, so it couldn't be him. Curious, I went to the back door. I stepped out onto the back gallery and glanced down. There was a dark van parked by the foot of the stairs, and a man was carrying what looked like an incredibly heavy oak table up the stairs on his back. Despite the size and bulk of the table, he was making good progress.

"I'll get the door for you," I called down, and stepped back out of the way, holding the door. The house wasn't level—no house in New Orleans was—so unless I held the door or propped it open, it would swing shut. I found the doorstop, a heavy cast-iron rooster, and propped the door open before going back to my desk. About five minutes later, the man carried the table through the door and into the workroom. Once past my desk, he knelt, resting the back legs on the floor, then leaned forward until the front legs also rested on the floor. He crawled out from under the table and smiled at me.

I inhaled sharply.

"Hi. You must be new," he said. There was a trace of what New Orleanians called a parish accent, but not as pronounced as others I'd heard. "I'm Doyle Landry."

"Valerie Cooper."

I knew I was staring but couldn't help myself. Doyle Landry was the best-looking man I'd seen since . . . well, since Tony. He was about five ten, with a thick head of curly bluish-black hair and eyes the deep blue of the Gulf of Mexico. His skin was darkly tanned, and there was a bluish-black shadow of razor stubble on the lower part of his face. He had a strong jaw, with a dimple in the center of his chin beneath slightly thick lips. His nose was a bit crooked, like it had been broken and not set quite right, and the smile was warm, open, and friendly. His teeth were white and straight. He was wearing a red-and-black-checked flannel shirt, open to reveal a white ribbed tank top, and tight black jeans that gripped his muscular thick legs like tights. The sleeves were rolled up above thick muscular forearms covered in curly black hair. The flannel and the T-shirt were stretched over a thick muscular torso, and his waist was ridiculously small. But that could have been an optical illusion because of the massive broad shoulders . . .

He pulled out a folded piece of paper from his right shirt pocket and held it out to me. "Randall around?"

"Randall's out in the field today, but Dee is downstairs," I replied, my mouth impossibly dry. *Stop it*, I chastised myself. *He's way too young. He looks barely older than the twins.* I unfolded the paper. It was an invoice for refinishing the table, and the name

111

of the business was Landry Furniture, 4221 Main Street, Bayou Shadows, Louisiana. Bayou Shadows was a small town out in Redemption Parish, upriver a bit from New Orleans, straddling the river. One of the few bridges across the river was located near there.

Doyle was still smiling that ridiculously handsome smile at me. He patted the table. "I had another delivery in town today, so I thought I'd bring this in to save Randall a trip out to the parish," he went on. "I had a devil of a time matching the original stain of the wood." He shook his head, the blue-black curls bouncing. "Now where are my manners? I guess lugging that table up them stairs wore out my brain or something." He held out his hand, and I placed my much smaller one inside his. It was dry and warm, calloused and strong. "Ms. Cooper, it's nice to meet you, ma'am." He bowed his head, those gorgeous sapphire eyes sparkling. "I mostly build furniture, but I also do restoration work. Randall gives me the stuff he thinks can't be repaired, but I just think he's trying to find a job I can't handle." He was still holding my hand, and I heard Dee coming up the stairs. I pulled my hand away from his, but I could still feel the burn of his skin on mine.

"I see you've met Valerie." Dee walked over to Randall's office. She unlocked the door and came back out with a binder of checks. She took the invoice from me with a raised eyebrow and sat down at the desk I'd been using, then carefully wrote out a check, which she tore out and handed to him.

"Thank you, Miss Dee." He bowed as he folded the check and placed it into his wallet before sliding it into his back pocket. His eyes met mine again, and the smile came back. "And I will see you the next time I stop in, Miss Valerie."

"Valerie is fine," I heard myself saying over the buzzing in my ears.

"Valerie, then." He gave Dee a big hug and kiss on the cheek, and before I knew it, he was clomping down the back steps.

I sank down into my chair. "I—"

Dee smiled at me. "Occupational hazard. I should have warned you about Doyle Landry, but I've found he has to be seen to be believed."

I picked up my bottle of water and took a big drink. "I—wow. I mean . . ."

"Trust me, girl, I know exactly what you're feeling. I remember the first time I saw Doyle." She shook her head, the beads in her braids clicking together. "That boy is far too good-looking for his own good. But he's the sweetest thing. I don't think he's even aware of the effect he has on women."

I took another drink of water. "I think I need something colder."

Dee laughed. "You'd think . . . well, handsome as he is, he has the worst luck with women."

"Really?"

She lowered her voice, even though there was no one else around to hear her. "He was engaged to his childhood sweetheart. They'd been together since puberty. He was raised by a single mom and had four older sisters, so he's . . . well, he was raised right. He'd not a wolf or a womanizer, even though he easily could be. He doesn't notice that women practically throw themselves at his feet; he just thinks they're being nice. Anyway, so he and this girl were engaged. He had opened his business by then, they were in their early twenties, and then three weeks before the wedding she eloped with his best friend."

"Oh my God."

She nodded. "Right? And *he forgave them*. They are still friends! Can you imagine? He says, 'I love them both and want them both to be happy, and if they make each other happy, that's good enough for me.'"

"So he's a unicorn?" I couldn't imagine either going through something like that or forgiving the folks involved. If Tony had run off with one of my best friends . . . well, let's just say the bodies would have never been found and leave it there.

Okay, that was a little extreme. But it would have taken me years to forgive them.

"His mamma raised him right," Dee said with a sniff. "But you'd best get used to him, if you're going to stick around. He's probably the best furniture repairman in the state. There's nothing he can't fix, and he also builds furniture. Prices are good too." She closed her right eye in a wink as she started down the steps. "You should check out his shop sometime."

"I might just have to do that," I muttered to myself.

"Don't forget to get those books packaged," she called back. The set of Nancy Drew mysteries had sold for nearly three hundred dollars. I spent the rest of the afternoon packaging them up, making an address label, and printing out the postage, arranging for them to be picked up the next morning, and put the box in the dumbwaiter to send it down to the first floor.

It was time to go home.

Chapter Eight

The week had passed a little too quickly for my liking. Randall stayed out in Redemption Parish, and on Friday morning the dagger wasn't on Randall's desk where I'd left it. I'd been late that morning—a teeth cleaning that left my gums feeling raw and abused—but when I was finished with invoicing the sales that had ended, I decided to spend some more time researching it. I rushed downstairs to ask Dee about it, only to get her patented eye roll.

"Collette came by this morning and took it." She looked up at the ceiling with a *Why me, Lord?* look. "Said she needed it for her Halloween costume, and Randall okayed it. It's not worth anything, anyway; you were just wasting your time with it."

The Saturday morning of the Boudicca ball dawned gloomy and gray. Rain was forecast for most of the weekend, with a chance of flash flooding later in the day. It was already raining outside when I opened my eyes. I looked at my alarm: 6:03 AM. Maybe, I thought, a day would come when I'd be able to sleep later.

I debated staying in bed—there are few things I love more than cocooning comfortably beneath a pile of warm blankets and listening to the rain—but it was useless. My brain had already started waking up and wouldn't be denied. I lay there maybe another half an hour with my eyes closed hopefully before deciding to give up and get out of bed.

The house was cold, and the wind was rattling the windows as the rain kept coming down. New Orleans houses are built to be cooler for the long, hot, sticky summer season, and cold weather rarely lasts more than a week or two at most. The high ceilings and enormous windows make the house felt like the inside of a refrigerator when the temperature drop. I rarely turn the heat on; I generally just put on more layers because it's cheaper than paying Entergy through my nose.

I pulled on sweats and dug out my slippers from the closet while managing to keep my bare feet off the cold floor and on the rugs. I pulled on a stocking cap over my *Bride of Frankenstein* bed hair and followed my morning routine before heading downstairs for coffee.

I checked the thermostat on my way to the kitchen. It was sixty degrees inside. Not that bad. I take great pride in holding out on the heat until it's fifty or less inside. *God, you really are a sad case*, I thought as I turned on the Keurig and popped two pieces of bread into the toaster. Next door, Lorna's kitchen lights were on. That . . . wasn't normal. Lorna got up at seven every weekday morning to write and take care of the business of being Felicity Deveraux, International Bestselling Romance Novelist. Weekends were a different story. She generally allowed herself the luxury of sleeping in.

I envied the way her body clock could reset so quickly.

So why was she up so early on a Saturday?

She couldn't be worried about the Boudicca ball tonight, could she?

I laughed at the thought and picked up my coffee mug from the machine. I'd never met anyone with the level of self-confidence Lorna had. She never worried about going to parties or public speaking, the kinds of things I dreaded. I wasn't as shy as Lorna claimed I was, but I always felt ill at ease at parties where I didn't know anyone. Maybe it came from being an only child? I'd always been more comfortable in a small group. Lorna could start a conversation with a total stranger and have them eating out of the palm of her hand within minutes.

She says it's the accent, but it isn't.

Be more like Lorna, I told myself. *Be more assertive. You can do it.*

The heated cup felt amazing against my cold hands, and I walked over to the window to get a better look. Maybe she'd just left her lights on by mistake? No; even when she was a bit over-served, Lorna didn't make mistakes that cost her money. She was too frugal to leave lights burning overnight. I walked back over to my desk and picked up my phone from its charger. I decided there wasn't any harm in shooting her a quick text to make sure she was okay. If she was asleep, she wouldn't answer.

Why you up so early?

I gave her a few minutes to reply before heading back to my desk.

I finished my coffee. The response came when the second cup was finished brewing. *I am so behind because of my wretched mother I have to work work work.*

I checked my email and read the news while eating my toast. The weather report was even more grim now than it had been last night: flash-flood warning the rest of the morning and through the afternoon, a further drop in temperature overnight. I might have to break out my fleece-lined tights to wear under my judicial robe tonight. I leaned back in my chair and stared at the screen.

Do some research on Arthur Cooper, I nagged myself as I got up to make another cup of coffee. *You've been too tired to do much of anything when you get home from the office, and what else are you going to do today? The ball starts at eight, and you know you'll be lucky to get Lorna into a Lyft by nine.*

Note to self—make a to-do list.

Maybe that was why I'd felt like I wasn't getting anything done lately, I reasoned as I reached for a small notepad. And if I was going in to the shop every day, I needed to be better organized. I sat for a moment, then wrote *Buy healthy things to take for lunch every day.*

Yes, perfect. A to-do list was just what I needed.

I'd already written off tomorrow. Even if I didn't have a drop of liquor at the Boudicca ball, I knew Lorna wouldn't want to leave if there was music playing she could dance to. She loved dancing. Whenever Captain Jack Farrow was in town, she was always dragging him to dance to live music. I wasn't much of a dancer; I could keep a beat, sure, but I wasn't going to be hired to twerk in any rap music videos anytime soon and had never been an *I'm going to a dance!* person. I hadn't dated much in high school and hadn't attended any of the dances—no homecoming or prom for me. I'd been too focused on playing soccer in the fall and running track in the spring and getting good grades to much care about being asked out. Well, I hadn't gotten that many offers either. I'd never been beautiful or a cheerleader or one of the popular girls at Sacred

Heart. I'd never been a femme fatale, dripping with sex appeal like Lorna, who drew every male eye the moment she walked into a room. I'd never been the kind of girl that stood out, that guys noticed.

When Tony was alive, I always imagined people looking at us and wondering how that mousy plain nobody had landed the gorgeous fireman-calendar model. I'd asked him once if we would have met that Fat Tuesday had I not fallen into his arms.

He looked deep into my eyes in that way he had that made me feel like the only woman in the world and said, "I was about to say hello when you fell."

No wonder I had fallen so deeply in love with him.

I'd never been serious with anyone before Tony, and I'd married him. We'd gone out a lot while we were dating and continued to do so after we were married, but once the twins were on their way, I became more of a homebody. Tony never seemed to mind. We were invited to any number of Mardi Gras balls by friends—Tony had so many friends—but rarely went. I was perfectly happy staying home with my gorgeous husband and my adorable boys. I wasn't big on dressing up in evening gowns and getting my hair and makeup done—which probably had something to do with my not ever being a femme fatale. I always felt like a little girl wearing my mom's makeup and clothes.

Costumes, though, were a different story. I loved wearing costumes.

Had the Boudicca ball called for black tie, Lorna couldn't have dragged me to it with a team of wild horses.

But I'd never pass up a chance to wear a costume.

I made another cup of coffee and sat back down at the computer. I typed *arthur cooper new orleans* into the search bar yet again, staring at the same entries that had come up every other time I'd done this search. The one sad obituary I'd found for him in the local paper was about three down on the list, and I'd already checked the other links. The ones to genealogical research websites were not for the same Arthur Cooper, and as I scrolled through more pages of results for other Arthur Coopers, I despaired of ever finding out anything about my benefactor. Therese had checked with Rafe and Louie and several older cousins, but no one seemed to know anything about the rift or Uncle Arthur. Tony had never mentioned him to any of his siblings, which also was weird.

Why? Why had Tony kept this a secret?

Why had he felt he *needed* to keep it from me?

I kept scrolling as I drank my coffee—and then saw a link I hadn't seen before. It went to an article in the *Avignon Daily Democrat* archive, a wedding announcement from about fifty years or so ago. *Arthur Cooper marries . . .* was all I could see without clicking on the link.

Like I wasn't going to click on that link.

I was immediately confronted by a paywall: *Archives only accessible to subscribers.*

I exhaled, irritated. A month's subscription was only $9.99. Ten bucks wasn't too much to spend to find out some new information about my mysterious benefactor, was it?

And even if it wasn't *my* Arthur Cooper, wasn't it worth ten bucks to find out?

I grabbed my purse and pulled out my wallet. I clicked on the *Subscribe* link, fished my debit card out of my wallet, and added

Cancel subscription to Avignon Daily Democrat online to my to-do list. The form popped up, and I filled it out:

> *Mother's maiden name: Rutledge*
> *Place you met your spouse: Marigny*
> *First pet's name: Skipper*
> *Where you went to high school: Sacred Heart*
> *Username: MotherofTwins* (The boys started calling me that
> while we were watching *Game of Thrones*. I liked it orig-
> inally, but after seeing how the show ended, I wasn't as
> fond of it as I had been.)
> *Password: Ilovetony1!*

I typed in the card number and the code on the back and tapped enter, watching the rainbow wheel spin.

Finally, the article loaded.

It was a wedding announcement written by someone with a flowery style common to lady society columnists of times past. This was certainly my Arthur; he'd been twenty-three at the time of the wedding, sixty years ago, so the age was right. "Arthur Cooper, 23, of New Orleans" had married "Elizabeth 'Bitsy' Saint-Simon, 67, of Avignon." The wedding had been a quiet family affair, with only friends and relatives, and held at Petitfleur, the Saint-Simon family estate in Redemption Parish.

I went back to the search bar and typed in *bitsy saint-simon, redemption parish*, and a long list of links popped up after a few moments.

Both Petitfleur and Saint-Simon rang some bells in my head—I knew those names, but my faulty memory couldn't bring up anything. The rainbow wheel in my head just spun pointlessly. I pulled up the first link, a piece published on the Historic New Orleans Collection website.

My coffee got cold as I went down the internet wormhole.

I got up to make another as I digested what I had read.

Bitsy had been the last scion of Redemption Parish's first family, the Saint-Simons. The Saint-Simons had been among the first French émigrés to Louisiana back in the eighteenth century, winding up owning most of what is now Redemption Parish. Petitfleur hadn't been just the name of the family's plantation and ancestral home but had also been a brand of products they produced— starting with sugar, then expanding into other areas, from canned seafood to frozen shrimp to pickles. The name had come from the first Saint-Simon's first wife, Fleur, who'd died in childbirth the first year they'd taken up residence in the New World.

The Petitfleur brands had been bought out by one of the major corporations in the 1950s for an insane amount of money, according to the article I'd found. Poor Bitsy had gone through a lot of her wealth by marrying several fortune hunters and having to buy her way out of her mésalliances. Arthur had been her fifth husband and had been over forty years younger than her.

Was that the scandal, the cause of the family rift? Because he'd married a rich, much-older woman?

Had he married her for her money?

But according to her obituary, they'd stayed married for fifteen years, devoted to each other. She'd died of pneumonia in her early eighties, peacefully in her bed at Petitfleur.

I went back to the home page for the *Avignon Daily Democrat* and typed *arthur cooper obituary* into the search form.

What came up was more detailed than what had been in the *Advocate*, but that wasn't a high bar to clear.

Arthur Baptiste Cooper, 83, passed away recently in his New Orleans home.

Mr. Cooper, an investor and businessman, was the widower of Elizabeth "Bitsy" Saint-Simon, of the Petitfleur plantation and museum. Shortly after his wife's death, Mr. Cooper donated the estate to the state of Louisiana, providing money for its upkeep and the establishment of a museum on the property. Petitfleur is now one of the more popular tourist destinations in Redemption Parish. Mr. Cooper also heavily invested in many businesses in Redemption Parish, and even after leaving the parish and taking up residence in New Orleans, he never lost his interest in Redemption Parish and its citizens. He donated the money for Bayou Shadows High School to build a new combination gym/auditorium, named for his late wife, ten years ago. He also made any number of private, anonymous donations to various organizations and nonprofits in the parish over the years.

He left behind no surviving family members.

Arthur had never married again.

Had Poppo and the rest of the family really cut him off because he'd married a wealthy much-older woman? That seemed a bit, I don't know, extreme?

That couldn't have been it, could it?

But it had been a different era, and even in our more enlightened times, a forty-year age difference between a rich older woman and her younger husband would raise eyebrows and get tongues wagging. But if Arthur had indeed loved her . . .

I thought back, remembering Poppo. Yes, I could believe that Poppo, with his strong work ethic and insistence that anything unearned wasn't worth having, might have said something so offensive that Arthur had found it unforgivable.

But that didn't make sense either. Sure, Poppo Cooper had a bit of a temper and sometimes said things way out of line that caused a flurry of yelling and screaming and shouting and drama. But he was always sorry once his temper passed and he always apologized later, tried to make it up to the person he offended.

No, that couldn't have been it.

And I'd gotten the impression no one had known Uncle Arthur had married money. That's the kind of family story that gets repeated regularly, feud or no feud: "Remember, Arthur married that old woman for her money. Well, at least he stayed with her until the end."

What did you do, Uncle Arthur?

I'd never been to Petitfleur. I'd taken field trips in high school to some of the other historic plantation homes out on the River Road—San Francisco, Houmas House, Oak Alley—but had never made it to Petitfleur.

When I pulled up Petitfleur's website, I recognized the house. *Everyone* knew that house; how many movies and television shows had been filmed there and in the magnificent gardens? I got dragged into another wormhole, with one website about Petitfleur leading to another about the Saint-Simons, but none of it was helping me solve the family mystery.

But in an interesting surprise, the movie company renting furniture from Rare Things was actually filming at Petitfleur.

I reached into my purse and found the card Doyle had given me. He lived in Bayou Shadows, didn't he? He was connected to Rare Things. Maybe he knew something?

Maybe you just want to call him because he's the first man you've really noticed in a romantic way since Tony.

"He's too young for me," I muttered to myself, making another cup of coffee as I debated calling him.

"You're not asking him for a date," I scolded myself as I dialed. And what if I was? There wasn't a forty-year age difference between us. As I waited for him to answer, I wondered if Arthur had pursued Bitsy, or had it been the other way around?

Sexist. I heard Lorna's voice in my head. *No one questions that kind of age difference when the man's older.*

"Landry Furniture, Bayou Shadows, Doyle Landry speaking."

"Doyle!" Now that he'd answered, I felt foolish for calling in the first place. I looked at the time on my computer screen. At least it was after nine—but still too early for a Saturday morning. "I'm sorry to call you so early. This is Valerie Cooper. We met the other day at Rare Things."

"I was already up, ma'am." The *ma'am* stung a bit but did remind me he was still in his late twenties. "I have a lot of work to get done today, but it can wait. What's on your mind?"

"Well, this is going to sound weird." I hesitated. "But did you know Arthur Cooper?"

"*Cooper.*" He whistled low. "Are you related to Mr. Arthur? I should have picked up on that the other day. My apologies, Ms. Cooper."

"Valerie. Please, Doyle, don't call me Ms. Cooper." I stopped myself from adding, *Mrs. Cooper is my mother-in-law.*

What was wrong with me? This was beyond my usual social awkwardness. "I know this is going to sound odd, Doyle, but Arthur—Mr. Arthur—was my husband's great-uncle."

"What's so odd about that?"

I nervously half laughed. "Oh, Doyle, you don't know the half of it. Are you sure you don't mind listening to me? Don't have something better to do?"

"I don't mind listening, Ms.—Valerie. My mamma always told me that a good man always listens to what a woman wants to tell him, so you go right ahead and tell me whatever it is you want to."

Was he for real? I felt like he was somehow casting a spell over me the more he talked. *How on earth did that fiancée leave him at the altar?* I wondered as I started telling him the story. He was a good listener—no surprise there; he was almost perfect—and with his encouragement, I began speaking more confidently, getting across my confusion and my weird sense of loss at having never met the man who was now making it possible for me to not have to worry about the boys' education. As I talked about the twins, I winced inwardly—*Nothing like letting the handsome young man who might be interested know that you have kids almost his age*—before reassuring myself again that I was *not* interested in him that way and of course he was too young for me and . . . soon I realized, to my horror, I was just babbling away, and of course he was too polite to interrupt or tell me to shut up.

So I wrapped things up, probably about five minutes after anyone besides Doyle would have stopped listening.

"Well, Valerie, that sure is some mystery you find yourself all wrapped up in, isn't it?" He whistled again. "Sure, I knew Mr. Arthur, and he was one of the best men I ever knew."

"Really?"

"Oh, I know there was probably a lot of talk about him when Miss Bitsy married him"—he couldn't be old enough to remember her, could he?—"but everyone in the parish knows that story, how she met him at the opera in New Orleans and how they fell head over heels in love with each other. Because of that age difference I'm sure people, being how they are, just automatically assumed Mr. Arthur married her for her money. But Mr. Arthur never talked about Miss Bitsy without getting this look in his eye, you know? He always sounded sad, too, whenever he talked about her. He still missed her, you know. He never married again. And he used her money to make the parish a better place. He paid for me to go to trade school and loaned me the money to set up my business. He's the one who introduced me to Mr. Randall, too, so I would have a place to sell some of my handmade furniture in the city. I don't think there's anyone here in Redemption Parish Mr. Arthur hasn't helped in some way—if not discreetly, then in some roundabout way, you know? He said he was going to spend the rest of his life using Miss Bitsy's money to help people."

"He . . . he sounds like a wonderful person."

"He really was, Ms. . . . er, Valerie. And he was awful fond of Tony—Tony must have been your husband, right?"

I sat up straight. "You . . . you met Tony?"

"Yes, a couple of times. A very nice man. I mostly saw him at Rare Things, and then one time Mr. Arthur brought him out here to my shop in Bayou Shadows."

What? Aloud I said, "So do you have any idea what reason they might have had to . . . not tell me they knew each other?"

"It doesn't sound like either of them, Valerie." He coughed softly. "I'm sure they had a reason, Valerie. I liked them both, and they struck me as straight shooters who wouldn't . . . I don't know, I don't think they were up to anything you need to worry about."

"Well, no. Can you think of anyone else out there who might have known Tony? Who knew them both?"

He thought for a moment. "I don't rightly know. But I'd imagine the people out at Petitfleur might know something."

Chapter Nine

It was still raining when the gray Honda Civic we'd summoned on Lyft pulled up in front of my house. Lorna and I were waiting on the front porch, sheltering from the wind and the rain.

"I should have gotten a fur-lined robe," Lorna groused as we dashed down the front walk and out the gate. I ran around to the opposite side of the car, avoiding the river in the gutter and the puddles in the pockmarked street. The plastic pumpkin Michael had placed on top of the cone in The Pothole That Won't Die must have blown off in the wind. I opened the door and slid into the seat, shaking out my umbrella before closing it.

The inside of the car felt deliciously warm.

Lorna slammed her door. "Besides, you're being silly," she said, continuing the conversation we'd been having on the porch. She pulled a compact out of her purse and started checking to make sure no hairs had escaped from the tight bun she'd pulled her hair into. "It's the easiest thing in the world to do. You'll be *amazed* at how easy it is to get people to talk about themselves." She snapped the compact closed and tossed it back into the purse. "In fact, good luck getting them to shut up about themselves." She smiled at the driver, who was fiddling with his phone before snapping it back into its holder on the dashboard. "Present company excepted, of course, Omar."

"You ladies going to the Boudicca ball? Municipal Auditorium?" he asked with a slight hint of an indeterminate accent. He smiled into the rearview mirror. "Supreme Court of the Two Sisters? Am I right?"

"Oh, well done, Omar. You just earned yourself a much-bigger tip and a guaranteed five-star rating," Lorna replied grandly. "Although I wish judicial robes allowed you to show a bit more cleavage," she said to me in a lower tone as she adjusted herself a bit in her seat.

"You don't need to worry, Lorna," I replied, glancing out the window as the car pulled away from the curb. "Even in unsexy black robes, there's not a man alive who won't notice your curves."

"Your lips to God's ears," she replied with a big smile. "But seriously, just call the main number at Petitfleur and ask to speak to whomever is in charge." She snapped her fingers and rolled her eyes. "Honestly, the stress of getting Boudicca to ask me to join while on *such* a tight deadline *and* my mother having yet another one of her patented meltdowns *and* Captain Jack being gone so long on this trip . . . anyway, like I said, just tell them you're doing the research for *me* and my next potential book, and if they want to check with me, you can certainly give them my number." She pinched the bridge of her nose between two fingertips. "Never, ever underestimate how willing people are to talk to a novelist—or her research assistant." She sighed. "Everyone wants to be in book."

"Will you put me in one?" Omar asked with a smile into the rearview mirror. "You're Felicity Deveraux, aren't you? My wife loves you."

"Obviously, she has excellent taste!" Lorna sparkled at him. She pulled out her phone and typed into the Notes app. "I think my next heroine just might be tempted away from her true love by a sexy man who drives for Lyft. It'll be out next fall, so look for it!" She dropped her phone back into her purse and turned back to me. "Believe me, Val, once you get them to start talking, you'll be lucky if you can get them to stop."

Traffic was heavy, but it was also the weekend. Halloween was next Sunday, but there were any number of costume balls and parties all over town. And it was a Saturday night in New Orleans. Even Prytania Street, usually a safe go-to when the main streets of the city were clogged with cars, was bumper-to-bumper in the rain.

The Municipal Auditorium was in Armstrong Park, located on the opposite side of Rampart Street from the French Quarter. There is just no easy way to get there from our neighborhood. The days when the Central Business District and the warehouse district were ghost towns after five on weekdays and on the weekend were in the distant past. The two neighborhoods, just on the other side of the raised approach to the Crescent City Connection twin bridges to the west bank, had been targeted by the gentrifiers early on and colonized with a vengeance. Empty lots in the CBD were a thing of the past. Even parking lots, a long mainstay of the neighborhood, had been replaced by tall condo/apartment buildings towering over the streets. The Quarter had always been difficult for traffic, but at least before, getting there had been a lot easier. The CBD now had restaurants and bars open until the wee hours every night, and of course, people *lived* there in those new modern residential buildings that promised luxury living. There were people out jogging or riding their bikes or walking their dogs at all hours. Poydras Street, the main artery running from the river out to I-10, was always packed with cars whenever I had the misfortune to try crossing it.

Omar did an amazing job navigating the city. He didn't make any rookie mistakes on the way to the Quarter and used the back roads and shortcuts only a local would know.

"I've been meaning to tell you," Lorna said, over the drumming of the rain on the roof of the car and the steady beat of the windshield wipers. "You're pretty aglow these days. Going to work at that shop has really worked some magic on you."

"Therese said something similar last weekend," I said, looking out my rain-spattered window. *The widow Cooper*, I heard again in my head, wincing a little bit. "Have I really been that bad?"

"I wouldn't say *bad*." Lorna dismissed my words with a wave of her hand. "Just—well, you've seemed, I don't know, more subdued since Tony died? And lately, well, you seem more like how you were *before* he died, if that makes sense?"

"The widow Cooper," I said without thinking.

"That awful woman." Lorna scowled. "Put that out of your head right now. Now don't take this the wrong way—"

"Oh boy." I braced myself. Lorna wasn't a cruel person, but she could be very blunt when she needed to be, and sometimes her bluntness was bruising.

"I was already established when I met Captain Jack Farrow." She fiddled with the lace collar at her neck, "And so, while I hate to even say it, if anything ever happened to him, yes, it would be horrible, and yes, I would mourn forever, but . . ." She exhaled. "You met and married Tony when you were barely out of high school. You weren't finished growing up, you know? And then you had the twins and the house and that became who you were. Oh, I know you had part-time jobs here and there and did volunteer work, but your entire identity was Mrs. Tony Cooper. When Tony died, you threw yourself into being the best mother on the planet. And when the boys left . . ." She reached over and squeezed my hand. "You've been kind of sleepwalking. But since you started going in to that store to work, you've woken up again, and it's *marvelous* to see."

I felt tears coming up in my eyes, so I looked out the window again.

"Oh dear, did I make you cry?" She looked stricken when I looked back at her. "Honestly, you'd think a writer would be better at communicating. I'm sorry, darling, forget I said anything. I could just rip out my tongue."

I started laughing. "No need for that." I squeezed her hand back. "Thank you, no, I appreciate it. You're a good friend." I took a deep breath. "I've actually felt better these last two weeks, you know?" I winked. "But I'm still not joining this krewe."

Traffic came to a standstill once the Honda crossed Canal Street, which was under about two inches of water.

There was also a flash of light, an eardrum-popping roar of thunder, and the sky opened yet again.

"I will get you as close to the entrance as I can." Omar looked back at us in the rearview mirror.

"That would be lovely." Lorna was using her Queen Mother voice on him. She placed her right hand on my arm. "Speaking of Boudicca, your friend Collette is quite a character, isn't she?"

"I wouldn't call her a friend," I replied, giving her a puzzled look.

"She stopped by again last Sunday, you know, as membership chair, saying she wanted to get to know me a little better, or so she said." Lorna made a little face. "Which . . . well, it was weird. First, she dropped off the invitations in person last week, and then she stopped by again?" She raised her eyebrows. "I mean, yes, she's the membership chair, I get it, but our attendance—our invitations—for tonight were sponsored by Chloe Hartshorne. You remember Chloe, don't you?"

Chloe was tall and gorgeous and had a laugh that could be heard in Baton Rouge. Her family money came from a long-gone chain of department stores, and she was a former Miss Louisiana and second runner-up for Miss United States. "Of course. Who could forget Chloe?"

"Chloe told me that she would be introducing us to the krewe members as well as the membership committee itself." Her face darkened. "Once I'm in, I'll be giving that Collette the back side of my tongue, let me tell you." She snorted. "The widow Cooper indeed."

"She must have stopped by my house after she left yours," I replied. "I promise, I'll be on my best behavior tonight, so I won't spoil your chances of getting a bid, or whatever they call it." *And if that means avoiding Collette, so be it.*

"She stopped by your place?"

I nodded. "It was weird. She said she wanted to check on whether I'd changed my mind about selling the house and asked to use my bathroom. She helped herself to a glass of water in the kitchen. I had to go check on her because she was taking so long." I frowned at the memory.

Come to think of it, I'd never heard the toilet flush.

How odd.

"I'll just avoid her," I went on. "She's the type who would hold being my friend against you."

"I'm not worried about you. If they don't want me because we're friends, well, I don't need to belong to their *little krewe*." Lorna gave the last two words a great deal of exaggeration. "And besides, she knows we're friends from the invitations. Not to sound arrogant, but they need *me* more than I need *them*." She gave me what she called her Mary Queen of Scots on the Scaffold look. "And the day I can't impress a group of women is the day I go to my grave"—I always have admired Lorna's self-confidence—"but I do not trust that Monaghan creature."

I smothered a laugh. Lorna's loyalty was one of the things I loved most about her.

"I've known women like her before—and I don't like them. I do not like women who don't support other women, you know? And that's who she is, mark my words. Always ready to tear other women down, just mean and self-absorbed to the core. And just like when she dropped off the tickets, what she was really interested in was *you*."

"Me?" I stared at her.

Lorna's eyes glittered. "At first, I thought she was, you know, trying to come through me to get to you, you know? Maybe I could convince you to let her sell your house for her. Anyway, I told her you weren't interested in joining and were merely coming with me to provide moral support—"

I laughed. If there were ever anyone who didn't need moral support from anyone, it was Lorna.

"—and she started asking me all sorts of questions about you again." She laughed. "Honestly, don't try to fool *me*." She scoffed. "Amateurs." She waved her hand. "I can always get more information than I give away."

"What did she want to know?" I was genuinely curious. I didn't like the idea of her going around digging for dirt on me, but . . . it was Collette. I wasn't the first person she'd done this to, I was certain.

And it probably had something to do with me inheriting Rare Things.

"Oh, yes, it was a scouting expedition." Lorna's voice was grim. "Why did you didn't tell me she was the daughter of your business partner?" She waved me to silence when I started to answer. "Maybe you did and I missed it—it's a lot of story. You're always saying this is a small town. Well, this is more evidence of it, even if I needed more, which I don't; it's insane how everyone really does know everyone here. Anyway, yes, she wanted to know all about you, Valerie. How you were fixed financially was really the bottom-line question." Lorna made a little gesture with her shoulders, a very Gallic shrug. "I gave her some wine and got her to start talking." She clicked her tongue. "Honestly, there's no better source than a snoop."

"What did she say?"

"Well, they were all—she didn't really specify who *they* actually all were, of course—expecting Arthur to hold up his verbal agreement to leave everything to do with Rare Things to Randall in his will, and so finding out what he actually did with it was quite a shock to the Charpentier/Monaghan clan."

"I . . . you know, I don't know how I feel about that, to be honest."

"*You* had nothing to do with it. You didn't even know Arthur Cooper existed before the lawyers reached out to you, so stop feeling guilty. You didn't cheat her and her children out of their inheritance, if that's where your Victorian little mind is going."

"It was," I replied, a little stung by the use of *Victorian*.

"I got the distinct impression that the Monaghans—especially Collette—have been living quite well beyond their means for a while now, and so the inheritance from Arthur was going to go a long way towards getting them out of the hole they've dug themselves into."

"Dee told me Collette basically bled Randall dry, which was why Arthur had wound up owning so much of Rare Things in the first place."

Lorna waved her hand again. "So she wanted to know if *I* thought you'd honor the original gentlemen's agreement between Arthur and Randall, let him buy you out."

"If they want to buy me out, they can make me an offer." I folded my arms. Sure, it wasn't fair of Arthur to change his mind about the will, but it was also not my fault or the twins'. Why should we cheat ourselves because Arthur changed his will?

Arthur's estate had been his to do with as he pleased, and he had pleased to leave it all to Tony's family.

"So I decided to do a little digging of my own about our friend Collette." Lorna's voice became even more serious. "I called some friends, called in some favors. She's a piece of work, that one. Do you want to hear?"

Nothing good ever comes from listening to or repeating gossip. Even if the gossip is true, inevitably it's spread or repeated by someone who relishes other people's unhappiness. My mother always warned me about gossiping when I was a little girl, admonishing me that "no one wants to be friends with someone who gossips." And almost every fight on every reality show comes down to gossip, doesn't it? *Don't talk about me behind my back?*

On the other hand, it was Collette. She'd always been so passively mean to me at the parents' group at L-High. I'd listened to her *Is it or isn't it?* insults for years with a cheerful smile and turning the other cheek. But now that she was snooping into *my* life? My finances? Maybe even implying that, somehow, I'd coerced Uncle Arthur into changing his will in my favor?

The widow Cooper.

No, I wasn't proud of myself for wanting to hear everything Lorna had to share—and a private eye could only wish to be as good at ferreting out intel on people as she was.

"Don't let me stop you," I replied. We were inching forward along Basin Street now, but the Chevron station at the corner of St. Louis was still at least a block ahead of us. It was obvious we were caught in ball traffic—the line of cars dropping people off at the doors at the Basin entrance or trying to get into the auditorium parking lot.

We had plenty of time.

"As you know, Chloe secured the invitations for us." Lorna buffed her nails on her judicial robe and examined them. "Chloe has been assistant membership chair since Boudicca was founded, but she's also a lieutenant."

I had never belonged to a krewe, but you can't live in New Orleans your entire life without getting an idea of how krewes are structured. Every Mardi Gras krewe has a reason for existing—some philanthropy they support, some kind of public service they offer. Some use the same dedicated charity every year, others rotate among a few, still others have more than one; it depends on the krewe. The krewe's captain is responsible for both the ball and the parade (if they parade). There's also usually an executive board as well as a regular board of lower-level officers. You have to be invited to join: some are incredibly secretive and require tracing your bloodline back to the original French settlers or the first Americans to come to New Orleans; others require no pedigree, only that you pay your dues and buy throws for a seat on one of the floats. Some work privately; others are more public. Some are more democratic; others are autocracies.

Boudicca was a mix of both. Their captain, Tracy LeStrange, had worked for the city—I remembered seeing that in an article on the krewe when they'd first launched several years ago—but had a middle-class background. But many young society women saw both Boudicca and its predecessor, Muses, as cooler and funkier, more irreverent, than Iris or the other older mainline krewes. I couldn't imagine Boudicca having an autocratic krewe structure if Collette was a member; she would never have joined anything where she didn't have a chance at moving up in the krewe hierarchy and taking over at some point. But Tracy had been running the krewe since its initial launch, and I believed she was also president of the krewe—something most krewes didn't permit.

So Chloe was assistant membership chair for the krewe *and* a lieutenant with parade duties. Maybe Boudicca allowed overlap between krewe officers and the parade officers.

"Chloe cannot *stand* Collette, and apparently, most people in the krewe can't either," Lorna went on, not bothering to lower her voice. I glanced at the back of Omar's head, but he was intent on watching the taillights in front of us.

Chloe was a source Woodward and Bernstein would have envied.

Apparently, Collette's money problems were no secret to her sisters of Boudicca—every year her dues were in arrears, but she always managed to get them paid. There was also always a question if she was going to ride every year—again, a question of money—but she always had an excuse about a house going into escrow or car repairs or something.

There were also rumors that Collette's husband was having an affair with a woman who owned a bistro on Chartres Street in the Lower Quarter. There was also a story about Collette getting appointed membership chair because she had "something" on Captain Tracy—that being why she'd never gotten moved to reserve on either parade or krewe, despite always paying late—but Chloe had dismissed that as a rumor.

"Maybe they have an open marriage," Lorna said as Omar drove the car under the porte cochere at the entrance to the auditorium.

Gossip makes time fly, apparently.

"Thank you, Omar," Lorna said airily as she climbed out of the Honda. "I trust you won't rat us out to the police when Collette turns up murdered tonight, right?"

He made a sign like he was locking his lip and throwing away the key as she shut the door and he pulled away.

"You'd better hope she doesn't turn up dead now," I said as we showed our invitation to the volunteer at the door and Lorna gave our names.

The volunteer, dressed as a green-faced Wicked Witch of the West, checked off our names and gave us directions. "Food stations and bars are set up all along the perimeter of the main auditorium," she said, pointing. "And seating inside the auditorium is for the tableau only, and the tables are for the krewe officers and royalty. After the tableau, there will be dancing."

"Marvelous. Thank you, darling." Once again Lorna was playing the Queen Mother. As we walked into the building, she steered me over to one of the bars. She got us both a plastic cup of white wine—which wasn't great, but it wasn't bad—and we stood to one side, watching the costumes as everyone entered.

"I wonder if anyone will notice if we stay out here and just drink during the tableau," Lorna groused. "I mean, I get that it's tradition, but you'd think a modern, new krewe trying to attract younger hipper members wouldn't put on something as musty and tired as a tableau."

I hated to agree with her, but the few times I'd gone to a Mardi Gras ball, the tableau—reenactments of some famous event, or simply people in costume posing like a painting of a famous event—was the least interesting part of the evening and always seemed to last far longer than necessary. I'd hoped that since this wasn't the "official" Boudicca ball—that was after Twelfth Night in January—we'd escape a tableau at this one.

No such luck, apparently.

But more people were coming in the longer we stood there. The costumes were splendid, I had to admit. And the music the deejay was playing while everyone milled around and noshed and drank was quite lively. Maybe—if I didn't get too sleepy—I'd let Lorna drag me out onto the dance floor later after all.

Lorna and I soon moved away from the wall—after our second glass of wine—and circulated. The goal of the evening was to earn her an invitation to join, and we couldn't make that happen skulking in corners sipping wine by herself. I soon realized why she hadn't picked out costumes that would have required masking our faces; this way everyone would remember her later. Our costumes also proved quite popular, and not everyone was as quick as Omar.

Or they were drunker, at any rate.

Chapter Ten

I've never been a fan of big parties like the Boudicca ball.

I've never liked crowds, and I like them even less in confined spaces. I hate going to any mall on the weekends during Christmas season, so I always try to do my shopping during off times when there isn't likely to be a mob of crazed, bargain-hunting shoppers.

The hallway around the main auditorium wasn't nearly as crowded as it was inside, but the strangely colored lights and the fog machines gave it an eerie, claustrophobic feel. All the people manning the food and drink stations were in costumes, their faces hidden behind masks. Most of the people at the ball were, in fact, wearing masks. Lorna and I were two of the rare exceptions. I've never been a big fan of masks—they're uncomfortable, they limit what you can see, and the feathers make my head itch. I also have trouble recognizing people I know when they have a mask on.

So it was possible the ball was filled with people I knew and just didn't recognize.

"Don't be a wallflower," Lorna hissed at me when she brought me another plastic cup of not-great white wine. "Circulate." She strode back into the crowd, starting a conversation with a man in a harlequin costume, which showed off quite a nice pair of muscular legs.

I took a deep breath and sipped my not-great wine. It was a good thing I wasn't interested in being one of the Ladies of Boudicca, I thought as I took a few tentative steps out of my darkened corner, ducking to avoid fake cobwebs hanging from a light fixture. This was why I didn't like coming to parties like this. How much longer would the infernal tableau go on before we got to the dancing part of the evening?

Lorna was, of course, in her element. I don't think I've ever known anyone with the astonishing level of confidence she possesses. Lorna not only believes she is witty and charming; she also believes everyone is better off knowing her. "Meeting people and making friends is a public service I provide free of charge, darling," she'd told me once grandly. "I change people's lives for the better."

I had to admit she wasn't wrong. As I listened to the unintelligible words the man playing tableau narrator was saying inside the auditorium, I watched her flit from the harlequin to a group of people dressed as courtiers from Versailles—given the towering heights of the women's wigs, I would guess the Louis XVI period—and make herself at home in the new group. I watched her charming them completely, knowing she was getting more information from them than one would think possible. (She believes she was Mata Hari in a previous life. I was never sure if she was joking when she said it.)

I joined her but didn't catch the names of her new friends, and then with our arms linked, she moved us effortlessly from one cluster of people to another, making introductions, quickly ascertaining whether or not the cluster would be of use to her either in her quest to become a member or in providing fodder for a future novel. "Life is material," she liked to say breezily, "and you never know where a great idea is going to come from, or when."

But I was getting tired. Mindless small talk was always awkward for me, and when I finally heard the deejay's voice from inside blaring through the loudspeakers—*"ARE YOU ALL READY TO PAR-TAY? EVERYBODY DANCE!"*—followed by the start of a hip-hop song I didn't recognize, I was relieved.

All the doors to the inside were flung open, costumed workers kicking the door stoppers down, and a crowd of costumed revelers came rushing out to hit the drinks and food tables. Others, like us clearly avoiding the Boudicca tableau, pushed the other way through the flowing currents of people to get inside to the dance floor. An excited look on her face, Lorna excused us from the little group of people she'd been entertaining—I hadn't caught their names either, but the entire group was dressed as the Scooby Gang—and grabbed my hand, dragging me through the crowd to the nearest entrance. We'd almost reached the door when she lost her grip on my hand, and she looked back in panic as more people crowded between us.

"I'll catch up!" I shouted, but it was a lie. Well, not completely a lie, but I wanted to sit for a bit before spending the rest of the night dancing. Lorna loved nothing more than to dance, leaving the floor only to use the bathroom or to get a drink. She would have worn me out if I'd known her when we both single.

She'd also talked me into higher heels than I usually wear, refusing to let me wear ballet flats, my go-to. The heels were wreaking havoc with my calves and knees, and I could also feel an ache starting in my hip joints and lower back. I wanted to slip the iron maidens off my crushed feet for a moment and let the poor things breathe. If I didn't, I wasn't going to be able spend much time, if any, on the dance floor.

I didn't want to ruin the party for Lorna either.

She disappeared into the crowd on the dance floor as I picked me way to an abandoned table in the back. It was covered with partially empty cups and paper plates and other debris from the evening, but it was also secluded. Being away from people for a few minutes seemed wonderful.

Once I sat down, I realized my chair was out of the light. With my black robe on, it would be hard for anyone to see me back here. Even better, I thought, sitting back with a relaxing sigh and slipping my aching feet out of the torture devices I'd let Lorna talk me into wearing. I closed my eyes. The first song faded into Billy Idol's "Mony Mony"—always a crowd pleaser—and I closed my eyes, stifling a yawn. I was a lot more tired than I thought, or the wine was hitting me harder than it should—

"I could kill her."

It was a male voice I didn't recognize. I sat up, my eyes wide open, and glanced around in the dim light.

Who'd said that, and who were they talking about?

This side of the auditorium, I realized as I situated myself, was the side that backed up to the parking lot and Armstrong Park beyond that. I also realized that, now that I was taking a better look, I wasn't seated in front of an actual wall. The decorations, all neon colors depicting your typical Halloween imagery—pumpkins, vampires, witches, ghosts, and varied other scary things—were in fact long pieces of fabric hanging from a runner suspended on ropes from the ceiling. Made sense, I figured. It was a multi-use facility, and the city would never have okayed painting the walls or doing anything to them that might require repairs. The runners were there so groups renting the place could hang decorations to go with the theme and make the auditorium look less like an auditorium. There was maybe about a foot or two between the runner and the actual back wall of the auditorium, so whoever I'd heard must be standing almost directly behind me, hidden by the draped cloth.

"Don't say things like that unless you mean it." This was a woman, the voice too low to recognize, but there was absolutely no mistaking the venom in the quiet, hushed voice. "It's about time Collette got what was coming to her."

Collette?

I cleared my throat loudly to let them know someone could hear them. The man responded to the woman, but I didn't quite catch his reply. The woman said clearly, "I need to get back now. Look for me in about an hour, and we'll find her then and make her see reason."

"And if she doesn't?" the man replied.

"We make her sorry."

My heart was pounding, my mouth was dry, and I wasn't sure what I should do. Had I just overheard two people talking about killing Collette? They had to mean Collette Monaghan. How many other Collettes could there be at this party?

I was peering through the gloom in the back of the room, trying to see who they were, when they emerged from behind the fabric. Sure enough, it began moving about three feet from where I was sitting as they groped for the place where the two separate pieces provided a way out. Two figures slipped through the opening. It was too dark to tell who they were or even what their costumes were at first, but as they moved forward, they stepped into a lit area. The man was masked but dressed as—well, I think he was Henry VIII, and I hoped that was padding—and the woman was dressed as a fortune teller. She was also wearing a mask that completely covered her face.

The only thing I could describe was their costumes.

Which, if they meant to harm Collette, wouldn't be much help.

And there were at least three other men dressed as the many-times-married misogynist, and fortune tellers were also clearly popular this Halloween. I could see at least four or five of them on the edges of the dance floor.

I slipped my feet back into my shoes. The two melted into the crowd by the time I got back to where the lighting was better, and I could see Lorna's head popping up and down on the dance floor not that far away. I squeezed my way past any number of masked, costumed dancers, muttering, "Sorry, pardon me, sorry, excuse me, pardon me," as a litany as I stepped and weaved and bobbed around them.

"There you are!" Lorna stopped bouncing as I finally reached her, both of us a little breathless. "I need to take a wine break. Come on, let's go."

She grabbed me by the hand, more firmly this time, and we started making our way to the edge of the dance floor. I breathed a sigh of relief when we reached the outside of the dancing crowd, but the area between the dance floor and the doors to where the refreshment tables were set up was also crowded. Not to be deterred, Lorna got a look on her face that would have quelled Patton in his tracks and started pushing her way through—it's amazing how charming her rude comments sounded when said in her accent—and before long we reached the outer hallway. We wandered away from the longer lines at the tables near the entrance to a drinks table where there was no line. She got us each a glass of white wine, and we moved away to two abandoned chairs by the fire exit and sat down.

She blotted perspiration off her face with a napkin. "Not the best deejay I've ever heard, but he'll do, I suppose. Are you having fun?"

"As much as I expected. What about you?"

She glanced at her watch. It was already after eleven. How had it gotten so late? Then I remembered we hadn't even summoned the Lyft until nine. "I figure I've done all the good I can do already. After twelve we can try to get a Lyft." She fanned herself with an abandoned program. "I have to write tomorrow anyway to make up for the days of work my mother cost me last week." She rolled her eyes.

"I overheard the strangest conversation," I said. "I don't know what I should do about it, if anything?"

"Spill!" she demanded. I filled her in quickly on what I'd overheard. Her eyes widened with every word I spoke.

"*Mon Dieu!*" she gasped when I finished. "That . . . doesn't sound good."

"I thought about trying to find Collette and warn her . . ." I started dubiously. "But then thought I'd probably sound kind of crazy to her, and since I have no idea who they were . . ." I could just imagine the look on Collette's face if I told her that Henry VIII and a fortune teller might want to kill her.

She already didn't like me. But didn't I have a duty to warn her?

Or had they just been talking the way people talk sometimes? People say they could kill someone all the time but don't do anything about it.

"Still." Lorna took a drink of her wine and made a face. "Honestly, why don't they just serve vinegar and be done with it? Although I do see both sides of your point. If someone means to harm Collette—and believe me, she's apparently made a lot of enemies—and you don't say anything, you'll feel guilty because you might have saved her. On the other hand, if they were just blowing off steam and you don't know who they were, nor do you know if she was the Collette they were talking about . . ." She opened her eyes even wider. "Wouldn't that be embarrassing?"

"I've not even seen Collette—or if I did, I didn't know it was her." I took a sip of the wine. The wine we'd had earlier hadn't been bad, but she was right. This was terrible. "I mean, everyone's in costume."

"I have seen her," Lorna replied, grimacing as she finished the wine. "I am switching to gin until we go home. She's dressed as a pirate wench, darling, and she has bigger hair than I've ever seen outside of a drag queen. How can you miss all that hair? Shall we go find her?"

"No, you don't have to come with me," I replied. "Go have fun, have some gin. I'm going to get a bottle of water and go look for her. Meet me here at midnight?"

"Absolutely." We walked back to the bar. I got my water while she ordered a gin and tonic, and I pressed my cheek against hers.

"Midnight, don't forget."

Searching for someone at a costume ball is like looking for a needle in a haystack or trying to meet someone at a Mardi Gras parade. While technically not impossible, it was certainly difficult enough to qualify. I wandered around the inside of the auditorium, asking people seated if they knew Collette and, if so, had they seen her? If not, had they seen a pirate wench with big red hair?

No one I asked knew her or had seen her—which would be a dashing blow to her ego, no doubt—and I was having no luck whatsoever until I went out into the hallway to get another bottle of water. It was past eleven thirty, and I had less than half an hour before I had to meet Lorna.

Well, probably more time than that. Lorna would be late. She probably wouldn't even think to check her watch until well past midnight. Deadlines she understood—appointments not so much.

As I came around a corner near the exit doors on the Rampart Street side, I froze.

Tony?

I shook my head. I'd had Tony on the brain too much lately. The man I mistook for my husband was about the same height and the same build and was wearing a *Flintstones*-style caveman costume. I smiled. He was Bamm-Bamm! There was something about the way he carried himself, the way he stood . . . I watched as he walked around the table set up as a makeshift bar. His sequined and feathered black mask was pushed up on the top of his head as I walked up to the table to get a better look.

His face was sort of shaped like Tony's, but his eyes were green and the jaw was all wrong. He smiled at me. "Can I help you?"

"Can I get a bottle of water?" I asked.

Lorna would have appreciated the way he managed to flex a muscle with every movement—a skill set I approved of, but not as thoroughly as she did—and I slipped a couple of ones into his almost empty tip jar. "Not much chance to make money back here, is there?" I said, taking a sip of the cold water.

He shrugged, and I noticed lines develop in his shoulder and neck muscles as he did. "Well, it's not that bad. I knew Collette was mad at me, and when she stationed me back here—well, it's easier to just accept the punishment than get into another argument with her, you know?" He laughed.

"Collette Monaghan?"

He smiled beneath his mask. "Is there another Collette?"

"Point." I toasted him with my water bottle. "My name's Valerie. What's yours?"

"King."

"As in your majesty?"

"Yes, as in your majesty." He held up his big, calloused hands. "My mom was a big Elvis fan, so she named me King Creole Tolliver."

"That must have been challenging in school."

"A bit. Nice to meet you, Valerie."

"I was actually looking for Collette, which was why I came around back here. You haven't seen her?"

"In that pirate wench costume, she's kind of hard to miss." He shook his head. He pointed with a thumb over his shoulder, like he was hitching a ride. "She just went out those doors with a guy dressed as Kermit the Frog." He shrugged. "I don't think it was her husband. I think he came as Henry VIII?"

Henry VIII?

"Thanks." I put another dollar in his tip jar, thinking as I headed for the exit doors that it was a pity he wasn't in a more traveled section of the auditorium. Lorna would have given him at least twenty dollars for that muscle-flexing trick alone.

"I'll let you back in," he called after me when I reached the door.

"Thanks!" I called back and waved, then stepped out into the cool damp of the evening. It had stopped raining, and the sky was clear. The almost full moon reflected off the wet surfaces—the sidewalk was wet, the trees and bushes glittered with water, and there were puddles in low-lying areas everywhere I looked. The ground alongside the walk was also wet and muddy. "Collette?" I called softly. I could hear cars on Rampart Street and see the neon glow of the Quarter on the other side, beyond the bushes and the trees.

I kept walking forward, toward the street.

I heard a cry from somewhere to my left, then running footsteps.

That can't be a good sign, I thought, as the hair on my arms stood up.

I walked over to the line of live oaks and started walking faster when I heard someone moaning.

Collette was lying on her back, the front of her costume covered in blood. She had been stabbed, the hilt of the knife driven upward beneath her rib cage. Her face was white underneath her makeup, and the lengthy extensions she'd added to her own hair fanned out in the mud around where she was lying.

It was the Lafitte dagger.

There were footprints in the mud and grass beyond her head. I looked in that direction quickly but didn't see anyone. Whoever had stabbed her was long gone—lost in the park, or back around the building to go back inside to the ball.

She was gasping for air, her bloody hands clenching and unclenching at her sides.

"R . . . r . . . r . . ."

She was trying to say something. Her strength was fading, but she wanted to tell me something. She tried to raise one of her hands, but it just fell back limply.

"Just calm down, take it easy, Collette, rest, okay, I'm going to call for help."

She blinked at me and shook her head from side to side only slightly, her face contorted with pain as she once again tried to form words.

"HELP!" I shouted. "I need help!"

I knelt down beside her in the dirt. "Collette, it's going to be okay." I fumbled in my purse and finally put my hands on my phone. I quickly dialed 911. "I need help. Someone's been stabbed on the walkway to the front of the Jackson Theater on Rampart Street. Please hurry! She's lost a lot of blood, and you need to hurry! We're about twenty yards in from the front gate to Armstrong Park!"

The voice kept talking, but I dropped the hand with the phone to my side. Collette's eyes were looking glassier by the second. Her breathing was becoming more labored, more raspy.

She whispered something I couldn't hear.

I leaned closer to her face. "Just rest, Collette. There will be time for talking later, okay?"

I could hear sirens in the distance.

She reached up and grabbed my arm with hers, her grip surprisingly strong.

"*Arrrrrrr . . .*" she managed to get out, so quietly I could barely hear her. "*Arrrr . . .*" Her voice trailed off as the sirens grew steadily louder.

Her breath rattled out of her one last time.

Her eyes went blank, her entire body relaxing, and her head lolled to one side.

Collette Monaghan was dead.

Chapter Eleven

Nothing will break up a party faster than ambulances, fire trucks, and the police.

The time between calling 911 and the arrival of the first cops on the scene seemed to take forever, but it couldn't have been long—there was a police station a block up the street. I was cold and shivering, but I also didn't want to leave poor Collette's body unattended and go back inside. We hadn't been friends, but it just seemed . . . disrespectful. And I had to meet the cops anyway to show them where the body was.

I vaguely remember the first car pulling up in front of the Rampart Street gates, lights flashing. I had my arms wrapped around myself for warmth but started waving with my right hand. I pointed out where the body was—the cops were an older Black man and a younger white woman—and the woman went back to the car to get me a blanket to wrap myself in while she took my information and my statement.

"Darling!"

I had just finished giving Officer Bourgeois my statement when I heard Lorna call my name. She'd texted me when she somehow

managed to hear the sirens over the loud dance music and realized she hadn't seen me in a while, so I was texting her back—*Out
front with a dead body*—just as an ambulance pulled up onto the
sidewalk in front of the gates. I waved at them to get their attention as my phone dinged with her reply: *On my way.* She came
running up in her high heels just as the EMTs started checking
out the—*Collette's*—body. She put an arm around me and started
rubbing the center of my back with her other hand.

"Darling, are you all right?" she whispered, glancing over to
where the Black cop was watching the EMTs check Collette's
vitals—which I could have told them was a waste of time but was
probably procedure.

I shivered. "I just feel so bad for Collette."

Lorna's eyes widened. "Collette *Monaghan*?" she whispered
back to me. Other cops were arriving. A fire truck pulled up
alongside the fence on the side street connecting Rampart to
Basin. A white van with the words NEW ORLEANS CRIME LAB sten-
ciled on the side pulled up onto the sidewalk outside the front
gates.

"Yes," I whispered back to her.

"So you were too late," Lorna replied grimly, gesturing with
her hand to the crime scene. Cops were blocking off the area and
weren't allowing partygoers to exit through the front doors of the
auditorium. There were flashes of light from where Collette's body
lay, crime techs taking pictures of the body and other pieces of
evidence around it.

"Just a little," I replied, watching a new arrival to the scene.
He wasn't wearing a uniform but had on a long jacket over a pair
of slacks and a Saints baseball cap on his head. He talked to the

evidence collectors, and the young woman cop pointed to me. He nodded and headed to where Lorna and I were standing.

"Mrs. Cooper?" he asked, holding out a hand for me to shake. He looked to be somewhere in his mid to late forties. Up close I couldn't really tell how he was built because of the long shapeless coat, but he was taller than he appeared—maybe it was some sort of optical illusion from the fog and the coat? "I'm Detective Guillotte, and this is my investigation now."

Or maybe I was going into shock.

"Yes, and this is my friend Lorna Walmsley," I replied, taking his outstretched hand. It was warm, strong, and calloused.

"Do you mind telling me what happened again?"

Out of patience and tired, I snapped, "I overheard a conversation that sounded like—I don't know, maybe I was overreacting—but it sounded like they were threatening Collette . . ." Yet again I went over the story of discovering the body while he scribbled notes in an old-time little spiral notebook. I could help but think, *Wouldn't it be easier to do that on your phone?*

"And you came out specifically to look for Ms. Monaghan, the victim?" he asked for what had to have been the thirtieth time.

"Yes, because I'd overheard a conversation about her and wanted to warn her," I replied again. "As I have told you and that other officer, I heard a man and a woman talking about her. The woman threatened her, and even if it was nothing, just talk, I thought . . . well, I thought she should know. And no, I still don't know who they were other than the man was dressed as Henry VIII and the woman was wearing a fortune teller costume, and yes, they were also wearing masks, so I couldn't see their faces."

"You took the threat seriously? You didn't think they were just"—he scratched his head with his pen—"talking, the way people do?"

I nodded. "It didn't sound like that to me." I shivered. "When they came out from behind the curtain, I saw their costumes and masks. Sorry I didn't see more."

He smiled slightly at me. "Nothing worse than something like this happening at a costume ball," he observed.

"I really just want to go home," I replied, shivering again. Lorna squeezed me tighter with the arm resting around my shoulders. I put my head against her shoulder. "And sleep for about a week."

"I understand, Ms. Cooper." He scratched the side of his head with his cheap pen. "Just one further question. You told the original officer than you recognized the murder weapon?"

I hear Lorna inhale sharply next to me. I knew exactly what that sigh meant, but I wasn't going to lie to the detective. "That's correct. It's . . . kind of a long story, but we had the dagger at Rare Things, where I . . ." *Work* was technically correct, but I was also an owner. "It's kind of a long story," I said again.

"Take your time."

Lorna's hand tightened on my arm warningly, but I had nothing to hide. I summed the last two weeks up as quickly as I could—the inheritance, how I came to be at Rare Things, how I hadn't known Collette's father was my business partner, and the Lafitte dagger.

"That's a lot of coincidences." He replied with a frown. "You and Ms. Monaghan were friends?"

"Maybe you shouldn't say anything more without a lawyer present," Lorna interrupted primly. Not Mary Poppins, not the

Queen Mother, but what she would certainly call a *posh* tone—like a Dowager Duchess, maybe? Yes, she sounded rather Maggie Smith regal.

"But I don't have anything to hide," I insisted.

"Darling, you *know* they always suspect the person who found the body first," she replied, "and anything you say can be used against you later, you know—if your story changes because you remember something you didn't say *because you were in shock*, for example."

"You watch too much television, miss," the detective replied, a smile forming at the corners of his mouth.

She gave him a look that had withered many a lesser man. "Are you quite finished with her? It's late and it's cold, and we'd like to be on our way."

He handed each of us one of his cards. "Ms. Cooper, we're going to need you to come down to the station to make a formal statement." He gave Lorna a look almost as withering as the one she'd just given him. "You know, once you've recovered from the shock. Anytime tomorrow will be good. Give me a call and we'll schedule it. I wouldn't want to waste any more of your time—it is cold out here." That last sentence was tinged with a bit of sarcasm, and no doubt directed at Lorna.

We walked out of the park and summoned a Lyft to pick us up at the corner in front of the police station on the next block. It was getting colder, and the robes we were wearing just weren't thick enough. I shared the blanket with her while we waited—I'd give it back when I went down to the station to make my statement.

Lorna said, "Well, I don't think I want to join this krewe after all—not that they'll ask me to join now." She laughed and linked her arm through mine. "Since my best friend is a suspect in the murder of their membership chair."

"You don't really think I'm a suspect?" I replied. "They can't seriously think I killed Collette?"

"Well, from what I've heard tonight, it was more likely the other way around, if anything," she went on, peering through the fog with a frown as a car approached, but it wasn't the blue Ford the app promised. "Collette would be at the top of my suspects list if you'd been found stabbed in the park."

"Why would you say that?"

"Darling." She stretched it out into five syllables at least. "You really need to start thinking less of the people you know! People are much more petty, and mean-spirited, than you give them credit for. You really need to read those Miss Marple mysteries I bought you. They'll show you what human nature is really all about."

"Why would Collette want to murder me, of all people?"

"Filthy lucre, for one. You said yourself she was livid when she found out that dear old Uncle Arthur had left you and the boys everything—I am sure she's been counting her chickens long before they hatched when it comes to Rare Things."

"But the store and everything wouldn't revert to Randall if she killed me; it would go to the boys." I remembered the will Stacia had dropped off last weekend and that I hadn't signed it yet.

"People who commit murder aren't rational," she went on grimly. "The Monaghans need money, and they need it badly. Collette wasn't as well beloved as she thought in the Krewe of Boudicca." She made a face. "Or they're all vicious gossips, which makes them more appealing than if they weren't, to be honest. But everyone I talked to tonight had a horror story about Collette, and no one really seemed to like her very much." She started ticking things off on her fingers. "She has three sons in expensive colleges. She has very expensive tastes when it comes to clothes and food and so forth. Neither she nor her husband makes enough money to support the lavish lifestyle she likes to flaunt in everyone's face. I think the husband—what was his name again?"

"Liam. He's on the city council."

"*Liam*." She made a face. "But no, Liam doesn't make nearly enough money to keep Collette the way she wants—wanted—to be kept. And I think there might also be a mistress." Her eyes glinted. "And some thought Collette herself had a guy on the side Liam didn't know about . . . a much *younger* man."

"Sounds like you should be working for the police or the FBI," I commented as a blue Ford materialized out of the fog and pulled over to the curb where we were standing. "It's uncanny what people will tell you. Seriously."

"I told you." She slid across the back seat. "People will tell you everything if you show an interest. Hello—Theo, is it?"

Theo, who couldn't have been more than twenty-five if a day, smiled back at us over the driver's seat. He had thin blond hair, pimples on his forehead and chin, and lovely blue eyes that seemed far too large for his remarkably slim face. "Yes, ma'am, and if you'll both just put on your seat belts, we'll be on our way."

I buckled mine. "Do you really think I should take Stacia with me to the police station?"

"Are you insane? Of course!" she said as Theo pulled away from the curb and began driving downtown. "The last thing you want is to be a suspect in this mess—that's what she's for, darling."

"Were y'all at the Boudicca ball?" Theo asked as he stopped for the red light at Canal. "Everyone's buzzing about that tonight. Someone was really murdered?"

Lorna gave me a warning look as she replied, "Yes. A terrible tragedy for her family."

Her family.

"Should I call Randall?" I whispered to Lorna. "I mean, I'd hate for him to hear about this from the police."

"I would imagine Liam will tell him," she replied as the car started moving again. "And that's probably for the best, you know. He'll probably have a lot of questions, *and* you don't really know him that well, do you? It's awkward enough that you found her body."

"You found the body?" This from Theo, looking back at us in the rearview mirror.

"Eyes on the road!" Lorna commanded, and made a slashing gesture across her throat with her index finger with a warning eye glance at Theo.

She was right—we shouldn't talk about this in front of our Lyft driver.

Once he let us out in front of Lorna's house, she took charge of me and led me inside. Lorna's house wasn't an antebellum double like mine but a Victorian built by someone with Garden District aspirations. There was a tower in one corner—her writing room was the second-floor tower room—and her gallery went around the entire house. When she and Captain Jack Farrow bought the place, they'd torn out most of the walls on the first floor to create an enormous open living space around the gorgeous hanging staircase in the center. Her floors were hardwood and polished till they gleamed. There was a sitting area near the fireplace, the back area behind the staircase was her kitchen with a wet bar and ice machine, and another corner was taken up by a baby grand piano, which, she admitted, she played terribly, though playing relaxed her. Sometimes when I was in my side yard, getting groceries out of the car, I could hear her discordant banging on the keys while she "sang" along; she was also a terrible singer, but she clearly enjoyed playing and singing so much I couldn't really tease her about how bad she was at both.

She went to the wet bar and grabbed an open bottle of Chardonnay from the wine fridge, pouring us each an enormous glass. We sat in the sitting area in the front corner of the house opposite the piano.

"I didn't want to say anything in front of that cop or the driver," she said grimly, "but you need to know that Collette despised you."

The wine was delicious. "What?"

I heard her voice sneering in my head again. *The widow Cooper.*

"The cops are going to hear it from any number of people—I certainly did," she went on, after taking a big gulp of her wine.

"Because of the inheritance?" I waved my hand. "I mean, I suppose I can understand that if it dashed her hopes of her money problems going away—but I thought she was a successful realtor."

Lorna barked out a laugh. "Actually, she wasn't. Yes, she showed a lot of properties, but she never closed on any of them. Her business partner was one of the women I spoke to tonight— what was her name?" She rooted around in her purse and produced a business card almost exactly like Collette's, only the name on it was *Lucy Dyer*. "Lucy and Collette had worked for another realtor, went out on their own a few years ago. Collette was quite successful at the other firm, which was why Lucy was eager to go into business with her. They basically used Lucy's money to set up the business—Collette's contribution was going to be her client list and her savvy as a saleswoman." She clicked her tongue. "But neither of those things ever materialized. Now the business is teetering on the edge of bankruptcy, and Lucy is about to lose everything."

"So Lucy has more of a reason to kill Collette than I do." I shook my head. "I can't believe you got her to tell you all of that."

"Well, she'd been drinking. She was a little the worse for gin." Lorna grinned. "There's also an insurance policy—that was one of the things they took out when they opened the business. Her exact words were 'Collette is worth more to me dead than alive.'"

"Lucy wasn't wearing a Kermit the Frog costume, by any chance, was she?" I took another sip of the wine. "That's the person the cops need to find. The caveman bartender saw her go outside with a man in a Kermit costume."

Lorna wrinkled her nose as she frowned. "You know, I don't remember seeing anyone in a Kermit costume."

"There were well over a thousand people there," I reminded her. "Boudicca itself has three thousand members. If they all brought a plus-one, and add to that everyone who was invited or bought a ticket—we couldn't have seen everyone."

"Did you get the bartender's name?"

I started to shiver a bit. The adrenaline and the shock were finally starting to wear off. Lorna tossed me a blanket. "King.

165

His name was King Creole Tolliver, of all things. You would have liked him, Lorna. He looked amazing in his caveman costume."

"Yes, well." Lorna yawned and stretched. "Anyway, there are lots of suspects, plenty of people who wanted Collette dead—and that's just the ones we know about. I imagine the police will find even more once they start poking around."

"Collette despised me." I'd always suspected Collette hadn't liked me very much, but she didn't treat me differently than any of the other moms at L-High. I'd always figured it was just her manner, how she was with everyone.

All that time she had hated me.

Why?

She had disliked me right from the start.

"That was Lucy again, along with some others," Lorna replied. "Maybe it was nothing, maybe she was just lashing out when she found out what Arthur Cooper's will said, but Lucy said Collette claimed you had influenced him to change his will in your favor—because you'd always been jealous of her."

"Jealous?" I gaped at Lorna. "I barely knew her!"

"My guess is she was projecting; women like her always do," Lorna replied helpfully. "She was jealous of you, so therefore she has—had—to act like the opposite is true."

"Jealous of me?" It didn't make sense. Collette had been a beautiful woman, happily married, a devoted wife and mother and a successful businesswoman—or so I had believed. It would never have crossed my mind that she might be jealous of me. It still didn't make sense, even though I now knew—or had heard gossip—that she wasn't happily married, she owed a lot of money, and her business was on the verge of collapse.

What did she see when she looked at me?

A widow—*the widow Cooper*—who didn't have to work and got to stay home to focus on raising my twin sons. A woman who didn't have a job yet owned a valuable property in the Irish Channel that was increasing in value with every year. She didn't see the woman who worried sometimes whether the money would stretch until the next profit-share check, who bought things in bulk at Costco to save pennies, who'd worried about her low value to prospective employers if she ended up needing to get a job.

And then that same woman had, in Collette's eyes, stolen her inheritance out from under her.

"I guess I never really thought about it."

"Of course you never did," Lorna observed. "No one ever thinks about how *other* people see them, you know. You know who you are, and you know your experience and what is going on in your family, your household. You don't see yourself how others see you." She smiled. "Of course, those of us who do know you are quite aware that you have little to no fashion sense, hate wearing heels, and don't like to wear much makeup. Other people see you as someone who doesn't care what other people think, doesn't dress to impress other people because you don't care what they think. I know you're almost painfully shy and kind of socially awkward, but that's because I know you. Strangers think you're distant and aloof and not interested in making new friends."

"Really?" I stared at her.

"And if you hadn't found Collette's body, you would have never known about any of this," she replied. "But the police are going to be looking at you, and so is everyone else. Everyone is going to have an opinion about Valerie Cooper now—and the whole Uncle Arthur inheritance thing is going to play a definite part in it. You know this whole city runs on gossip." She exhaled. "So get used to it—everyone is now going to be talking about you."

Great, I thought, and held out my glass for a refill.

Chapter Twelve

The ringing of the doorbell dragged me from a fevered half sleep of vague nightmares I couldn't remember.

I opened my eyes blearily. I hadn't made it upstairs to my bed, falling asleep on the couch in the television room instead. I reached for my phone to see what time it was, but it was dead. I swore under my breath as I wiped my eyes and looked at the clock on the wall above the television.

It was past noon.

So much for getting up at six every morning.

I got to my feet groggily and stretched. The couch was comfortable, but not for sleeping. I'd made this mistake before, so I knew better than to sleep there, which meant I'd had too much wine after Lorna walked me home last night. I was still in my costume. A half-empty wineglass still sat on the coffee table, and an empty bottle lay on its side on the floor. I vaguely remembered getting a glass and the bottle before coming in here to relax and clear my head before going to bed. I'd found an old Doris Day comedy on TCM and must have finished the wine while watching. Beyond that I didn't remember anything. I must have dozed off. *Passed out*, my mother's voice said in my head.

Hey, I stumbled over a dead body last night, I scolded the voice. *I could have gone for tequila.*

My neck was stiff from the couch cushions, and my back ached from the awkward position I'd slept in. I cracked my neck and stumbled through the double doors into the front room. The blinds on the front door window were open. I could see gray light outside, became aware of the soft patter of rain on the roof and water gushing out the drain spout on the side of the house. I caught a glimpse of myself in the mirror on the wall next to the front door (Lorna's advice: always have a mirror next to the front door so you can make sure you didn't miss something on your way out of the house) and recoiled from the Gorgon visage I saw staring back at me. My makeup was smeared all over my face, mascara giving me raccoon eyes, my lipstick bleeding off my lips and onto my cheeks. My hair was sticking up in every direction . . .

And of course, the pièce de résistance that pulled the look together: my judicial robe from the Supreme Court of the Two Sisters.

It was too late to pretend not to be home, since he could see me through the door window. He smiled and waved at me.

I left on the chain when I opened the door and said through the crack, "Yes, what?"

"Ms. Cooper, it's Detective Andy Guillotte. You remember we met last night at the Municipal Auditorium? I gave you my card? I said I might have some more questions for you? Is this a bad time?"

"Do I look like this is a good time?" I gestured to my face.

"I can come back later—"

I sighed and closed the door to remove the chain. I opened the door wide and gestured for him to enter. "Come on in, Detective." The front room is more for show than anything else. When the shutters on the big front windows are open, people can see everything from the street, so Tony and I did it up as a showroom—nice furniture, always spotlessly clean, always organized and neat— but we primarily lived in the kitchen and the television room or upstairs, away from prying eyes of pedestrians walking past.

I led the detective to the television room where I'd been sleeping, grabbing the glass and empty bottle. "Make yourself at home. I'm going to run upstairs and do some damage control." I gestured toward my face. "I'm sorry, I fell asleep on the couch after I finally got home last night. I promise I won't be more than five minutes."

"Thanks, Mrs. Cooper. Sorry to bother you."

"I usually don't let people see me looking like this," I said.

He had the decency to smile at this. "I've seen worse, Mrs. Cooper," he said, sitting down on the couch I'd used as a bed.

"I'll be back in a few minutes. Can I get you some coffee or anything?"

He held up a PJ's cup. "Maybe a little later."

I smiled and closed the door behind me. I put the bottle and the glass on the island in the kitchen and took the back staircase up. I scrubbed my face clean, then wet my hair and ran a brush through it to give it a little bit less of that charming rat's nest look I'd apparently been going for while I slept. I stripped off the costume in my bedroom, pulling on a pair of LSU sweatpants and a purple hooded LSU sweatshirt, and slipped my feet into my lined slippers. It was chilly in the house this morning—*afternoon*—and I hurried back downstairs.

Detective Guillotte was where I'd left him, paging through a copy of *Architectural Digest* that had been resting on the glass-topped coffee table. "Come into the kitchen," I said, beckoning him to follow me. "I need coffee. Are you sure you don't want a fresh cup?"

Had I been asked to identify Detective Guillotte without seeing him again, I wouldn't have been able to. Everything from last night had kind of jumbled together in my mind. As I put a pod into my coffeemaker, I took a better look at him as he sat down at my kitchen table.

"I'm good, but thanks."

Last night I hadn't been able to put my finger on what seemed off about him, so I took a good look.

I guess the best way to describe Detective Andy Guillotte was *rumpled*. Everything about him was rumpled. His navy-blue suit didn't quite fit his body, his dark-brown hair (with a hint of gray at the temples and an occasional gray strand scattered through the thickness covering his scalp) looked mussed, and there was a cowlick in the back. He hadn't shaved for at least a day or so, and the scruff on his face was salt-and-pepper. There was a scar right above his right eye. He had the body of someone who had probably been athletic when younger and was just starting to let the muscularity go a little bit. There was more padding around his waist than there had been when he'd bought the beige dress shirt he was wearing—the buttons at the bottom seemed a little more stressed than the higher ones. His yellow-and-blue-striped tie had a stain of some sort about halfway down. His tie clip was gold, with a blue stone—probably glass—set into it. His eyes were wide set, brown, and bloodshot, and he looked a little tired, like he'd been awake for too many consecutive hours. He wasn't unpleasant looking, even though his facial features seemed a little out of proportion—his eyes too big for his nose, his lips too thin for his big, crooked teeth, his cheeks collapsing inward below the bones supporting his eyes—but despite the overall impression of rumpled-ness, he also radiated an energy of competence and efficiency.

I added some half-and-half and dumped a packet of artificial sweetener in my coffee. I took a big drink. It was marvelous and just what I'd needed. It was warming me up on the inside, and the caffeine sent a jolt of energy through me. "You sure you don't want a cup?"

He took a drink from his paper cup. "No, thanks. I've probably had enough coffee to me for a while." He hid a yawn behind his hand.

"Have you been on duty all this time?"

He winked at me. "Crime doesn't take a day off, Mrs. Cooper."

I sat down across from him at the table. "You said you had some more questions for me, Detective?" I asked, as my stomach growled. I'd never had a police officer inside my kitchen before. What was the protocol? If I made myself something to eat, did I need to offer him something? Was he a guest? I glanced out my windows over at Lorna's house, which was still dark. Lorna would know the answer.

I decided to wait to eat something until he was gone—if I could hold out that long.

He pulled out his crumpled little spiral notebook from an inside pocket and uncapped the pen. "Yes, Mrs. Cooper, that's correct. I do have some more questions. I hope that's all right? I can come back if you like—"

"Well, since you're here, might as well get it over with. I'll take your word for it that I don't need a lawyer." I stirred my coffee absently. "Although my lawyer and my friend Lorna would tell me that's a bad idea."

He smiled at me. "Your friend watches too much television," he said, taking another sup of his coffee.

"Isn't it always the person who finds the body? Or the spouse?" I decided that a blueberry muffin would hit the spot, so I got up and retrieved the ones I'd gotten at the grocery store on my way home from work on Friday. I offered him one—he demurred—and I opened the packaging. "Or is that a television thing too?"

"Most murder victims are killed by someone they know—and yes, it's often a spouse," he admitted. "Television shows don't always get everything wrong."

"That lets me off the hook, then?"

"Not entirely." He held up his hands. "I'm not going to lie to you, Mrs. Cooper. You did find the body, and you've admitted that you were looking for Mrs. Monaghan when you found her body. But I don't think you could have stabbed her without getting blood on you, and there wasn't enough time for you to clean any blood off before the first cops arrived on the scene." He tilted his head to one side. "Sure, you could have had something on over your costume that you took off, but I don't think you did."

"I didn't."

"Of course, it's possible that you killed her, but I don't think it's likely. I've been wrong before, but . . ." He smiled again. "No offense, but you don't strike me as the murderous type."

"Thanks, I think?" I finished my coffee. "I'm going to make another cup. You sure I can't tempt you?" I was feeling better. Maybe I wasn't being bright talking to him without my lawyer present, but he didn't seem to seriously consider me a suspect.

He crumpled the PJ's cup. "You know what, sure." He shook his head. "It seems all I live on these days is coffee."

I carried the steaming cups back to the table and got the creamer from the refrigerator. "I seem to recall being told once that anyone, under the proper circumstances, could kill another human being." Lorna had said that, when we were watching another of those true crime documentary shows she'd gotten us both addicted to. "But I didn't have any reason to kill Collette." I shrugged. "I didn't care for her, but I never interacted with her. Like I said, I only knew her from the Cardirents group . . . and until the other week, I hadn't seen her in months."

"So, what exactly was your falling-out with Mrs. Monaghan about?"

I stared at him, confused. "I never had a falling-out with Collette. I told you, I didn't know her very well."

He looked at me for a moment without blinking. "Are you sure about that, Ms. Cooper?"

"Pretty sure. I never had much contact with Collette other than through the parents' group at L-High—Loyola High," I amended. "I didn't even know her before I joined the parents' group."

"So maybe it had something to do with the parents' group?"

"I told you, I never had a falling-out with her." I started picking at the blueberry muffin, slowly peeling the wrapper off its sides. "In fact, I'd completely forgotten about her until I ran into

175

her last week at Big Fisherman Market. I'd gone to get shrimp because I had friends coming over for dinner." I was overexplaining, which was something Lorna had warned me about with the police: *Just answer their questions and don't offer new information unless specifically asked.*

"You're sure of that?"

I took a deep breath. "Detective Guillotte, I swear to you, Collette and I never had a falling-out. I know there were—are—rumors circulating about the two of us." Lorna had touched on this in the Lyft last night, though I hadn't taken her seriously. "But I can assure you, Collette and I barely knew each other. If we hadn't had sons at L-High in the same class, we would have never met."

He scratched his left eyebrow with his pen. "Ms. Cooper, I'm telling you, I spoke with a lot of Mrs. Monaghan's friends, her husband—she absolutely did not like you. You're saying you had no idea how she felt that way about you?"

I shook my head, my heart sinking. "No. No clue at all. I mean, she was unpleasant, but she was the same with everyone, as best I could tell."

He flipped through the pages of his notebook. "In fact, some people were surprised *you* found her. One of her best friends—a woman named Ashley Barrett—said she would have thought it far more likely that Collette would have killed you than the other way around, given how she felt about you."

The coffee began turning to acid inside my stomach. "You . . . really aren't joking about this, are you?"

"I'm not."

I got up from the table and walked over to the French doors to the side gallery. It was more of a patio than a gallery, just a small roofed porch accessible only from the house. I'd turned it into a sitting area, with a love seat and some chairs and tables. I always preferred sitting on the back gallery because it couldn't be seen from the street. I opened the blinds. It was still drizzling and gray outside. Lorna's house was still dark. *I may need to talk to Stacia about this after all*, I thought.

I didn't like the direction this investigation was taking.

I thought back to when Father Ambrose had convinced me to join the parents' group at L-High. I'd just lost Tony, and I needed, well, *something* to help take my mind off my grief. Getting more involved with the boys' school, especially with them starting high school, had seemed like a great idea. Lorna and Stacia had both approved—although Lorna had started hinting at me getting a job or going back to college myself, now that I thought about it—and the parents' group at L-High was very active. I hadn't liked Collette when I met her either, but most of the other moms seemed to share that feeling. I couldn't have been the only mom who'd thought Collette was pushy and passive-aggressive and mean-spirited? That her compliments were backhanded?

The widow Cooper.

But now, as I remembered that first time I'd met her . . . hadn't she been rude to me?

She had been.

She'd made some sort of tasteless joke about "widows and orphans," hadn't she?

I'd smiled and not let her see how her words had stung me— and I'd never liked her after that. But we'd been able to work together. I just thought that was who she was.

"Any animosity between us was entirely on her side," I said stiffly, sitting back down at the table. "I'd never really thought about it before, Detective, but now that I am . . . she always seemed to have something against me from the very first. And before you ask, no, I don't know why. She used to make little jokes, you know, at my expense, all the time. Backhanded compliments, that sort of thing. I just—well, I just thought she wasn't nice. I didn't like her because she wasn't nice to me, but I didn't take it personally. I just thought, you know, she wasn't a nice person, so I never tried to get to know her better."

"You said you'd not seen her since your boys graduated from Loyola High, until you ran into her recently?"

"At the Big Fisherman Market, yes." I thought back to that afternoon. "She approached me when I was at the cash register. She made some small talk about me being missed around L-High and the Cardirents—she still has a son there, I think—and then . . . well, she offered to sell my house."

"She told me she could get over a million dollars for this place—even said she had a potential buyer for the house." I tried to remember what exactly she'd said. "A couple with small kids moving here to work at University Medical, I think is what she said. I didn't really think much of it. I wasn't really interested in selling the house."

Not true, a little voice reminded me. *You were concerned about the new tax assessment after she told you what the house was worth.*

"But that was also the same day I found out about the"—it sounded so weird saying it out loud to a stranger—"*inheritance* from a relative of my late husband's."

And that inheritance had brought me even deeper into Collette's orbit, hadn't it?

He gave me a wry, if rumpled, smile. "And that inheritance was actually something Collette Monaghan was expecting, wasn't it?"

He *had* done his homework. "As it turned out, yes."

"Is it possible that day at the fish market, when she ran into you, maybe she *wanted* to run into you? That she already knew about the terms of Arthur Cooper's will?"

"I don't see how she could have known I'd be at the market," I replied slowly. "And I guess it's possible she knew about the contents of the will—it was the same day I found out, after all. And since Arthur had been in business with her father . . . I suppose Randall could have known that Arthur had changed his will, cutting them out." Now that I was thinking about it, Randall hadn't seemed terribly surprised when I showed up at the store. "If anyone would have wanted me out of the way because of Arthur's will, her father had more motive than she did, I'd think. I was told Arthur had always planned to leave his share of the business to him, and leaving it to me and my twins had to be a shock."

"Mr. Charpentier claims he wasn't surprised by Mr. Cooper's will," Detective Guillotte went on. "That Mr. Cooper had made him aware when he changed the will that he was doing so and did so with Mr. Charpentier's blessing."

"I don't understand." Hadn't Randall told me he'd been surprised by the will?

He smiled at me slightly. "I think you'll have to take that up with Mr. Charpentier, Ms. Cooper." He stood up and held out his hand for me to shake. It was warm, dry, and firm. "Don't forget to come by the station and sign your statement—feel free to bring your lawyer with you." His left eye closed in a lazy wink.

I walked him to the front door, my mind racing.

But as I was closing the front door behind him, he paused one last time and turned back for another question. "You never saw the man in the Kermit costume?"

I shook my head. "No. I heard running footsteps, but it was too dark and foggy for me to see who was running away. I never saw anyone all night in a Kermit costume."

"You're certain?"

"Pretty certain, why?"

He tilted his head to one side. "No one else seems to remember seeing anyone in a Kermit costume."

I held up my hands. "That's what Bamm-Bamm told me—she'd gone outside with a guy in a Kermit costume. I never saw him." I shivered. "But thank you for not considering me a suspect."

He shook his head. "Just between you and me, Mrs. Cooper—"

"Valerie."

"A lot of people didn't like Mrs. Monaghan. According to her business partner, she was embezzling from their company." He smiled at me. "And then there's the husband . . ."

I waited for him to say more, but instead he just gave me a salute and headed down the front steps.

I closed the door.

Kermit had to be the killer.

But who was Kermit?

Chapter Thirteen

I was getting out of the shower upstairs when I heard the alarm system beeping.

My heart racing, I grabbed a towel from the rack and wrapped it around me. I crept to the bathroom door and opened it, listening.

I swore under my breath. I'd left my phone downstairs, but the landline had an extension on my nightstand. I could probably get there and call for help.

I tiptoed back into the bedroom. The master panel for our security system was mounted on the wall by the closet door. Just seconds before the alarm started blaring, I saw the red light flash three times and turn green.

Someone had disarmed it. Which meant—

Still dripping, I stepped out into the hallway and shouted down the front stairs, "BOYS?"

"Hey, Mom!" the twins chorused from somewhere downstairs. "Surprise!"

Relief flooded through me, although I was tempted to wring both their necks. "I just got out of the shower—give me a minute and I'll be right down. There's cookies and muffins in the kitchen." I walked back into my bedroom and toweled off quickly. How had they known I could use a visit? I didn't care; I was just glad they'd come home for however long they could stay. I slipped on a pair of jeans and a sweatshirt and went down the back stairs, my hair still dripping.

The twins aren't identical, but they're pretty close to it. Taylor, older by five minutes, is an inch and a half taller than his brother and slightly stockier—I think Tay outweighs Ty by maybe about ten pounds or so. Their hair is the same color as their father's was, so black it has a blue sheen in the light. But Tay's hair is curly like his father's, while Ty has straight hair like mine. Tay's face is also rounder than Ty's. Ty had slightly visible cheekbones, with a gentle hollow below them. Tay's smile is more crooked, upturning more on the right side than the left. Ty has a chipped front tooth and a chicken pox scar on his nose.

I've regretted naming them Taylor and Tyler almost from the first. What seemed adorable and cute when they were newborns got tired quickly as they grew up.

"What a great surprise! But if you'd given me some warning, I could have had something ready for y'all to eat," I said as I walked into the kitchen. Tay was eating a blueberry muffin at the table, while Ty was rooting around inside the refrigerator. I kissed the top of Ty's head and gave Tay a hug. "Did you bring your laundry with you?"

"Already got a load going," Ty said over his shoulder as he continued searching through the refrigerator. I reached past him and got the lemonade.

I poured myself a glass. "Are you boys hungry? If one of you wants to run over to Breaux Mart, I'll make mac and cheese, but

I don't have everything I need." My mac and cheese was a special favorite of the twins. All that cheese was too fattening to eat regularly, so I only made it as a treat for special occasions—like their birthdays.

"Make a list and I'll go," Tay said, crumpling the muffin wrapper and tossing it into the garbage can. It hit the rim and bounced away. He scowled and got up to pick it up. "But the bigger question here is, how are you doing, Mom? As soon as Aunt Lorna called us, we jumped in the car to come check on you." He was smiling but sounded concerned. "You are okay, right?"

I really was a lucky mom. "Yes, I'm fine. A little shaken up, but . . . what exactly did Lorna tell you?" I glanced over at her house, which was now lit up.

"Oh, just that you found a dead body last night and it was Rodger Monaghan's mom," Ty said, standing up with a plastic container of plain Greek yogurt in one hand and my bowl of raspberries in the other. He dumped the yogurt over the raspberries and sat down at the island. "Seriously, Mom, can't we trust you to be on your own without getting in trouble?" His eyes twinkled.

God, how like his dad Ty looked when he teased me! I felt sudden tears coming up in my eyes.

"Cute." I sat down at the kitchen table with my glass of lemonade and reached over to brush a lock of hair out of Tay's eyes. "Well, I'm sorry Lorna got you to come down here on false pretenses, but seriously—I'm fine. I was a little shaky earlier when that cop came by—"

"Hold up." Ty straddled a chair on the other side of the table, a mockingly stern look on his face. "Now you have cops stopping by the house? Come on, Mom, what gives? First you tell us about this weird inheritance from an uncle we never knew we had, and now Auntie Lorna says you're working and going to costume balls and finding murder victims, and you're telling us there's nothing to worry about?" He folded his arms. "What would you say if either of us told you this story?"

The gate between our yards opened and Lorna popped through, carrying a covered basket. Lorna loved baking and had probably made rolls once she knew the twins were on their way down.

"And you didn't tell us everything about the inheritance, Mom," Tay went on as Lorna rapped her knuckles on the back door before letting herself in. She *had* made fresh rolls. I could smell their doughy goodness the moment she stepped through and shut the door behind her.

"Thank *God* you boys are here," she said dramatically, setting the basket down on the island and uncovering the rolls. "I thought it was about time we had a council of war." She opened the refrigerator and grabbed the butter. "We need to combine forces."

"You didn't tell us the cops came by to see Mom again," Ty replied.

"I didn't know." She turned to me, her eyes open wide. "Care to fill us all in on that one, Val?"

I grabbed a roll, pulled it open, and spread butter on its warm insides. "Well, a lot *has* happened since I last spoke to you boys." Had it only been last weekend?

When the boys first went off to Baton Rouge, I'd spoken to one or both of them every day—usually to answer a question of some sort: "How much dishwasher stuff goes in before you turn it on?" or "It says sixteen to twenty minutes to heat this frozen pizza; which is it?" or "Do you really have to separate the colors from the whites?" There were so many of what I had come to call the *Mom didn't prepare them as well to live on their own as she thought* questions that I began questioning my parenting skills. But better they ask than try to experiment and find out how horribly wrong things could go, right? Maybe I hadn't done such a terrible job . . .

But as the days passed and became weeks, the texts and calls had tapered down to the one call every Sunday in the early evening. It had stung a bit when I realized that, despite how close Baton Rouge was, they weren't going to be coming home every weekend for me to do their laundry for them and cook their favorite meals and spoil them so much that they'd reconsider LSU and transfer to Tulane or UNO and move back home.

A mom can dream, can't she?

I got up and walked over to the refrigerator. What did I need for the mac and cheese? I needed colby and pepper jack cheese. I had eggs and sour cream, and I had noodles . . . looked like all I needed was the different cheeses. I got my purse and handed Ty a ten-dollar bill. "I need eight ounces of colby cheese and eight ounces of pepper jack, and yes, no stories will be told until you get back."

"Come on, Tay," he said, snatching the bill from my hands and a roll with the other, "the sooner we get back, the sooner we'll find out what she's been up to."

A few moments later the entire house shook when they slammed the front door. When they lived at home, I would have chased after them about it, but I was so happy to have them here that the sound of the slamming door was music to my ears.

It didn't hurt that there hadn't been the corresponding crash of something falling off the furniture in the living room afterward.

"You're not mad I called them, are you?" Lorna asked, licking melted butter off her fingers and reaching for another roll with her free hand. "I've been worried since we hung up."

"No," I replied dubiously, getting down my food processor. I cubed the sharp cheddar and started feeding it into the processor, talking louder to be heard over the grinding of the blades. "I mean, I was going to have to tell them anyway, and it's easier to do it in person than over the phone or, God forbid, on text messages. And I do need to give them more details about Arthur's legacy." I shook my head. "I sound like a heroine in one of those old Gothic suspense novels my mom used to love. You know, the ones with the woman with long hair in a gown running away from a spooky house with a lighted window?"

"If you've never read Victoria Holt, don't knock the books." Lorna wagged a finger at me. "The detective stopped by again?"

I nodded as I dumped the shredded cheese into a bowl. The recipe said to just use the cubes and they would melt when mixed with the hot pasta, but in my experience, this left you with massive blobs of semi-melted cheese, like buried treasure hidden inside the noodles, rather than a nice creamy blend of cheese sauce covering all the pasta. I filled my pasta pot with water, added some salt and olive oil, and put it on a burner turned to high. While the water heated, I got an onion down from the hanging copper baskets over the island and started dicing it. "I think I'll wait till the boys are back before I say anything about *that*," I said as I put the onion heels and skins down the garbage disposal, "so I don't have to repeat myself."

"You'll be pleased to know I received an official invitation to become a member of the Krewe of Boudicca this morning—well, this afternoon," Lorna replied, buttering another roll. She took a big bite and moaned in delight. "I'm going to have to do an extra hour of spin class this week to make up for these rolls and your mac and cheese," she said, pouring herself a glass of the lemonade. "The krewe also cut the initiation fee for me by fifty percent." She brushed imaginary dust off her shoulders proudly.

"Clearly, the Krewe of Boudicca needs the celebrity boost of having Felicity Deveraux, international bestselling author of steamy romances involving the rich and famous, as a member," I teased as I started mixing the rest of the ingredients in a bowl. Sour cream, egg, nutmeg, cayenne pepper, black pepper—now what was I forgetting? Dry mustard, half-and-half . . . damn, I didn't have any heavy cream. I quickly texted Tay to ask him to get a container before I started whisking everything.

"Yes, well, I imagine having their membership chair getting murdered during their costume ball wasn't exactly a key recruiting experience for them," Lorna replied, putting back the roll she had just picked up and scowling at it. "I guess they probably wanted to get me to join before I found out anything about the murder happening." She rolled her eyes. "Little did they realize."

"But if Collette was membership chair, who—" The water for the pasta was starting to boil, so I opened the package of elbow macaroni and dumped it into the rolling water, which ceased boiling instantly. "I mean, they had to move pretty fast. She was killed last night and already they have an acting membership chair?"

Lorna pulled out her phone, and her thumbs started flying over it. "Here it is—acting membership chair Gillian LaCroix." She frowned. "I don't think I met her. Did you?"

"No, I didn't. Given the situation, yes, I would imagine their board moved pretty fast." The front door opened and closed—more gently this time—and the boys swarmed into the kitchen. No wonder, I thought, the house seemed so empty without them here. How did they take up so much space?

With a flourish, Ty presented me with the two packages of cheese, a small carton of heavy cream, and change for the ten. I started cubing the cheese after adding the heavy cream to the mixture in the bowl and got down a long glass baking pan from a cabinet.

"So tell us everything, Mom," Ty said as he helped himself to the last roll in the basket. He pointed at me with a sly grin. "From the very beginning, and don't leave anything out."

I raised my eyebrow at him. Quoting my own stern words back to me from the last time he was in trouble? Well played, son. So, while I shredded cheese and drained the pasta, I told them the story of the inheritance again from the very beginning—from the moment Michael told me he'd accepted a delivery for me from a messenger service through the meeting with the lawyer and what I'd found out since starting work at Rare Things, finishing with the call from Doyle that led me to Uncle Arthur's marriage to Bitsy Saint-Simon. "And that is where I assume his money must have come from," I concluded. "He married a much older heiress and inherited her fortune when she died."

"Saint-Simon," Taylor mused. "They used to be a pretty prominent Louisiana family."

"I don't see why marrying a rich old lady would make the family mad at him," Tyler added.

"There's probably more to the story—a lot more," I replied as I stirred the shredded cheese into the hot pasta. As the cheese melted, the pasta became stickier, so I started spreading it into the glass pan with a wooden spoon. Once it was evenly spread out, I poured the heavy cream mixture into the pan. I covered the entire top with what was left of the shredded cheese and slipped it into the oven. I set the timer for fifty minutes—which was when I'd have to take it out to sprinkle bread crumbs over the top to toast for the final ten minutes of cooking time. "I've just started looking into it. My source—Doyle the furniture guy—knew Uncle Arthur but isn't old enough to have known Bitsy Saint-Simon. I'm sure there are some people out in Redemption Parish I can talk to who might know more. You boys are sure you never met Arthur Cooper? I won't be mad—you can tell me."

They shook their head in unison, which made them look more identical than they were.

"That's all for the one mystery," I said. "Now, for the other." I told them how Collette had been trying to get me to let her sell the house, how it turned out she was Randall's daughter, and what I had overheard at the ball last night from Henry VIII and the fortune teller. "I went looking for her. I knew she was dressed as a pirate wench—"

"With gigantic red hair. She must have teased it and used a gallon of hair spray on it," Lorna interrupted.

"—so I didn't think it would be too hard to find her. A bartender saw her go out the Rampart Street doors to the auditorium with a guy wearing a Kermit the Frog costume, and I went out the front doors. It was dark and foggy, and I heard a cry, then running footsteps. I walked over to where I heard the cry, and that's when I saw her. Lying there, with the dagger in her chest. She was trying to talk—she kept saying, '*Arrrrr . . . arrrrr . . .*'" I shuddered. "And then she died, and I called the police, and here we are."

"And what did the detective want today?" Lorna asked.

"Apparently, Collette hated me and made no secret of it," I held up my hands. "It was news to me. I had no idea she ever gave me a second thought, let alone hated me."

Ty and Tay looked at each other for a moment and started laughing.

"I fail to see what's so funny," I said coldly.

Ty wiped at his eyes. "Oh, *Mom*. One of my favorite things about you is how oblivious you are."

"You honestly didn't know Mrs. Monaghan hated you?" Tay blurted out before dissolving into laughter again. "Oh, Mom. That's so you."

"What?"

Lorna was trying very hard not to smile but not succeeding. "It's actually one of your more endearing qualities, you know," she said, shaking from the visible effort of not laughing out loud. "I envy you your single-mindedness sometimes! Really, I do."

"Well, I'm glad you're all amused by my inability to see what's going on around me," I replied grimly. "I mean, I've been racking my brain trying to figure out what I did to make Collette hate me so much. At least Detective Guillotte had the decency to not think it was quite as funny as you all do. I can't believe she hated me so much and everyone knew but me. What did I ever do to her?" I sat down at the table, wishing there was another roll in the basket. "I don't think I even said anything negative behind her back to any of the other moms." I sighed, remembering that first time I'd met her. "But now that I am thinking about it, she did have it in for me from the very start."

"Seriously, Mom, Rodger used to apologize to us *all the time* because his mom was so nasty to you," Tay said. "It must have really driven her crazy that it didn't bother you in the least. I mean . . ."

"It probably made her hate you even more," Ty chimed in. "That you didn't care. Mrs. Monaghan was the kind of person who would hate being ignored more than anything else. There were probably all kinds of people who hated her a lot more than you ever could."

"The detective did say she'd been embezzling from her business partner." He'd also told me to keep that quiet.

Lorna smiled. "Wait—that cop said she was stealing from her business partner? Their realty business?"

I nodded.

"Maybe she figured if she could turn your house around quickly, she could replace the money she'd stolen."

"But why me? Why my house?" I frowned. "And for the life of me, I cannot remember anything awful I could have done or said—even innocently—that would have made her hate me so much." I scratched my head. "I wish I knew what I did, you know?"

"Collette was clearly not the most stable woman." Lorna shook her head. "I could tell the day she dropped off the invitations—"

"Wait, that's right. I forgot Collette dropped off the invitations!" I thought back to the night I'd run into her at the Big Fisherman. "Collette was here, at your place, before she ran into me at the market?"

"Yes. I told you, didn't I?" Lorna made a face.

"What time did she come by?"

"It was around four." Lorna frowned, thinking. "Yes, because I'd planned on writing until five and my mother called . . . I was actually grateful she came to the door, because it gave me an excuse to hang up on Mum. Then after she left, I couldn't get back into the story, so I just answered my emails until it was time to come over."

"I left to walk over to the market around four," I replied.

Collette must have seen me as she was leaving.

She'd followed me to the Big Fisherman.

But why? Getting me to sell the house couldn't have been it.

It didn't make sense.

Why go to that much trouble to work with someone you hated?

Unless . . .

"I wonder if she already knew about Arthur's will," I said slowly. "That day when we 'ran' into each other at Big Fisherman. She followed me there. Listing the house—I think that was just an excuse."

What had she been up to?

Chapter Fourteen

I was taking the mac and cheese out of the oven when my cell phone started ringing. The caller ID showed *Dionne*. I took off my oven mitts, grabbed the phone, and went out onto the side gallery.

Lorna was entertaining the boys with the story of That Time She Did Shots With Keanu Reeves in Florence, so I closed the door before taking the call. "Hey, Dee."

"Valerie, I'm so sorry, but we're going to close the store for a week. There's been a—" She paused for a moment before continuing. "Randall's daughter died last night." She sounded subdued and sad.

I wasn't sure how to answer her, so I just said, "Oh no. Is Randall okay?"

"She was his only child, and he was devoted to her." Her voice broke again, and I could hear her sharp intake of breath. "He's devastated, of course. Have you read the paper this morning?"

"It's probably still on the front porch," I replied, "or in my rose beds. Why?" I knew why and I thought, *I'll probably regret playing dumb with her, but what do I say?*

What was the proper etiquette in this situation?

"She was murdered last night at the Boudicca costume ball."

I took a deep breath. "I know, Dee. I was the one who found her and called the police."

She was silent for a moment. "Well, if that's not irony, I don't know what is." She half laughed, a little hysterically. "Collette— well, I'm not sure I know how to say this to you—"

"It's okay, Dee. Since last night I've become very aware of how much Collette hated me." I sighed. "It's also become very clear to me that I am completely oblivious." I looked back into the kitchen, where Lorna had the boys crying laughing. "Is there anything I can do for Randall? I assume he doesn't want to see me."

"It's not like that. Tell you what, I'll let him grieve for a bit and call him tomorrow, see how he's feeling, and I'll let him know you offered. I know he'll be touched. And I'll let you know about the store opening again."

"What about the auctions?"

But she'd already hung up. Maybe I could get a key from her tomorrow and just stop in, see if invoices needed to be sent. I knew I'd set up some online auctions ending Monday morning.

The boys left for Baton Rouge around nine, with the leftover mac and cheese safely in plasticware I felt confident I would never see again.

Since I didn't have to work the next morning, Lorna and I opened a bottle of wine the moment they'd pulled away from the curb. We watched some classic films from the 1940s, with Lorna keeping up a running commentary about misogyny in old Hollywood that got more and more slurred by the time we finished *The Philadelphia Story* and moved on to *Gaslight*.

I woke up at my usual time the next morning. My head ached a bit—okay, a *lot*—so I rolled over and managed to fall back to sleep. I finally woke up around nine. My head and stomach felt fine, but I'd slept too much. I brushed my teeth and washed my face. By my second cup of coffee, I was awake, alert, and raring to go. The kitchen sinks were cleaned and the dishwasher running as I toasted a bagel and checked Lorna's windows. It was a bright day, with few clouds in the sky, and felt a little warmer than yesterday.

I couldn't stop thinking about Collette hating me, nor wondering what her deal was with my house. She'd purposely run into me at Big Fisherman with her sales pitch. She'd even managed to talk herself into the house for a little while last Sunday.

What had she been up to?

Maybe I could stop by her office with her business card? She *had* approached me about selling the house, after all. I checked the reports about her death online; I wasn't named in any of the stories I could see—everything said "another ball attendee" or some variation. That was a relief. There was no reason I couldn't make a quick stop at her realty office, pretend a bit, see what I could find out. If Detective Guillotte was right, there had been no love lost between her and her business partner . . . and everyone in New Orleans loves to gossip. My mother used to say, "New Orleans is a block long, and everyone is on the same party line."

Yeah, that pump probably wouldn't need much priming.

And her office wasn't far from Whole Foods. I could pop in on my way to get groceries. That was believable, right? I just had to dress the part.

Besides, what else did I have to do?

I had to dig through two purses before I was able to put my hands on Collette's business card, which I slipped into my wallet. I took a shower, styled my hair, and put on what Lorna and I jokingly called *Uptown New Orleans mom with a purpose* attire: a loose-fitting white cotton blouse over black yoga pants and ballet flats. (I didn't own a tennis skirt, which was the other de rigueur outfit choice for species *Uptownus new orleanianus*.) I checked my makeup one last time, adding a bit more powder to my cheeks and another layer of lip gloss.

I decided to drive up Magazine Street, since I wasn't in a hurry and didn't need to be anywhere—which, I thought as I made the left turn onto Magazine at the corner, was kind of a sad statement about my life. What would I be doing if I hadn't inherited Rare Things or found a dying murder victim? Probably rearranging the bookshelves in the television room or cleaning chandeliers—something like that.

You've really let yourself go since the boys left, I thought while I waited for the light at Louisiana Avenue to turn green. *Once you get to the bottom of all this crazy stuff that's been going on lately, you're going to need to figure out what to do with the rest of your life. You're not even forty yet.*

I'd put my life on hold to be a wife and mother. I hadn't minded. I loved Tony, and the twins were a joy most of the time. And one of the curses of buying an old house was there was *always* work to be done on the house. Those first years when the boys were babies, I'd spent a lot of time sanding walls and painting and refinishing floors. I would always be a mom. I'd probably be a grandmother before I was ready for it. I'd just been drifting aimlessly through my life, slightly depressed and feeling sorry for myself, since the boys had left for Baton Rouge.

I felt more alive now than I had in years.

I laughed at myself as I cruised up Magazine Street. I mean, what does that say about me?

I turned right onto Jefferson Avenue and found a place to park about halfway down the street. New Orleans Lifestyles was located on the river side of Magazine, across the street from Lippert, Abbott & Sloane, Uncle Arthur's lawyers. I remembered seeing the realty shop sign two weeks earlier after I met with Lucas Abbott. I locked the car and walked back down to the intersection. I crossed Jefferson and resisted the urge to go into CC's for a cappuccino. Instead, I stood on the corner smelling brewing coffee while I waited for the light to change again.

The Whole Foods was only a block or so farther up Magazine Street. I remembered what a big deal it had been when it first opened. The only location in town prior to this big new store opening was a small place on Esplanade Avenue near the fairgrounds. The beautiful new Whole Foods was in a building that was once a streetcar barn. This part of Magazine used to be a lot seedier—well, the whole city used to be a lot seedier. The new Whole Foods had led to higher property values in the neighborhood. With the higher property values, rents went up, and older businesses closed and were replaced by what the twins would say were "more bougie" shops. There used to be a bank branch on the opposite corner, but it had moved to the corner closer to the river at Tchoupitoulas. Its old building was still empty. New Orleans Lifestyles was next door, right before the buildings with actual storefronts lined up on the rest of the block. There was a PJ's coffee shop closer to the far corner. The next building housed a boutique for women's clothes—probably far too expensive for me to even look inside, let alone buy anything—but the business space sharing the building was also for lease.

I crossed the street and stood in front of New Orleans Lifestyles.

The building looked like a double shotgun that didn't have columns, using brackets instead to support the gallery roof. The front gallery had a black iron table and matching chairs in the center between the two doors on opposite sides. The far door was clearly not the one to be used, as there was an OPEN sign on the door in front of me. The building was painted white, the shutters a pale blue.

I opened the gate and walked up the steps. When I opened the door, a bell rang as I stepped inside. The front room had been arranged as a reception area; the matching front room on the other side had been converted into an office. There was a woman seated at a desk in that office space talking on the phone; she had spun her chair around so her back was to the door. The reception room had been painted a beautiful shade of azure, with melon highlights. Framed photographs of houses lined the walls behind the reception desk, which was really a computer table in an L shape with a filing cabinet back in the far rear corner. A bouquet of roses rested in a green glass vase on a side table beside an overstuffed black vinyl chair.

I was debating whether to knock on the open door to let the woman know someone was here when another woman appeared from the hallway just beyond the reception area. "Oh, I'm sorry, were you waiting long?" she chirped in a professional, *How may I help you?* voice.

"I just walked in," I replied with a friendly but businesslike smile.

She smoothed her black silk skirt as she folded herself into the chair behind her desk. "Are you looking for a new home?"

"Well—" I pretended to fish around in my purse before pulling out Collette's card. "I was wondering if Ms. Monaghan was in?"

On a closer inspection, the woman was younger than I had originally thought. She couldn't have been older than thirty at the most. She had short blonde hair cut pixie-style, big brown eyes, and a heart-shaped face. She was wearing a black blouse over that black skirt, wedding and engagement rings bedecked her left hand, and a nice watch draped her slim wrist. She was slender— maybe too slender; another couple on her would help her look a bit healthier. Her eyes were bloodshot, and they opened even wider as I handed her Collette's card. Her face flooded with color underneath her makeup, and her eyes filled with tears. "Oh," she said in a very small voice.

"I ran into Collette a couple of weeks ago, and she asked me if I was interested in selling my house," I said in a rush, not giving her a chance to interrupt. "And while I wasn't at the time—it hadn't crossed my mind, to be honest—but with my kids off at school, it is an awful lot of house, like she said, and the more I've thought about it, the more I'm thinking it's probably not a bad idea, and it doesn't hurt to explore the option, and I . . . I'm sorry, are you all right?"

She nodded, reaching for a tissue and daubing at her eyes carefully so she didn't smear her eyeliner. "I'm sorry," she gulped, reaching for her CC's coffee cup and taking a drink. "I don't really know how to tell you this—"

"Collette is dead." The woman in the office had finished her call and was leaning against the doorframe. She made a slight shrugging movement. "No way to sugarcoat it, I'm afraid. Collette was murdered on Saturday night, so it's still a little fresh for us all." She didn't sound or look upset. "Jill, why don't you go get yourself another cup of coffee? And why don't you come into my office and have a seat?" She stepped aside and made a grand welcoming gesture to invite me into her office. "I'm Lucy Dyer."

The bell rang again as Jill left to get her coffee, and I walked into Lucy's office. Her desk, like the reception desk, was clear glass. A laptop was open in the center, and a phone with multiple lines was sitting on the two-drawer black filing cabinet next to the desk. A photograph of Lucy with what must have been her husband and three teenagers (two boys and a girl) sat next to the phone. The walls were yellow and covered in framed posters of New Orleans scenes—Café Du Monde with the obligatory tourists with powdered sugar all over them, the Crescent City Connection bridge at sunrise with the sky exploding into multiple colors beyond, Bourbon Street crowded with costumed revelers on Fat Tuesday.

I offered her my hand. "Valerie Cooper."

Her facial expression didn't change, but I noticed a nerve twitching in her left cheek as she shook my hand. "You said Collette approached you about selling your house?"

"Well, yes." I smiled at her. "I actually know—*knew* her. We were in the parents' group at L-High. My twins were in the same class as her son Rodger."

"And if I'm not mistaken, you already knew she was dead before you came by." Her voice was emotionless and cold. "What precisely are you up to, Ms. Cooper?"

I was clearly terrible at this sort of thing, which meant I had no future as an international spy. She'd seen right through me instantly. "She really did offer to sell my house." I replied. "I ran into her at Big Fisherman on Magazine, and she told me she could get me over a million for it."

She smiled, shaking her head. "You actually found the body." She nodded. "You and Lorna Walmsley were Supreme Court of the Two Sisters. I thought you looked familiar. We met at the ball on Saturday, actually."

"Oh, you're in Boudicca also?"

She nodded. "Valerie Cooper." She gave me an appraising look, up and down. "Funny, you don't look like the devil incarnate."

"Thanks, I think." I shook my head. "All of this is . . . well, it's so weird, Lucy. I hadn't thought about Collette since the boys graduated, and then she bumps into me at Big Fisherman and offers to sell my house for me. Then she gets murdered, and the police are telling me that all her friends are saying that she hated me, and God help me, I don't know why." I held up my hands. "So I figured maybe I could come by here, where she worked, and see if anyone here knew what was going on."

Lucy looked at me for a long moment before getting up and shutting the door. "Saying Collette hated you is like saying water is wet, Valerie—is it okay to call you Valerie?" I nodded. "Collette . . . had issues." She sighed. "Trust me, Valerie, Collette and I have—*had*—known? Knew? Each other for a long time. We used to work together at Melancon Realty." Melancon Realty was the society realtor in New Orleans, with an office at the corner of Prytania and Washington, across the street from Lafayette Cemetery No. 1. "We got tired of making money for them instead of for us, so we decided to go into business together, open this place up. The market was booming here, and we figured with a little spit and elbow grease, there was no reason why we couldn't become one of the top realtors in Orleans Parish." She tapped her fingers on the desktop. "Collette talked a big game, though—she was great at talking, she was great at organizing, but she wasn't so great about not offending clients." She exhaled. "I was trying to save up the money, or find an investor, so I could buy her out." She made a face. "Turns out she'd been helping herself to business funds and covering it up—borrowing against her commissions and then keeping her commissions. Never let someone else do the books for you, Valerie." She smiled sadly. "Always check the accounts, always check the books." She harrumphed. "Let me guess, you own a big old antebellum raised double in the Irish Channel?"

"How did you know that?"

"We have a client who is looking for that same kind of house. It's exactly what they want." Her face turned grim. "We don't have any listings for those. Collette said she'd find one. And if she thought she could get a million for your place . . ." She pulled out her phone and opened the calculator function. "Yes, that commission would pay off what she owed the business."

"I'd heard you were going to file embezzlement charges with the police."

"I told her that, but I didn't really mean it." Lucy ran a hand through her hair. "I just thought it would wake her up, snap her out of it, you know? And I was seriously angry at her. I thought we were friends, not just business partners. She broke down in front of me, claimed she was being blackmailed."

"Blackmailed?" I stared at her. "About what?"

"I don't know. I'm not sure I even believed her." She shook her head. "She said she was good for the money—she was due an inheritance—and once the will was probated . . ."

She was due an inheritance.

Of course.

Collette had believed Arthur was leaving the business, and everything to do with the business, to Randall.

Arthur's lawyers' office was just across the street from New Orleans Lifestyles.

She'd known Arthur had left his estate to me that day she "accidentally" bumped into me.

And I also just happened to own a house that was exactly what her clients were looking for.

"Do you have any idea why she hated me so much?" I asked, as thoughts raced through my head. I couldn't quite grasp any of them. There was something there—something about my house and the inheritance, something Collette had been up to—but my mind just couldn't get there. "I mean, other than the parents' group, I didn't know her at all."

Lucy laughed. "Really? Oh my God . . . the irony." She leaned forward, resting her elbows on her desktop. "Collette and Liam have been married for almost thirty years now, but they've had some rough patches over the years."

"And?"

"After her third child, Collette threw him out. She was done. She was getting a divorce and that was all there was to it. She'd fallen in love with another man, you see, and she was done with

Liam. She was madly in love with this new guy and was ready to throw everything away for him." She raised her eyebrows. "None of this is ringing any bells for you?"

"No."

"But before she could file for divorce, the new love of her life met someone else and fell in love with her. He broke things off with Collette—who was *wrecked*. I don't know that she ever got over him, you know. She left town for a while—'to get her head together' was what she said—left Liam in charge of the kids and just went away. When she came back, she wound up taking Liam back. They had another two kids, but I don't think they ever were like they were before, you know? She felt like she'd settled." She shrugged. "I always got the impression she went back to him, well, because of his political career."

"But what does any of this have to do with me?" I asked, even though I was beginning to get a sinking feeling that I already knew the answer.

"The man she fell in love with was a fireman named Tony Cooper." Lucy's eyes glinted. "And I believe he left her for you."

Chapter Fifteen

I couldn't have heard that right.

Lucy kept talking—I could see her mouth moving, some gesturing with her hands, the occasional change of expression on her face or the tilt of her head—but I wasn't hearing anything she was saying. I could hear myself responding to things she was saying, making the appropriate noises and short sentences in response, but I wasn't there with her.

Collette and my Tony?

My Tony and *Collette*?

Collette Monaghan?

Bits and pieces of what she was saying somehow managed to get through the roaring in my ears and the fog in my head. My vision grew cloudy on the edges, everything around and behind Lucy getting blurry. It was like having tunnel vision. Lucy was three-dimensional and vivid to my eyes. My peripheral vision was gone, replaced by gray darkness. I could hear my heart beating loudly, the breath going in and out of my lungs. I kept seeing Tony's face, smiling at me, his beautifully white even teeth, the thickness of his lips, his voice telling me over and over again how much he loved me. I was getting flashes of memory from our life together, playing like one of those movie falling-in-love montage things with some beautiful Celine Dion ballad playing in the background.

My Tony and Collette Monaghan?

In the distant reaches of my memory, I could hear Therese throwing her arms around me and whispering in my ear, after Tony and I had told her the news about our engagement and I'd shown her my modest diamond ring, "I don't have words for how happy I am. Before you, Tony had the most *terrible* taste in women. We were all terrified he'd want to marry his last girlfriend." She'd shuddered delicately. "Thank God that's all over."

His last girlfriend.

Therese had said she was . . . stalkerish, hadn't she?

I could see Collette being like that.

I'd never cared about Tony's past girlfriends, never wanted to know because they didn't matter. He married *me*, after all.

Therese had been talking about Collette Monaghan.

I felt a little sick.

I heard Lorna saying grimly, *The wife is always the last to know.*

I licked my lips and focused on what Lucy was saying. She was telling me that Collette and her oldest son Raymond weren't on speaking terms because she didn't approve of the young woman he'd married, but Lucy didn't know precisely what Collette's objection to her daughter-in-law was. "All she would say was she was wrong for him. They got married by a justice of the peace, and Collette would just get that look on her face whenever the subject came up."

"How sad," I heard myself replying.

Lucy also believed Collette was currently having an affair—she didn't know with whom—but Collette had been getting calls from a man, had been acting very secretive over the last few months. That was a pattern for Collette. Lucy had, over the years, begun to recognize the signs when Collette was having an affair.

She had an affair with my husband, I thought.

"I used to think of her as one of my closest friends." Lucy frowned. "I mean, we went into business together. I told her everything. But she . . . was always hiding things from me. And then over the last couple of years something was going on with her. I mean, I knew the signs, and I heard enough of her side of calls to know she'd found some other man she thought would give her a better life than poor Liam could. Poor Liam—she always believed she'd married down and was always looking for something better."

"But they had five kids together." The shock was beginning to dissipate some, but I was still kind of numb.

"Collette believed in being fruitful and multiplying." Lucy smirked. "But she was a good mother, I'll give her that." She made a face. "About a year ago, something happened that was strange—and I've wondered, you know, if it was related to her stealing." She drummed her fingers on her desktop. "Listen to me, speaking ill of the dead! These last few months we've been avoiding each other . . . but about a year ago, this young man stopped by here looking for her." Lucy looked off into the distance. "He was too young for her, but he was good-looking, which made me wonder. Anyway, she wasn't here, and he wouldn't leave a message or anything for her. When I asked her about it later, she was even more secretive than she'd ever been before, so it set off a red flag for me, you know? And it was right around that time she started 'borrowing' from the accounts." She glanced at her watch. "Oh, look at the time. You must think I'm a terrible gossip, but I have some things I have to get to right now."

"Well, thank you for your time," I replied, standing up.

She pressed a business card into my hand "in case you change your mind about selling the house" and walked me to her door, closing it behind me.

"Are you okay?" Jill asked from the front desk, putting down her cell phone. "You look like you've seen a ghost or something."

"Something." I smiled at her. "Thank you for your help." I went out the front door. But before I got to the gate, Jill called, "Ms. Cooper? Can you wait a moment?"

My hand on the gate latch, I turned back as she hurried down the front steps and along the brick walkway. Her face was turning red. "I just wanted . . ." She blushed even darker. "I just wanted to tell you—that guy Collette was having an affair with?"

"You heard us talking?"

"The walls are thin." She shrugged and smiled, her skin returning to its normal hue. "Lucy wasn't being completely honest with you—although I don't know why."

"You weren't a fan of Collette?"

She rolled her eyes. "No one was. She treated me like—well, I felt like Andy in *The Devil Wears Prada*." She hugged herself. "I'm studying for my realtor's license. Lucy encourages me, pushes me to work harder and make something of myself, you know? Collette acted like receptionist was the best I could ever hope for. She had a way of saying things . . ." Her face twisted.

"Oh, yes, well aware." I smiled back at her. *The widow Cooper.* "I was on the receiving end of her scorn more than once. It's funny, I knew Collette didn't like me, but had no idea how deep it went with her. I've been finding out how much she hated me, which . . ." I swallowed. "I thought it might be easier to deal with if I knew why. But now that I do know . . . maybe I was better off not knowing?"

She gave me a curious look.

"I guess"—it sounded so *Days of Our Lives* I was reluctant to say it out loud—"she thought I stole my husband from her?"

"If you married the guy Collette considered the great love of her life—she still talked about him, you know." Jill shivered. "I guess there's not any harm in talking about it now, since she's, you know, gone, but yeah, she used to talk about your husband every now and then. Usually when she was complaining about Liam and what a letdown marrying him had turned out to be."

"Do you know who she was having an affair with before she died?" I suspected Lucy had known the name, but discretion won out in the end. *And was he at the Boudicca Ball dressed as Kermit the Frog?*

She took a deep breath and whispered, "No, but I was here the day that young man stopped by to see Collette. I don't think she was having an affair with him; Lucy's wrong about that." She blushed deeply. "She was giving him money, I think."

"He was a gigolo?"

Jill shook her head. "No, but I . . . he called for her once on the office line. I recognized his voice. When I transferred it to her, before I hung up, I heard him say, 'Did you get the money?'"

"Do you know his name?"

"He told me, when I asked who was calling, to tell her it was Hunter."

Hunter. That wasn't any help.

Jill looked back over her shoulder nervously. "And the reason she wasn't on speaking terms with her son?" She fiddled with her phone for a moment, then held up the screen so I could see it.

It was a wedding photo. The groom was redheaded and handsome, with golden skin and golden highlights flashing in his hair when the light caught it. The bride was beautiful, with a stunning smile and a curvy figure.

She was also Black.

"Collette refused to speak to him after he got engaged," Jill whispered. "They've been married for two years now and have a child Collette had never seen. Can you imagine being that awful? Cut off your child, never see your first grandchild, because you didn't want your son to marry a Black woman?" She shoved her phone back into her pocket and stalked back up the stairs.

I crossed the street. CC's was practically empty, so I got a cappuccino to go and walked back to where my car was parked.

A lot of people, it seemed, had a motive for wanting Collette dead.

Including me, apparently.

But did I? Sure, she hated me, but it had been one-sided. Detective Guillotte wouldn't be able to find anyone who could say I'd ever said anything negative about her. And if she'd been in love with Tony . . .

The thought made me shudder as I put the keys in the car ignition. Tony and *Collette*?

When we'd started dating after meeting on Fat Tuesday, he'd told me he was "sort of" seeing someone else but wanted to break it off. About a month or so after we'd started seeing each other, he told me he'd dropped the other woman and wanted us to be exclusive—which I already was.

Tony had been four years older than me. He'd disappointed his parents by not wanting to go to college, and after a summer working for the family construction company, he'd applied to become a firefighter and gone through the training. (He'd also managed to get into two New Orleans firemen calendars before we met.) Tony was by far the best-looking man I'd ever seen (although Doyle the furniture guy gave him a run for his money). Those first few years we were together, we'd occasionally run into someone he'd dated before he met me. I wasn't jealous of them; I'd won the prize, after all, and never really cared. He'd told me I was the first woman he'd been serious about, and that was all that mattered.

But *Collette Monaghan*?

Seriously, dude?

To be fair, Collette had been pretty—and twenty years ago, when they would have dated, she'd probably been a knockout.

But . . . it still didn't sit well with me.

Because she'd been married? Or because the thought of them together turned my stomach?

She wanted to leave her husband for Tony.

No wonder she'd hated me. But it also sounded like Tony hadn't been her first affair, nor her last.

I'd always believed Collette was happily married. I mean, five kids usually serves as a sign of a strong, happy marriage, and there was all Collette's talk about husbands and wives and women's duties to their husbands . . . did the other Cardirent moms know about any of this? There was definitely a public persona Collette liked to put on for other people—perfect wife, hardworking supermom holding down a successful full-time job while raising five sons and being active in the parents' group and . . .

And all that time she'd hated me for marrying Tony while she smiled in my face. Maybe those little digs I'd thought were passive-aggressive had been meant to be aggressive-aggressive.

And I'd never risen to the bait.

For twenty years, she'd hated me. What an incredible waste of time and energy! I remembered that time she'd come to the house, when I'd had all the moms over for whatever reason it was I'd had them over. Tony was still alive then, but he'd been on duty at the fire station—that was when he worked at the station in the Quarter—and I remembered how she'd turned up her nose at the house. I'd even joked to myself that if I waited long enough, I'd probably catch her running a finger along surfaces to see if there was dust (spoiler: there would have been) with one eyebrow raised critically. It didn't bother me—that sort of thing never did—and having been to Collette's house before . . .

A condolence call.

I could pay the Monaghans a condolence call.

But I didn't have a casserole.

I whipped out my cell phone and called Reginelli's, ordering two pizzas for pickup. *Girl, what are you doing?* I asked myself as I pulled away from the curb. Casseroles might not be the thing anymore. When Tony died—

When Tony died.

It hit me again, the way it sometimes did, and as the tears suddenly filled my eyes, I pulled over to the side of the road again. I gripped the steering wheel and did the breathing exercises the therapist I'd seen all those years ago had taught me to use whenever I felt overwhelmed.

It never gets easier. No matter what they tell you, it doesn't. What becomes easier is living with it. What remains hard is how it sneaks up on you when you aren't expecting it and sucker punches you: grief saying, *Remember me? You thought it was over, didn't you?*

But those times do become further and further apart—and it really wasn't a surprise that the grief would come back again now. Collette was dead, murdered; I'd found the body. Even just thinking about selling the house we'd renovated together and made our own brought up all those memories I'd thought were buried deep inside my psyche or wouldn't be painful when they resurfaced.

I swung by Reginelli's and picked up the two large pizzas before heading over to the Monaghan place on upper Nashville Street in Uptown. The Monaghan place was a big old house between St. Charles and Freret Streets, near Lusher High School. I remembered wondering the first time I went there for a Cardirents meeting why Collette hadn't just sent her sons to Lusher—they were within walking distance. L-High was a good school, one of the better Catholic boys' schools in the city, but Lusher was also a respected school with a strong academic reputation; you were even more likely to get into an Ivy had you gone to Lusher rather than L-High. Maybe it was a Catholic school/society thing? I had no idea. I knew that Sacred Heart, where I'd gone, was considered a debutante school, but not to the degree that McGehee in the Garden District and Ursuline on Claiborne were. It was that sort of thing that seemed silly to me but still mattered to people in New Orleans. Our boys had gone to L-High because that was where the Cooper boys had always gone; Therese had also gone to Sacred Heart.

Where'd you go to high school? was a New Orleans thing—it was a way of finding out where someone ranked on the social scale without coming out and saying so. I wasn't Catholic, and neither were the Coopers, but we'd all gone to Catholic schools because most people in New Orleans thought our public schools were terrible.

I couldn't park anywhere close to the Monaghan place, which I'd expected. I didn't know much about the family. I'd gotten the impression Collette had been an only child, but there could have been more siblings. The Monaghans were clearly Irish Catholic, so there could be more of them than you'd find in a polygamous Mormon family. Just because I didn't much like Collette didn't mean she didn't have an extended group of close friends.

I wondered where Collette went to high school as I walked the two blocks from where I'd parked to her home, carrying two hot cardboard boxes of pizza.

The house itself was what you'd expect from Collette: two-story brick, with upper and lower galleries boasting round white columns to give it that graceful antebellum air so many architects and homeowners tried to recapture. I was a little surprised she didn't have a lawn jockey statue holding a lantern in her front yard, though. The two-car driveway was filled. The house's lawn was immaculately kept, and I mentally girded my loins as I walked up the sidewalk to the front of the house.

I'd just stepped on the lowest step to the porch when the front door—with a black wreath prominently centered on it—opened and a young woman dressed entirely in black stepped out on the porch. Shakily she lit a cigarette, waving away the smoke when she saw me. "Sorry," she called over to me, "I probably shouldn't smoke near the house anyway."

She could have been any age between eighteen and thirty-five, really; she had amazing skin. Her hair was cut in a bob that was shorter in the back and parted in the center; the last inch or so of each strand had been dyed a lovely shade of electric blue. Her brown eyes were large and round, her face was perfectly made up, and the black turtleneck clung to her curves, as did the knee-length black wool skirt. A strand of pearls around her neck was the only relief from all the black she was wearing.

"Oh, it's okay," I said, nodding at the pizza boxes. "I'm Valerie Cooper. I'd offer to shake hands—"

"God, it's so nice to see pizza," she said, taking another drag off the cigarette. "If I see another casserole dish, I can't be held responsible." She rolled her eyes. "I mean, I get it—they're easy to warm up so don't require much effort—but don't people think that maybe the family might *want* to cook, to take their minds off their grief?"

"I'd never thought about that," I said, putting the pizzas down on a small iron table on the front porch. "And you are?"

"God, I am so sorry. You must think I'm the rudest woman." She dropped the cigarette to the porch and ground it out under her shoe. She turned her head away from me and blew the smoke out the side of her mouth, then turn back and held out her own hand. "Giselle Monaghan, wife of Rodney, the oldest Monaghan boy."

I shook her hand, giving her a better look. She was quite beautiful. "I didn't know her that well," I admitted, once she let go of my hand. "My sons were in the same class with Rodger at L-High, and I knew her from the parents' group." I gestured with my head at the pizzas. "And I work with her father."

"Wait—you said *Cooper*, didn't you?"

I nodded. "Yes."

She laughed. "Wow. You might be the one person on the planet the old witch hated more than me."

"I'd heard . . ." I hesitated. "I honestly didn't know until she was . . . until she died how she felt about me." I shook my head. "It's a little disconcerting, to be honest. And since I work with her father now—"

She smirked at me. "You mean her father works for *you*, don't you?"

"I—"

"It's okay; don't worry about it. I may not have been welcome in her house—and she may not have ever wanted to meet her grandchild, at least the one I gave birth to—but I know all about the ins and outs of Rare Things. Over the last week or so, poor Raymond has had to listen to chapter and verse on how you screwed her family over."

"Screwed her over?"

"She thought you screwed her out of her inheritance somehow." She rolled her eyes. "Like Arthur Cooper couldn't see what a monster she was on his own? You might as well come on in and meet the family, pay your respects, so you can get out of here." She reached for the doorknob. "I can't thank you enough for not bringing another casserole."

She opened the door, and I followed her inside.

Chapter Sixteen

Collette's house was decorated in a style that Lorna would describe, with an upturned nose, as *nouveau riche tacky*. I could see her lip curl as she contemptuously snapped out the words.

The front door opened into a center hallway. There was a heavy dark mahogany coat-tree immediately to my left and a ceramic planter for umbrellas on the other side from it. The floor was checkerboard tiled, alternating black and white squares giving the hallway the illusion of being much bigger than it was. I could hear the low murmur of voices coming from the rooms on either side of the hallway. A hanging stair toward the rear was covered in what looked to be a durable but inexpensive indoor-outdoor carpet, worn thinner and balder in the center. At the far end was a door leading out to the backyard.

It was hot inside, the air thick and heavy and cloying. Incense was burning somewhere, and the smell hung in the air like a thick cloud of odor.

And if I wasn't mistaken, someone was smoking marijuana somewhere in the house. I'd know that smell anywhere—John and Michael next door indulged from time to time.

Once inside I felt my throat close in panic. What in the actual hell was I doing here? This was a mistake. The woman had hated me and made no secret of it, since apparently everyone she knew was aware. Her husband and children and friends—everyone here— would also know about her antipathy toward me. But, I rationalized, as Giselle closed the front door behind me, *I* hadn't known.

And that was going to be my fallback position, if it came to that.

Given the circumstances, they'd probably all have the decency to wait until I left before whispering about me showing up.

"Come on, you probably want to talk to the widower," Giselle whispered, leading me into a dining room. The big table in the center of the room was covered with casseroles and other dishes, the tinfoil peeled back to make the food easily accessible. There was a silver bucket of ice on a sideboard beside several bottles of drinks, both soft and hard. I was slipping the pizzas into an open spot on the table, managing not to have to move anything aside, when someone grabbed my arm.

"What are you doing here, Valerie?"

"I came to pay my respects and drop off some food for the family, Randall," I replied in a matching whisper. "I figured no one would think about kids preferring pizza to casseroles, you know, so I stopped by Reginelli's. How are you doing? I'm so sorry for your loss."

His tight grip on my arm lessened, and his eyes softened. "Oh, Valerie, that was . . . that was actually very thoughtful." He visibly sagged. "Forgive me, I'm not myself." He brought a hand up to cover his eyes for a moment before wiping at them and giving me a weak smile.

"You lost a child, Randall, and no matter what age the child, it's still a horrible loss." I shivered a bit. "Parents aren't supposed to outlive their children. I can't imagine how you must be feeling." Even the suggestion of anything happening to either of the boys was all it took to bring tears to my eyes. Poor Randall. I softly rubbed between his shoulder blades.

"She wasn't the easiest child," he replied softly, his voice shaking. "Bu there were times when I wanted to throttle her. She could be infuriating . . . and you . . . you didn't know how she felt about you, did you?"

I nodded. "I . . . I've only just been finding out." I dry swallowed. "I just found out about her and . . . and Tony."

"Oh." His voice was small. "I . . . I didn't know how to tell you, Valerie. I hope you can forgive me?"

"Is there somewhere we can sit and talk?"

He nodded. Taking me by the hand, he led me through a doorway into another room—a masculine den, with a television, couch and chairs, the walls covered in everything New Orleans Saints imaginable—and through yet another door into a smaller room. The room was spare. There was a small desk with a closed laptop sitting on it and a file cabinet shoved into one corner, and the walls were covered in framed photographs, presumably family. Centered squarely in the wall above the desk was what had to be Collette's wedding picture, in an ornate gilt frame. Collette was beautiful, I thought as I looked at her happy, smiling face, her shining red hair cascading down beneath the veil and past her shoulders. She was gazing up into Liam's eyes. Liam was still young and handsome in that first flush of masculine virility that slowly fades. Lorna would say, *Age hit him in the face with a two-by-four, didn't it?*

I sat down in a wooden rocking chair while Randall took the desk chair, spinning it around so he was facing me. Heartbreak was written all over his face, his eyes reddened and swollen. My heart broke again for him, so I reached over and clasped his hands with mine. "Seriously, Randall, if there's anything I can do—"

"She hated you." Randall smiled sadly, the rest of his face barely moving. "All those years . . . I thought you were a monster, you know. All the things Collette told me about you and all the things she claimed you did to her . . . she was my daughter, so, of course I believed her. And then of course when we found out the contents of Arthur's will . . ." He shook his head gently. "She lost it, absolutely lost it. She was *certain* you had convinced Arthur to change his will, just to screw her over again. Her words, not mine."

"Is that what you thought too?"

"The difference between Collette and me was I actually knew Arthur. He was my friend. To her he was a checkbook." He clutched my hands with his. "Oh, I know a lot of people would say she saw me the same way, and sometimes I've wondered myself."

"I'm sure she loved you, Randall."

He laughed brokenly. "I guess I need to believe that, so thank you."

"I never knew about . . . her and Tony."

He gave me a sad look. "I thought that might be the case." He cleared his throat. "Arthur was many things—and in some ways he was a terrible person—but no one could influence Arthur into doing anything. Arthur made up his own mind. And after Tony—I'm sorry, I know it's been years, but I also know it can still hurt after all this time—died, she was so out of control . . ."

"I never knew, Randall. Tony never told me." I replied. "We never talked about our exes, you know? Now I kind of wish we had."

"My dear, I realized that when I first met you." His eyes softened. "It was so clear to me you had no idea who I was, or who my daughter was, hadn't known Arthur . . . that's so typical of Arthur, you know."

"Do you know why . . . do you know why he was estranged from the family? Was it because he married Bitsy Saint-Simon?"

He laughed. "That I don't know. I met him shortly after Bitsy died, actually—that was how we met. He tried to make a go of things at Petitfleur, but despite the age difference, he truly loved her, and he just couldn't stay there without her. So when he decided to get rid of Petitfleur, I handled the estate sale for him. I'd handled some pieces for the Legendre family at Chambord"— Chambord was one of the more famous plantation houses out in Redemption Parish—"so when he wanted to sell everything at Petitfleur, the Legendres recommended me to him. He wasn't the type to talk a lot about his personal life, Valerie. You could ask, but he wouldn't answer. He used to say he liked to live in the present, not in the past, and he knew Bitsy wanted him to leave Petitfleur to the state as a museum, so he figured since he couldn't bear to live there without her, he'd just go ahead and do it and move back into the city."

"He really loved her?"

"He really loved her, despite the age difference. I know a lot of people thought he was a gold digger or a fortune hunter, but I know how much he loved that woman. After the estate sale, he never spoke about Bitsy to me again. A piece of him went into the grave with her, and she was the last Saint-Simon. Her death,

I remember him saying when we were starting to get everything together for the estate sale, was the end of an era, and so it was only right that Petitfleur belonged to the state."

"I . . . I wish I'd had the chance to know him."

He patted my hand. "He would have liked you, I think. I'd been under the impression he didn't have any relatives, so the first time he brought Tony around, you can imagine how surprised I was." He swallowed. "I liked Tony. A lot. Arthur was crushed when he died."

"Why didn't he reach out to me?"

"If I had to hazard a guess, I'd say he was probably afraid to get close to you and your sons." He held up a hand. "As he got older, he became a lot more . . . a lot more reclusive. After Tony died, he hardly ever left that house." He squeezed my hand. "I don't envy you having to clean out that house on Harmony Street. He became a bit of a hoarder in those last few years."

"Well, that was left to the trust for the boys, so once the probate has cleared, that's their problem," I said, knowing as I said the words that I would be the one who'd wind up having to handle it. "Although I am sure they can be persuaded to let Rare Things handle the estate sale."

He smiled sadly. "He does have some wonderful pieces I'd love to sell. And some I sold him I could get a good price for at auction."

"Do you have any idea why Arthur changed his will?"

"Collette." His face got sad again, and he paused as his eyes got wet again. "I was her father and I loved her, but that girl—that *woman*—had such a penchant for getting in trouble.' He sighed. "She was completely wrapped up in who we—the

Charpentiers—*used* to be. The problem with family history is it's easy to become obsessed with it. Her mother, God rest her soul, didn't care about any of that, of course, so Collette made her life miserable. She wasn't New Orleans gentry, you see, and I'd married beneath myself."

"Oh, how awful for your poor wife."

"Connie knew what Collette was like." He sighed. "And she never took it personally. The Charpentiers ran out of money during my grandfather's lifetime. I started Rare Things because I loved antiques and history. Collette always believed I should have married money to rebuild the family's stature in the city. It was hard, but I tried to give her everything she wanted."

"Is that why she married Liam?" I was a bit confused. The Monaghans were a political family, but did that count as high society in New Orleans?

"She married Liam Monaghan because he got her pregnant when they were in college." He made a face. "Oh, we went all out for her. She was a debutante, and I even managed to afford Rex for a few years so she could be a maiden of the King's court and participate in all of that. You can imagine how shocked her mother and I were when she ran off and married Liam." He sighed again. "She was pregnant and of course couldn't have an abortion as a Catholic. I put up the money for them to buy this house as a wedding gift. I put up the money for any number of Liam's business ventures—which all failed, I might add—and for his political campaigns, and she just kept taking and taking until the point I was going to lose the business. That's when Arthur stepped in and bailed me out. He wanted to just loan me the money, without any strings, but I insisted." He made a face. "I insisted that I couldn't just take an unsecured loan from him, so I sold him the business and the building on St. Charles—he was the one who bought the warehouse, so we could expand the business—but the problem was always Collette. She always needed more money, for clothes and jewelry and to send the boys to the right schools and . . . I know Arthur was worried if he left everything back to me, she'd just spend it all and I'd be bankrupted. Again." He pursed his lips. "They'd had a horrible fight—Arthur and Collette—about six months ago? That was when he changed his will, I think."

"What did they fight about?"

"Money." He held up his hands. "What else? She needed money and I didn't have it. So she asked Arthur for it. I guess since she thought it was going to be her inheritance, he could give some of it to her then. Arthur told me about it. The will change wasn't a surprise to me, honestly. But Collette convinced herself you were behind it, which of course was ridiculous."

"And Collette met Tony through you and Arthur?"

He nodded. "Collette had just come by here to get yet another check when Arthur stopped by to check on something, and he had Tony with him . . . Collette was smitten immediately. I know—*knew*—my daughter well, and I saw the look on her face when Arthur introduced her to us both. I'm not sure when they started the affair; I myself didn't know about it until Arthur told me. By that time Tony had met you and was planning on marrying you. The only reason I even found out was because Arthur wanted me to make sure Collette didn't do anything to interfere."

"Interfere?"

"He was afraid she'd do something to stop your wedding from happening."

"Oh." I could see that, like something out of an old-time soap: Collette appearing at the end of the aisle as the minister asked if anyone had cause for us not to be married, then dramatically making some melodramatic announcement. "But Tony wasn't . . . Tony wasn't seeing her anymore by then?" I heard my voice lilt upward at the end of the sentence, making it sound like a plea.

It was bad enough finding out Tony had been involved with her—could I handle hearing that it had continued after he met me?

"Tony wasn't that type. I thought you of all people would know that."

"I didn't think he was the type to sleep with a married woman either," I retorted. I held my hands up to my face. "I'm sorry, Randall. I shouldn't be bothering you. I shouldn't even be here. I don't know what I was thinking. Obviously, I wasn't." I started to get up, but his grip on my hands became stronger.

"I shouldn't have kept any of this from you," he said softly. "Please, don't go." His voice caught and he took a deep breath, closing his eyes and holding it for just a moment. "You aren't . . . you aren't bothering me, Val. To be honest, when Dee told me you'd shown up at Rare Things and were taking an interest in the business, yes, I was worried about what you might do." He held up a hand sadly. "I'm not any closer to having the money to buy you out than I ever was with Arthur, but please don't sell the business."

"Sell the business?" I gaped at him. "Why would you . . . I would never." Now it was my turn to squeeze his hands. I took a deep breath of my own. "Randall, Rare Things—all of this—came along at just the right time for me. Had I known any of this before? I might have sold the business, liquidated everything, and gotten out. But I *like* working at Rare Things. I like you. I like Dee. I'm so sorry about everything with—you know, Tony and Collette and everything—I don't know where you got the impression that I wanted to sell the business."

"Collette thought—" He winced. "I am beginning to realize that I probably shouldn't have believed everything she said to me."

"She was your daughter, Randall." I squeezed his hands again. "I hope she realized how lucky she was to have you as her father."

"That's very kind of you to say." He shook his head. "She needed more money, of course. I think she'd been borrowing money from New Orleans Lifestyles—"

"She was." Embezzling, actually, but this wasn't the time to break that bit of news to him.

His face twisted. "And she thought—since I didn't have any to spare for her—she thought she'd kill two birds with one stone. If she could get you to let her sell your house, the commission was enough to pay back the business and leave her with some extra, and she figured if you sold your house, you'd have enough money—"

"I wouldn't have to sell Rare Things." I shook my head. "It's kind of harebrained, don't you think?"

"Collette had her own logic." His smile was sad. "She had clients who were looking for exactly the kind of house you own, and she was convinced she could get you to sell. She really was obsessed with you."

I got to my feet, and he stood up as well. He gave me a hug. "Thank you for coming by, and thank you for understanding . . .

it was very difficult for me not being honest with you. But I didn't know what you knew and what was appropriate—"

"Just know I have no plans on selling Rare Things any more than I would sell my house," I replied resolutely, reaching up to kiss him on the cheek. "And even if wanted to, I would talk to you about it first, okay?"

"Thank you," he said, opening the door to the outer room just as Liam Monaghan appeared in the doorway.

"Giselle told me you were here," he said awkwardly to me as Randall squeezed past him without a word, "and I wanted to say thanks for bringing the pizzas."

"I'm very sorry for your loss," I said, trying very hard not to look him in the eye.

Liam wasn't taking Collette's death easy, that was clear. He looked terrible. He had several days' worth of salt-and-pepper stubble on his face, his eyes were bloodshot, and he smelled of day-old sweat and sour liquor. His graying hair, combed across a forehead that reached back on his skull past his ears, looked greasy and unwashed. There was a spot of something on his white dress shirt; his dress slacks looked unpressed and sloppy.

"You were the last person to see her alive," he said, and I could smell cheap whiskey on his breath. "You heard her last words."

"Well, yes, although she didn't really say anything."

He grabbed my hands and crushed them in his sweaty grip. "What did she say?"

I struggled to get my hands free. "You're hurting me," I said sharply, and when he relaxed his grip, I wrenched myself free. "She tried to say something, but she didn't have the strength to get the words out," I replied, shaking my aching hands.

"What did she say?"

"She just said *r*," I replied. "A couple of times. She said *are*. I don't know if she meant *our*, or *are*, or just the letter . . . but that was all she said."

"You're sure?"

Those two words clicked in my head.

I knew that sound, I recognized his voice.

"You went to the ball dressed as Henry VIII," I said slowly, backing carefully toward the door. "I heard you, talking to the woman in the fortune teller's outfit—that was why I went looking for Collette in the first place. You both . . . you both threatened her."

"I would never have hurt Collette." His entire body sagged. "Yes, I'd asked her for a divorce, because I'd fallen for Gina and she was delaying . . ."

"Gina?"

He swallowed and licked his lips. "Gina Brandon. The fortune teller. We've . . . we've been involved for a little over a year. But we—"

Gina Brandon?

Gina was another one of the L-High moms I knew from the parents' group.

He sank down into one of the chairs and started sobbing.

I took this as a sign to make my exit as quickly as I could.

Chapter Seventeen

I somehow managed to get out the front door with my composure intact.

But once the door was closed behind me, I leaned back against it and tried to get a grip on my breathing.

Had Liam killed Collette? He had a motive, and I'd heard him threatening her right before she was murdered. But he'd been dressed as Henry VIII; Bamm-Bamm the caveman had told me she'd gone outside with a man in a Kermit costume.

I shivered as the wind picked up. Clouds had blown up out of somewhere while I'd been inside, and the air felt cold, wet, and heavy. Rain again, for sure.

I was able to make it back to my car before it started coming down, but just barely. The drops started splatting against the car, hard, almost the moment I shut the door. I started the car and switched the heat to a higher level. I hugged myself as my teeth started chattering while I waited for hot air to start blowing through the vents.

I also kind of knew it wasn't just the rain and the cold. I was still feeling the vestiges of the nonstop shocks of the past few weeks.

I tried to organize my random thoughts into some sort of order.

Had I been a bit bored just a few weeks ago? I shook my head as the rain kept pouring down, feeling the warm air caressing my cold arms. My teeth stopped chattering.

Tony had been involved with Collette when he met me. So what? Maybe I wasn't comfortable with the thought of my Tony having an affair with a married woman, but did it really matter now? Sure, it would be great to sit him down and talk this out— okay, maybe I really wanted to shake him a bit and yell, "What were you thinking?" at him—but that wasn't going to happen. They were both dead now, and no one would ever know what had gone on between them now.

I remembered our first date clearly. He'd picked me up at my parents' home in Broadmoor, and he'd taken me to an early dinner. We'd gone to Straya on St. Charles, a gaudy place with a menu as thick as my Betty Crocker cookbook, before heading to the movie theater at Canal Place to see *Bring It On*. Straya had been loud and crowded, making it hard for us to hear each other over the cacophony of other voices, utensils scraping against plates, and the tinkling of glasses. I do remember him asking me if I was seeing anyone else, shortly before our entrees arrived.

"No," I'd replied. After I said it, it crossed my mind that maybe I was handling this the wrong way. My best friend from high school, Kylie, was constantly telling me I didn't know how to handle men and therefore was doomed to die a spinster. I always retorted that it was better to die a spinster than not be honest with a guy I might want to spend the rest of my life with: "What kind of relationship can it be if it starts with us lying to each other?"

Kylie would always roll her eyes at my response—"He'll think there's something wrong with you if you aren't dating someone else"—but I didn't care. I didn't want to play games with a guy or try to guilt him into committing to me. My parents had been born two days apart in the same hospital, started kindergarten together, gone steady in junior high, and gotten married after college. They'd been together most of their lives and they fit together so well; it was hard to imagine them not being together. I knew they were special and it wasn't likely I'd wind up that lucky, but I refused to believe that relationships were part of some stupid battle of the sexes with winners and losers. I didn't want to be with any man who didn't want me as I was. If that meant dying single, so be it.

"I'm free, no prospects of any kind." I'd smiled back at him that night. "What about you? I'd think a handsome young firemen would be beating women off him with a stick." I could hear Kylie's moan of disgust in my head.

"I'm sort of seeing someone, but it's not going anywhere," he'd replied, reaching across the table to take my hand. "But now that I've met you—I won't be seeing her anymore."

I'd thought it was an incredibly sweet thing to say at the time, and I never thought about it—*her*—again. Sometimes his older siblings teased him about a past girlfriend—the girl he'd gone to prom with, a neighborhood girl who'd had a big crush on him, that sort of thing—but I never caught names. I figured there was no need. Tony wasn't the type to sneak around; for one thing, he was a terrible liar, and he'd been devoted to me and the twins. I'd never once suspected him of even looking at another woman, let alone cheating.

Well, I'd thought Tony wasn't the type to sneak around.

He'd had an affair with a married woman.

And he'd sneaked around and never told me about Uncle Arthur either.

I couldn't be mad that he'd never told me about Collette. If he hadn't died, he would have gotten involved with the Cardirents along with me and he would have had to tell me about her.

Get a grip, I chastised myself. Sure, it was a surprise. No, he hadn't kept it from me, because I'd never asked about his past girlfriends.

I'd never asked because they didn't matter to me, and that hadn't changed.

Poor Collette, I thought as I started the car. What an awful existence she'd lived.

I put the car in gear and pulled away from the curb. What game had Collette been playing those last few weeks she was alive? She'd hated me for years. How she must have ground her teeth having to deal with me in the parents' group! She'd been running—dominating—that group for years, and then one day I show up? The woman she thought had "stolen" Tony from her, taken away the man she thought was the love of her life?

Funny that she *had* been my nemesis—well, at least she'd seen me as hers, anyway.

"What were you up to in the weeks before you died, Collette?" I whispered as I stopped for the light at Claiborne Avenue.

I turned right. Claiborne was clogged with cars driving slowly because the rain was coming down so hard. Visibility was negligible and the gutters were filling with water. Thinking I needed to stop at the grocery store, I turned right at Napoleon—the Rouses was down Napoleon at Tchoupitoulas. What was it I'd needed any-way? Berries and fruit, some fresh vegetables . . . I still hadn't got-ten used to shopping for just one person, so I tended to make lists that adapted and changed so I wouldn't wind up wasting food.

"Okay," I said aloud. "Organize your thoughts. What are the facts as you know them?"

Fact number one: Collette was being blackmailed and had embezzled money from her business, and she'd needed to repay it.

Fact number two: I'd overheard her husband talking about killing her at the Boudicca ball with his mistress, Gina Brandon, right before someone did kill her.

Fact number three: She'd tried to push me to sell my home. I assumed her motivation was for the commission to pay off her debt to New Orleans Lifestyles, so Lucy wouldn't press charges against her.

But that was an assumption, not a fact. Forget why she was pushing to sell the house.

Fact number four: She'd been stabbed with the Lafitte dagger.

They always say on cop shows and movies that coincidences never happen, but how could any of this have been some kind of master plan? Even getting me to sell my house had been a dra-matic long shot—what would she have done in the very likely event I wouldn't want to sell it? Where else could she have gotten money from?

The terms of Arthur's will must have been a shock to her. She must have been furious.

What game were you playing, Collette?

Something was missing. I was missing something important and had no idea what it could be.

Just forget about it all, I told myself as I pulled into the Rouses parking lot. *The police can find who killed Collette, and it's not your problem.*

Of course, it bothered me that she'd hated me so much. I didn't like that someone could hate me so passionately with me being blissfully unaware. That probably made her hate me even more. The real coincidence was that she'd been membership chair for Boudicca and Lorna wanted to join.

But that kind of coincidence was normal in New Orleans and happened every day.

But it still didn't make sense, I thought, wheeling a cart through the front doors. It was a long shot, but—

Desperate people will play long shots, won't they?

Solving murders was a lot easier on television, I reflected as I added a pack of white button mushrooms to the cart and pushed the cart over to where the berries were stocked. I liked having raspberries or blackberries with plain yogurt for breakfast, but with the summer season now over, the cost was going up. *You're an heiress now; you don't have to worry about the cost*, I reminded myself with a slight smile, putting two cartons of blackberries into the cart and heading for the coffee aisle.

I'm glad it's not my job to solve these crimes, I thought. *I hope Detective Guillotte is having more luck than me trying to figure this all out.*

It was still raining when I pushed my cart over the wet pavement. My feet got soaked in a puddle and the wind made me shiver. What had I been thinking not taking a jacket with me when I left the house? After putting the bags in the back, I dutifully returned my cart to the nearest corral despite the rain—I think it's a sign of civic commitment to return your cart to the corral, just like you should dump your trash in a fast-food place—and ran back to the car. I grabbed a paper towel from the passenger seat and blotted the wet off my face. I wrang some excess water out of my hair. Lightning flashed, and the crack of thunder that followed was so close and loud it sounded like the sky was breaking in half. I turned on the lights and drove down to Louisiana, where I turned left to head for home.

It started coming down so hard again by the time I reached my driveway that a slight river about two inches deep was running down into the street from my backyard. I could barely make out the pumpkin head on top of the orange cone in the sinkhole—the cone was still sinking, despite Michael's best efforts—and while I was waiting for the gate to open, I noticed something strange about the house.

The lights were on in the living room. I didn't remember turning them on.

Had I? No, it was bright outside when I'd left the house, and I hadn't been in the front.

It couldn't be the twins, because they would have parked their car in the driveway—especially in the rain, and they had classes this afternoon anyway.

A chill went down my spine as I dug my phone out of my purse and dialed Lorna.

"Yes, darling?" She sounded breathless—but she always did whenever I committed the crime of interrupting her while she was writing.

"I'm sorry to interrupt you while you're writing—"

"Actually, you saved me from yet another call from my horrible mother. I told her it was my agent so had to go." Her words flew like bullets from a machine gun, which meant she was still in manic writing mode. "What's going on?"

"Well, for one thing, the lights in my living room are on, and I didn't turn them on this morning," I replied, trying to see through the gloom if there was any movement in the house. "Have you noticed anything strange around my house today since I went out?"

"Oh, there you are, in the driveway. I can see your headlights." The fence between our two properties hid the driveway from her windows' line of sight. "And it's raining too hard for me to really see anything inside your house. Are you sure?"

"I didn't even go into the living room this morning," I replied. "I came down from the bedroom to the kitchen and then out the kitchen door to get in the car. I can see the kitchen lights are on." The gate finally finished opening, and just as I was getting ready to pull forward, out of the corner of my eye I noticed that my front door was ajar. I'd set the alarm on the way out, and it wouldn't have set if the door had been open.

A chill went down my spine. "Lorna, call the police and then call me right back, okay? I think someone's broken into my house."

"Are you sure, darling?"

"The front door is open. Call the police!"

"Don't go insi—"

I cut her off by disconnecting the call. I turned off the car and opened my door, my heart thumping. *This is what you scream at stupid women for doing in movies* dashed through my mind as I hopped across the lawn from flagstone to flagstone until I reached the front walk. The front door *was* ajar—it hadn't been my imagination. I crept up the front steps to the front gallery. "Hello?" I shouted inside the house, poking my head through the doorway and taking in the front room. I didn't see any watery footprints, so whoever had come inside the house had done so before it started raining, but that didn't help me at all. It could have started raining here earlier than it did over at Collette's neighborhood, or it might have rained there first. New Orleans was weird that way with its weather; one neighborhood could be getting so much rain the streets were flooding while another neighborhood not far away had bright sunshine and stayed completely dry.

I stepped inside the house. The front room was clear, as far as I could see, and there was no one in the television lounge just off the front room on this side. I grabbed a fireplace poker and clutched it as I walked around into the dining room area on the side of the house closest to Lorna's. My phone vibrated. It was Lorna.

"I've called the police and they are on their way, and they specifically said for you to *not* go inside. . . . so let me guess, you're inside already?"

"Of course," I said. "The front room is clear, and so is the dining room."

I wandered through the hallway by the stairs and dropped my phone in shock.

There was a body lying next to the island in the kitchen.

Scooter was sitting beside the body, cleaning his paws.

There was blood on the floor pooling by the head.

Kneeling down, I reached for my phone. "There's a body in my kitchen," I whispered into the phone, aware my hands were shaking nearly as much as my voice. "Call an ambulance. Let them know the police are on their way."

"Do you know who it is?"

Lightning lit up my darkened kitchen, and I reached for the light switch on the wall. I flipped it up, and the room filled with warm light.

"It's Michael." I knelt beside him and put my fingers on his wrist. I could feel a strong pulse beneath the skin, so I let out a breath I hadn't known I was holding. There was a lump on the back of his head, and his hair was wet around it—drops of blood dripping from his hair had created the small puddle next to him. He moaned, and I whispered, "Michael, are you okay?"

He'd been lying on his stomach, sprawled arms and legs akimbo, and he shook his head. "Man, I've got a headache," he said in a shaky voice as he tried to sit up.

"Careful, Michael, you've been injured," I said, slipping my arm around his shoulders and helping to anchor him in a sitting position. "Let me get you some water."

"Thanks." His voice sounded better. He put a hand up to the back of his head and winced. "Ouch." There was blood on his hand when he pulled it away.

I got some ice from the freezer and poured him a glass from the filtered pitcher in the refrigerator. "What are you doing in my house?" I asked as I handed him the ice water, kneeling beside him. "But are you okay, more important?"

"My head hurts, but I think I'm okay other than that." He took another drink of water. "I was out in the street, trying to figure out how much gravel I needed to add to the sinkhole to get make the cone visible again." He gave me a weak smile. "I'd just gone back into the house and come out with the bag of gravel when I noticed your front door was open—and it hadn't been. I walked over to see if your car was here, and when I saw it wasn't, well, I thought I'd take a look around and make sure everything was okay." He touched the back of his head again and winced. "I probably should have just called the police."

I could hear sirens over the sound of the rain and got up to get him an ice pack from the freezer for the back of his head. As I handed it to him, I heard a tapping on the back door and saw a drenched Lorna standing there, her face pressed against the glass.

"It's Michael," I said as I let her in, filling her in quickly. "You stay back here with him, and I'll go let the cops in. And close Scooter up in the downstairs guest room."

Chapter Eighteen

Detective Guillotte arrived while the paramedics were checking out Michael in the kitchen.

It was still raining, and everyone was tracking in water and mud all over my hardwood floors. Everywhere I looked, I saw little puddles of dirty water. I tried keeping up with my trusty mop at first but finally acknowledged defeat. It would have to wait until everyone had gone and I was alone in the house. I also recognized that my obsession with making sure I mopped up every single drop of dirty water, and now the distress not wiping it up was causing, had everything to with feeling like everything had somehow gotten out of my control. I was trying to process the nightmarish shock of having my home broken into and my dear neighbor, who was practically a member of my family, being attacked by some monster who'd violated my private space. Knowing Michael seemed okay and was in good hands with the paramedics helped some, but not much.

How would I ever feel safe or secure inside my house again?

Maybe I should sell the place.

Lorna had sensibly grabbed an umbrella, once she knew the paramedics and cops were on their way, to go around the neighborhood and let everyone on our street know what was happening so the sight of police cars, a fire truck, and an ambulance wouldn't alarm them too much. Michael's partner John and John's mother, Mrs. Domanico, had come rushing over to check on Michael, which meant we had to keep them in a contained area inside the kitchen so they didn't destroy or muddle up any evidence. (Lorna breezily pointed this out to me when she brought them by, full of apologies: "Darling, you know I could hardly tell them Michael was injured and expect them to stay home and *wait*, do you?" I had to admit she was right, and if Detective Guillotte got angry about his crime scene, well, I'd deal with him.)

Once I'd spoken to the cops who'd arrived in their patrol car—tracking more water through the living room into the kitchen to talk to Michael—I had to deal with the crime scene technicians when they arrived in their van. Then came the joy of walking through the house with one of the officers, a nice young Black man, while I checked to see if anything was missing. I wasn't sure nothing was missing, but that didn't mean they hadn't taken something. The nice young Black man seemed to understand and gently told me to let Detective Guillotte know if I discovered something missing later. The techs started dusting that nasty black fingerprint powder all over everything.

Which meant I'd have to clean all that up at some point too.

Lorna must have known what I was thinking, because she muttered, "Hire a cleaning service. It'll take forever to clean all this mess up."

The techs also took my fingerprints, as well as Lorna's and Michael's, so they could "eliminate" ours from ones that didn't belong in my house.

"My sons were home last weekend," I said to the older man who seemed to be in charge, "but they're back in Baton Rouge at school." I hated the thought of the twins needing to be fingerprinted.

"Process of elimination, ma'am." One of the techs, a young blonde woman, smiled at me like she'd read my mind. "Their fingerprints will be all over their bedrooms, so . . ."

Detective Guillotte arrived shortly after I retreated to the front gallery with a blanket wrapped around me. There were too many strangers inside my house, I couldn't hear myself think, and I felt—well, *violated*. Someone had broken into my house. It didn't make sense. There was nothing of value in the house to steal; it wasn't like I had jewels scattered all over my dresser or stocks and bearer bonds and piles of cash locked in a safe somewhere. But someone *had broken into my house.*

My home.

My castle.

My safe space.

Just the thought of someone pawing through my underwear drawer or touching my clothes, whether the burglar had done it or not, made my skin crawl. I would have to wash everything, I thought, just so I'd know my clothing was clean and unsoiled.

I remembered turning on the alarm on my way out. I distinctly remembered disarming and rearming it to give me the three-minute window to go out and close it before it finished rearming. It was a habit so ingrained I could do it in my sleep. But I *remembered* doing it. I remembered the light switching from red to green back to blinking red again, the beeping noise it made to remind me of the ticking clock before it armed again.

How had they gotten in without setting off the alarm?

Another mystery.

I needed a glass of wine. I was going to drink an entire bottle once all these strangers were gone and some semblance of normalcy was restored to my poor house.

I had a bad feeling that was never going to happen.

I wasn't sure I'd ever feel safe and secure inside my house again.

Well, you can have Lucy sell it if you decide to get out, I thought hysterically. *And at least Collette won't be getting the commission.*

"I'm very sorry this happened, Ms. Cooper." Detective Guillotte said, gesturing toward the police cars and ambulance and fire truck with their lights flashing in the street in front of my house. He indicated a metal chair on the other side of the table I was sitting beside. "Do you mind if I have a seat?"

"Make yourself at home," I said wearily, shaking my head. It had finally stopped raining, and the gallery chairs were relatively dry. The air was chilly and damp. Every so often, I noticed one of the neighbors peering out their windows at the scene in front of my house. John and Mrs. Domanico were in the kitchen with Michael while the paramedics continued making sure he was okay. "They're going to be here a while, aren't they?" I was tired. I wrapped the blanket more tightly around me. The wind was bitterly cold, and every blast seemed to go right through me to the bone. "I need a drink."

"You and me both, Ms. Cooper," he said, pulling out his inevitable notepad from an inner jacket pocket. "Do you mind taking me through what happened when you got home?"

Tonelessly, I went through it all again while he took notes. When I was finished, he said, "And you didn't see or hear anything else when you got home?"

"The house was quiet." I shivered, remembering the shock I felt when I saw Michael lying there on the kitchen floor and the horrible feeling that he was dead. "Plus I had Lorna on the phone with me, and she was keeping me company. She'd already called 911 on her landline."

"You know you shouldn't have gone inside the house, Ms. Cooper?" He said it kindly, not chidingly, not judgmentally. "You should have gone next door and called the police and waited for them to check out the house before you went inside."

"I know, I know, I knew it then, but I couldn't help myself." I shivered uncontrollably for a few moments again. "It wasn't the smartest thing I've done, I know. But you know, it's my *house*, Detective." I heard my voice shaking. "I've always felt safe here, you know what I mean? I don't . . . I know it's an illusion, but you should feel safe inside your own house!" My voice cracked, and I choked down the sob.

My house. The house Tony and I fell in love with when we were first married and living in his horrible little one-bedroom apartment on Magazine Street in the lower Garden District. Well, it wasn't horrible, just small, but once I knew I was pregnant, we needed a bigger place. I'd loved that little old apartment—don't get me wrong. A former burlesque dancer on Bourbon Street with the stage name of Cherry Jubilee (her real name was Rhea Gittelstein) had lived there for thirty years before dying of cancer at Charity Hospital. It was on the third floor of a Creole townhouse—the entire block was made of townhouses—with a skylight over the bed so you could see the stars and moon and the velvety dark-blue sky at night. There was nothing more comforting than lying in that bed with Tony's arms around me during a thunderstorm, watching the rain and the lightning and the clouds overhead while safely warm in our double bed covered in blankets. The place was small for two people, but I liked all the touches Cherry Jubilee had added over the years to the ceiling and walls.

I remembered the day Tony's brother told us about the house for sale on a block where Cooper Construction was renovating an old double shotgun. I'd driven by to get a look, my baby bump not even noticeable yet, and something about the old raised Creole cottage-style house spoke to me. It needed work, for sure. It looked like it hadn't been painted since Hoover was president, and the porch sagged a bit to one side. One of the columns supporting the front gallery roof was missing, but it seemed like the perfect place for us. Once the realtor had shown us around—and quoted us the ridiculously low asking price—we decided to take it.

Three months later we moved in and started renovating our house.

Our house.

I knew then I would never sell the place for as long as I could afford to keep it.

It was *my* house. Most of the memories of my marriage—and all the memories of my twins—were a part of this house.

It might take me a while to feel safe in it again, but I was never selling.

"And you set your alarm when you left the house?"

I exhaled. "Yes, and before you say it, it's not something that's become such a habit that I don't remember whether I did it or not. Okay, sometimes that happens, yes, I don't remember if I've set it or not. But I do remember setting it before I left." I shook my head. "I remember waiting for the beeps to let me know I could go out the kitchen door. I remember watching the light go from green to blinking red, Detective. Do I remember doing it Saturday night before we left for the Boudicca ball? No, I don't. But I definitely do remember today."

"Who all knows your passcode?"

I blinked at him. "You think it was someone I know?"

"If you set the alarm, Ms. Cooper, it stands to reason that whoever broke in must have known the code as well. Otherwise it would have gone off, right?" He gave me a sad smile.

At least he believed me. "Well, that would be me and the twins, of course, and Lorna. Michael and John next door, and . . ." Had we ever given the code to anyone else? I didn't think so. "I think that's it."

"Of course, any of them may have given out your code."

"Why would they do that?"

He smiled gently at the sharpness of my tone. "Was the code a combination of numbers that someone might have been able to figure out? Like your sons' birthday?"

"I—" I paused. I didn't really think about it anymore—it had become just a series of numbers to punch in, but *one-zero-one-two-zero-one* was Tony's and my anniversary: 10/12/01. "It's my wedding anniversary. But whoever broke in would have to know that, and you only get three chances before the alarm goes off. I figured"—I swallowed, avoiding his eyes—"that the odds against someone breaking into my house and knowing my anniversary were in my favor. I mean, it's not like someone online trying to hack into my accounts or something." *Note to self: Change all your online passwords.*

He flipped the notebook closed and put it back into his inner pocket. "Ms. Cooper, I'd advise you to change that password as soon as you can tonight, once the crime lab has finished with the house." He took a deep breath, and his face got very stern. "Now I have to ask you why you have been playing detective."

"What are you talking about?" I looked at him. "I've been trying to figure out the mystery around this inheritance I received recently, if that's what you're referring to. Why wouldn't I try to find out why my husband never told me about this uncle and the family feud?"

"You've been asking questions about Collette Monaghan." He raised his eyebrows. "I can't have you interfering with my murder investigation." He nodded toward the house. "Has it not occurred to you that maybe this break-in has something to do with you going around asking questions about Collette?"

I stared at him for a moment before I started laughing. Really, it was all starting to get to be too much for me to deal with, and maybe I needed to just pack a bag and go sleep on Lorna's couch for a couple of weeks. "Detective, I'm not trying to solve Collette's murder." I shivered again. "*You* were the one who told me Collette hated me. *That's* what I was doing. I was trying to figure out why she hated me so much."

"You honestly didn't know?"

"I didn't even know she hated me until you told me."

The front door opened before he could say anything, and the crime scene guys in their coveralls emerged. The Black woman who was in charge apologized to me, then told Guillotte they were finished and would be heading back to process everything. He thanked her, and they piled into the lab van. They were followed by the EMTs and firefighters—I didn't recognize any of them, but they were from a different station from where Tony had worked. The lead fireman tipped his hat to me.

"The victim is refusing to go to the hospital to be checked for concussion, but his partner and mother-in-law will be keeping an eye on him. Are you sure you don't need to be checked out yourself, ma'am?"

"I just had a shock is all. Thank you."

Guillotte and I stood there watching as the vehicles departed, their flashing red lights turned off, and when I shivered again, he asked, "Shall we go inside?"

"Let me check on Michael." I got up and moved inside. I pointed to the television room. "I'll be right in. Do you want some coffee or anything?"

"Water would be nice."

The kitchen was a disaster area. There was black powder all over every surface in sight, and all my cabinet doors were open. Michael was sitting at the kitchen table. He looked better, if pale, and was holding an ice pack to the back of his head. Mrs. Domanico was sitting across from him, her old face glowering at him. "Are you sure you don't need to go to the hospital?" I asked as I got a bottle of water for Guillotte from the refrigerator. I was tempted to make myself a vodka-and-anything but figured that should probably wait until Guillotte was finished with me.

But that vodka bottle was very tempting.

"I think he should," John said.

"I'm fine," Michael replied. "I just should have brought a baseball bat with me." He grinned wanly. "Next time for sure."

"Hopefully, there won't be a next time. What exactly happened?" I opened a bottle of Pellegrino and poured myself a glass. "I mean, I appreciate you watching out for the house for me, but Michael, you shouldn't ever put yourself in danger like that.

Anything anyone would take is—well, it's just a thing that can be replaced. You, on the other hand . . ."

"I know." He had the decency to look ashamed of himself. "I just knew you weren't home, and when I saw someone in the house—"

"Did you get a good look at whoever it was?"

As soon as the words came out, I could hear Detective Guillotte saying, *Why are you interfering in my investigation?* But this was different. This was my house.

"No." He looked unhappy. "You know how our kitchen windows look right into your front room? I was in the kitchen making red gravy, and I saw someone move past your window. I didn't get a good look, because it was out of the corner of my eye, you know, when you're not really looking or paying attention? I wasn't sure I was right that I'd seen anyone, and I couldn't be sure it wasn't you, of course—although I knew you'd gone out. Maybe I just hadn't seen you come home, you know, but there was something wrong about it, you know what I mean? He or she seemed kind of . . . I don't know, *furtive.* So I stopped what I was doing and came over. I thought, well, if Val's car's in the driveway, that's the end of it. But it wasn't, and your front door was open." He swallowed. "So I came inside and called for you. I heard a noise in the back of the house, and you know, I thought maybe you'd fallen or something and might need help—I wasn't thinking clearly. I mean, this is the thing you always yell at people for doing in scary movies and you think they deserve what happens to them for being so stupid, but you know, I couldn't stop thinking about you possibly needing help, and so I walked into the kitchen, and that's the last thing I remember until the paramedics were talking to me."

"You're lucky you weren't killed," Lorna said grimly as she entered from the side gallery door. She placed her umbrella in the stand beside the door and crossed her arms. "You should have called me. I would have brought over my gun."

"Lorna." I started to tell her again I didn't want her gun in my house but remembered the detective in the television room waiting for me. "I have to finish talking to Detective Guillotte, but y'all wait for me in here, okay?"

I didn't wait for an answer, carrying the water bottle and my glass through the door that opened out under the staircase into the little hallway and into the television room. I handed Detective Guillotte his water.

"Thank you. You said you were trying to find out why Mrs. Monaghan hated you?" He took a drink and recapped the bottle. "What did you find out?"

"Well, apparently—" I stopped myself. It was still hard to wrap my mind around it. "My husband was involved with her when he met me. I mean, I knew he was seeing someone when we first started dating, but I didn't know anything about the woman. He said she didn't matter, it was really over, and he'd just been waiting for the right time to break it off with her. Now that he'd met me, he would. I never knew who she was, or that she"—I took a deep breath—"was married. So, when I joined the parents' group at L-High, she must have . . . to be honest, I always thought she didn't like me, but she didn't treat me any differently than she treated anyone else." I shrugged. "It never occurred to me she hated me . . . Detective Guillotte was right—she must have followed me there." It all sounded crazy saying it out loud. "My neighbor, Lorna, wanted to join that krewe Boudicca. Collette was the membership chair, and she brought the invitations over and dropped them off at Lorna's that day. She must have seen me walking to Big Fisherman and followed me there. I guess . . ." I hesitated. I hated talking smack about her, but she *was* dead and she'd hated *me*, so did I really owe her anything? "You were right. She needed money. She took a chance that I might be willing to sell the house. I guess she also knew that Arthur Cooper had left the store and everything she was expecting to go to her father to me and my sons. I can't think why anyone would think I knew anything that made me a danger to them, you know?"

"Ms. Cooper." He stood up. "Please stop asking questions. I don't know that this break-in was related to your asking around about Mrs. Monaghan, but I don't believe in coincidences. Can you stay with your neighbor until we get to the bottom of this, or somewhere else?"

"I will not be driven out of my house." I set my jaw. "My neighbors—we're all very close, and we watch out for each other."

He held up his hands. "It was worth a try." He stood up. "Thank you for the water. I'll be in touch as soon as we know anything further."

I walked him to the front door. I was just shutting the door behind him when he stopped me. "Oh, by the way—you're sure the guy who was working the bar back by the Rampart Street doors to the auditorium was dressed as Bamm-Bamm?"

"I guess it could have been some other caveman." I frowned. "Tarzan, caveman, something like that. Why?"

He shrugged. "The volunteer who was supposed to work that bar setup never showed up that night. He was sick with food poisoning."

Chapter Nineteen

With an exaggerated sigh, Lorna uncorked a bottle of Chardonnay she claimed she'd smuggled into the country on her last trip back from Italy. She poured out a glass and placed the bottle on the kitchen table with a dramatic toss of her head. "Drink up, kids."

Michael reached for the bottle, but Mrs. Domanico slapped his hand. "No liquor for you until we know there's no concussion, and you really should be at the hospital." She scowled at him disapprovingly. John was the youngest of her seven children—and Michael was about ten years or so younger than John, so he'd become her baby the moment he moved in.

Michael gave her a frown. John took his hand, and they smiled at each other. I poured out another glass of Pellegrino for Michael, which he accepted gratefully, and I helped myself to the Italian Chardonnay with the shrimp on the label (Lorna always called it "shrimp wine"). "It's going to take me forever to clean this place," I grumbled, looking over at the clock on the wall. It was past nine—which meant it would have to wait until the morning, which meant . . . I wouldn't be able to sleep, which meant I needed to stay up until the house was clean.

"Well, you're spending the night at my place," Lorna replied after taking a big swig from her glass. "I'll come over and help you clean up tomorrow. I still think you should hire a cleaning crew, though." She glanced over at the island, covered in fingerprint dust. Mrs. Domanico had wiped the kitchen table clean the moment the cops had okayed it. "No objections. I won't be able to sleep a wink if I'm worried about your intruder coming back. So you're coming home with me tonight."

"Did the detective think this was related to the murder?" John asked. He accepted the glass of wine Lorna offered him, which Michael looked at wistfully. "Or was it just another coincidence?"

"I don't believe in coincidence," Lorna replied airily, waving her right hand around. "No such thing. It's all connected somehow—we just don't have all the pieces." She raised an eyebrow and looked at me. "It's just a matter of figuring how it all connects together." She held up her hand. "Count them off: Colleen comes by my house to drop off the invitations to the ball. She then runs into Val at Big Fisherman. Okay, that one I can sort of believe in—she stopped by Big Fisherman because she was in the neighborhood, and Val just happened to be there."

"No, that wasn't a coincidence either." I shook my head. "Detective Guillotte seems to think she followed me there on purpose. She didn't *have* to drop those invitations off in person. I mean, do you really think all those people there Saturday night had their invitations dropped off personally by the membership chair? No, she knew Lorna's address was on my block, so she made a point of dropping them off in person. I think she wanted to scope out the place. She already knew Arthur Cooper had changed his will and so the money she was expecting to get through her father wasn't happening."

Michael put the ice pack down on the table. Mrs. Domanico cleared her throat with her eyebrows raised, so he meekly said, "My head is frozen, Mom. Let me have a few minutes to let it thaw out a bit, okay?" He cleared his throat. "Do you think Collette really wanted to sell your house?"

"She'd embezzled money from her business, and her partner was threatening to press charges." I took another drink of wine. I was tired, exhausted, and knew I'd be asleep the minute my head hit the pillow, regardless of how messy my house was. *Thank God I don't have to go in to the store tomorrow*, I thought. *It's going to take me hours to clean up this mess.* "But even so—even if the clients who were looking for something like my house would have made an offer, it would have taken a while for her to get the money, so I don't know how that would have benefited her at all?"

"That's easy," John replied. "If I had to make a guess, her plan was to let the company keep whatever her commission would have been to make up for the money she 'borrowed'"—he made air quotes—"and so knowing the money was being repaid, her partner wouldn't have pressed charges—and would have fired her once the check cleared."

"I think they were actually partners in the business, but it doesn't matter how that would have worked out," I replied. "Collette was desperate; she was being blackmailed and was grasping at straws." I shook my head. "But *why* was she being blackmailed?"

"I don't think the partner would have ever pressed charges," Mrs. Domanico nodded. "They wouldn't want any scandal." Mrs. Domanico had, before she retired, worked in real estate herself. I wasn't precisely sure whether she'd been an office manager for a realtor company or if she'd shown houses and sold them herself. She was now in her eighties, and her mind was sharp as a tack. She was an excellent resource when it came to anything involving property in the city—taxes, zoning, or getting a handicapped spot for your house—and she was your best adviser in dealing with the city. "You have that kind of scandal and no one wants to use you—it drives away business. Who wants to use a realtor who might steal their money? Might cheat you? Everyone suspects the salesperson to lie and be dishonest as it is to try to get the sale— and some of them, unfortunately, are, whether they are just lazy or incompetent or really crooked. And everyone here knows everything about everyone else, you know. It would be bad for business for that to get out. The partner actually wanted to file charges?"

"She didn't sound like she wanted to," I replied, reaching for the wine bottle. My glass had magically emptied, and I could feel a headache starting to form between my eyes. "She sounded like she was sad and more disappointed than angry at Collette. It was more personal for Lucy. She felt betrayed. I can't imagine how she felt. She'd thought they were friends—and friends don't do that to friends." I finished filling the glass and pinched the bridge of my nose. "I also got a lecture from Detective Guillotte because I was going around asking questions. I wasn't interfering with his investigation. I don't want to find out who killed her—I mean, that's the police's job, not mine; I'm not Miss Marple or Jessica Fletcher. I have no idea who killed Collette nor any interest in finding out who it was. All I wanted to know is why Collette hated me so much." I sighed. "And now I know." *And kind of wish I didn't, honestly.*

I didn't say that out loud.

"What did you find out?" Michael asked. "Although with Collette, it wouldn't take much. That woman held grudges like a clutch purse."

I hesitated, looking around my kitchen table at the faces of my friends and neighbors. They might not be blood, but they were family. We'd all lived next door to each other for years. Michael, John, and Mrs. Domanico had been in their place when Tony and I bought ours. Lorna had moved in next to us just before the boys started kindergarten. They'd been there for me when Tony had died—keeping me going, reminding me that I needed to be there for the twins. They'd babysat the boys and watched them grow up, gone to watch their games and plays and choir performances at L-High. They'd become an extended family for all three of us—even more so after my parents retired and moved to Florida.

And if I couldn't be honest with family, who could I be honest with?

"Apparently, when Tony and I first met, he was involved with Collette," I said slowly. Their collective intake of breath made me feel a little better—they were just as shocked as I'd been. "I never knew about it. All Tony said to me was he'd been seeing someone he'd been intending to break up with but had been putting it off, or something like that; I don't really remember. I was falling in love with him, and so . . . well, it wasn't hard to believe that someone like Tony would be involved with someone, you know? I mean, it wasn't hard for me to believe every woman he met would fall in love with him."

"He was hot." Lorna nodded. "And he was a great guy on top of it."

"Well, I thought he was perfect." I gave a halfhearted shrug. "I mean, I knew about some of his past girlfriends, because sometimes his family would talk about them and tease him, and me, a little, but . . . I never really asked. I never wanted to know, because what he did before he met me never mattered." I took another drink. I did love shrimp wine. "And I still don't care about it. Maybe I should have asked him more questions. But how would that have helped me, knowing about him and Collette? If she hated me for 'stealing' Tony from her, me knowing about it wouldn't have changed that." I shook my head. But would I have been different, more understanding, with Collette? I'd never know. "The weird thing is I keep thinking . . . in trying to find out why Collette hated me, all I am finding is that a lot of people seem to have had a real motive for killing *her*." I held up my hand and started ticking things off my fingers. "She hated me because I stole Tony from her—at least that's what she thought, true or not—and I wound up getting the inheritance she thought would be hers, or rather, would have gone to her father, so of course she could access it, and she needed money. Her office manager thought she was being blackmailed. And she was having an affair with a younger—much younger—man. And . . ." I shook my head. "Well, I found that Henry VIII and the fortune teller, who I overheard talking about killing her, were her husband and his mistress."

"Interesting." Michael sipped his sparkling water. "What happens to the inheritance if something happens to you?"

I knew he meant *if you died*, but I appreciated him not saying it out loud. "Collette wouldn't have been able to get her hands on it, if that's what you're asking." I remembered I still hadn't signed my will. But I knew enough Louisiana inheritance law to say, "If

I don't have a will, everything will go to the boys. Even with a will I can't disinherit them before they're twenty-four without just cause—incarceration, physical violence against me, and there are a couple of others but nothing that would ever happen. I would never have cause to disinherit the boys, anyway."

"Didn't you say that Arthur didn't name you in the will, though? Do you have your copy of it?" Lorna asked, an eyebrow going up. "I mean, I'm not a lawyer, but I can read a will."

"Sure." I got up and walked over to my desk. The packet of papers I'd gotten from the lawyers included a copy of the will. I pulled it out and handed it to her. She scanned it quickly. She looked at me with a triumphant smile.

"*I bequeath the bulk of my estate to the heirs of my grand-nephew, Anthony Francis Cooper*," Lorna quoted. "The will was written *after* Tony died . . ." She tapped her forehead. "We're missing something here. That wording . . . Tony died intestate, didn't he?"

"Yes." Tony had died on the job, a four-alarm fire in the Warehouse District. It had never occurred to us to have wills done. It had been a headache—and I'd been very grateful to Stacia for guiding me through that period and the division of property.

Sign your damned will, I reminded myself, *so the twins won't have to deal with that same mess.*

"Why would Arthur make his will so cryptic?" Lorna wondered, tapping the will against the island. "He knew your names. He knew Tony was dead. Why Tony's heirs?"

"Is no one going to mention the elephant in the room?" Mrs. Domanico asked.

We all turned to look at her.

She made a face before continuing. "The break-in. If this break-in is related to Collette's murder, *why*?" She finished her glass of wine and held it out to Lorna for a refill. "There are only two reasons why someone would break into your house, Valerie, that have to do with her death. Either *you* have something here in the house the killer wants or needs or might expose them—"

"She's watched a lot of *Law & Order*," John said in a loud fake-whisper.

She shushed him and went on. "Or the killer thinks you know something—something you may not even realize you know—that could expose them."

"But that doesn't make any sense!"

"It does," Lorna said. "The night of the ball—you overheard Henry VIII and a fortune teller threatening her, right? That was why you went looking for her, right, to warn her?"

I nodded. "And Henry VIII turned out to be Liam Monaghan. The fortune teller was his mistress, Gina Brandon."

Lorna's jaw dropped. "Gina? Who owns that cute little boutique in the Quarter?" She shook her head. "Just goes to show how you never really know anyone . . . so you walked around to the back—front, whatever—of the auditorium, and asked the bartender there if he'd seen a pirate wench with big red hair?"

I nodded. "And he said she'd just gone out front with Kermit the Frog."

"I still don't remember seeing anyone dressed like Kermit," Lorna replied grimly. "And you went outside into the mist and heard footsteps running away, and a moan, and that was what led you to where you found Collette."

"Yes," I agreed. "She'd been stabbed with the fake Lafitte dagger. And she said *ar* two or three times before she died."

"Are?"

"Like a pirate. *Arrrrr.*" I thought back to that night, how chilly and damp it had been out there, the shock of finding Collette lying there with the hilt of the dagger sticking out of her chest, the pirate wench costume bloodied, the strange look on her face.

"Maybe she was trying to tell you her killer was in a pirate costume?" John suggested.

"Or it was Randall," Michael pointed out. "His name starts with an *r.*"

"I can't imagine Randall killing his daughter," I replied. "And what was Collette up to, anyway?" My headache was getting worse. I didn't know how cops did this sort of thing for a living.

"I still think Collette meant harm to come to you," Lorna insisted. "That's the kind of woman she was—narcissistic, sociopathic. Trust me, I've researched enough for my books to know one when I see one." She shuddered. "I keep the *Diagnostic and Statistical Manual of Mental Disorders* on my nightstand."

"I don't think I ever want to know what kind of pillow talk you and Captain Jack Farrow indulge in," John replied. He yawned and stretched. "I'm thinking maybe we should head on home. Mom, Michael? It's been quite an evening."

"I just want to be sure that Val isn't planning on spending the night here alone," Michael said, raising his eyebrows at me.

"Fine." I held up my hands. "I'll spend the night at Lorna's, but I'd be fine here with the alarm on. Detective Guillotte said they'd have a squad car go by every half hour or so all night too." I closed my eyes. I was going to have to tell the boys what happened—and they'd probably insist on driving down from Baton Rouge on a school night, with classes tomorrow morning. No, I could call them in the morning—it could wait until then.

"The burglar knew your alarm code," Michael pointed out. "How?"

"I don't know." I was feeling tired myself, drained of all energy. The entire day had been an emotional roller coaster. "I've changed the code, anyway. Detective Guillotte suggested it."

Lorna had an odd look on her face. She was thinking about something, but I was too tired to process any more information. I just wanted to drink some more wine and lay down.

No one had any reason to hurt me, so it had to be some random kind of thing, right?

Maybe I was wrong about the alarm. Maybe I was remembering another time recently when I'd set it on the way out. Setting the alarm had become second nature, like locking the door.

I needed to start paying more attention when setting the alarm in the future . . .

I hated not being certain that I'd set it.

Although I preferred to believe I hadn't than that someone had come looking for me and knew the code.

Which wasn't possible, I reminded myself.

Tony and I should have listened when the security company tried to upsell us cameras on the property. But we'd thought it was too much money, and a bit of overkill—did we really need cameras hooked up to a computer recording a livestream saved in a cloud system somewhere?

"You're an idiot," I told myself.

One of the options we *had* paid for was alarm history.

I pulled my phone out, opened the alarm app, touched the button for *HISTORY*.

I *had* turned on the alarm when I'd left.

Someone had turned it off around four.

Which was just before Michael noticed the front door was open.

So whoever had broken in had known my code.

But—what could possibly have been inside the house that someone could have wanted?

I walked John, Michael, and Mrs. Domanico out, then locked the door behind them, closing the blinds. I had already closed the shutters before the police left, and I really didn't want anyone seeing into my house from the street. I'd never thought about it before, but when the shutters were open, my life—my house, my family, everything—was on display to anyone driving or walking by. If not for the alarm, my house could so easily be broken into. Massive windows lined the front gallery; even the front door was half glass.

Yes, I would always be making sure the alarm was on from now on—especially when I was home.

Lorna and I carried our wineglasses upstairs to pack an overnight bag for me. I just tossed some clean underwear, clean sweats, and my travel kit into a gym bag and slung it over my shoulder. I grabbed the cat carrier and handed it to her to put Scooter in.

I set the alarm and we went out the back door, locking it behind us. As we went through the gate between our yards and Lorna latched the gate behind her, I said, "Detective Guillotte mentioned something odd before he left." Her backyard was dark. The lights from her house didn't illuminate her yard much, and there were pockets of shadows everywhere I looked. I chose to focus on her back door as we went up the back stairs. "He said that back bar—you know, where I saw Bamm-Bamm, who sent me outside after Collette? Bamm-Bamm wasn't working that back bar; the guy who was supposed to had food poisoning and didn't show up, so according to the volunteer chair, no one was supposed to be bartending back there. I guess Bamm-Bamm was just helping himself." I closed my eyes and could see him vividly. Muscular, good-looking, his eyes hidden behind that small black mask. The thick bluish-black curly hair, the politeness, the mannerisms.

He reminded you of Tony, didn't he? You just thought you had Tony on the brain. You thought when you first saw him it was Tony.

Tony had gone as a caveman for Halloween when the boys were kids.

It wasn't just the costume, though, was it?

Think, Valerie, think—the answer is right in front of you.

Lorna flipped a switch, and her big open downstairs floor plan flooded with light. Her shutters were closed, thankfully—I didn't think I could stand looking out into the dark and seeing shadows. She turned the deadbolt on the door behind me. She finished off the shrimp wine bottle and grabbed another from inside the wine cooler.

Bamm-Bamm was the only person who'd seen Collette go outside. *He* was the only person who'd seen her with Kermit.

Maybe . . . maybe the running footsteps I'd heard in the distance had been unrelated? Someone running along the sidewalk of Rampart Street from some reason and not the killer getting away?

Didn't it make more sense for the killer to go back inside and get lost in the crowd?

I tried to remember.

I'd been thinking about finding Collette, warning her. I was lost in my own thoughts and wasn't really paying attention to anything other than looking for someone in a pirate wench costume . . . but hadn't Bamm-Bamm been *in front* of the bar when I came around the corner?

I remembered hearing Detective Guillotte telling me that the volunteer for that back bar had been sick; the bar hadn't been manned.

So who was the caveman?

"Just picking up some trash," he'd said, giving me a big smile, and I'd been distracted—I was looking for Collette and he'd reminded me of Tony, which had shaken me; I'd thought he actually *was* Tony at first. And why wouldn't he be picking up litter when he was bored?

He could have just as easily been coming back inside—from stabbing Collette.

Who was he? Why would he have killed her?

Why had he reminded me of Tony?

Another memory flashed through my head. When I'd dug out my copy of Arthur's will . . . *the envelope from Stacia with mine hadn't been there.*

My will.

The burglar had taken my will.

Lorna popped the cork out of the bottle and reached for my glass as I said slowly, "Lorna, I think I may know who killed Collette—"

And that's when all the lights in her house went out.

Chapter Twenty

"*Bloody Entergy*," Lorna shouted, following that up with a string of curse words that would have made a sailor blush.

"Um, I don't think it's Entergy," I said into the darkness. But the streetlight in front of her house was still shining—I could see the rays through the slats on the shutters. That meant it wasn't the neighborhood. I turned to look back at my house, and I could see the glow of my kitchen lights.

It was *just* Lorna's house.

A chill went down my spine.

Sure, it was an old house and old houses often had fuse issues . . . but the *whole* house?

Was it my imagination, or had a shadow just moved across the gallery in front of that shutter?

Was someone out there?

Your house was just broken into. It's just your imagination. The cops checked out your backyard and Lorna's before they left, so there can't be anyone out there . . .

Aloud, I whispered, "Lorna, be quiet!"

There was a stumbling sound from the back and a crash, and Lorna swore some more. "Where's that flashlight?"

I stood completely still, afraid to even breathe, waiting for my eyes to adjust. There wasn't much light from the moon—still too much of a cloud cover. I could see the glow of my kitchen's lights on the other side of the fence. It was too dark for me to see.

Something about this didn't feel right.

Scooter started yowling in his carrier.

Instinctively, I dropped my overnight bag and reached into my purse for my phone. I moaned as I remembered Detective Guillotte's card was still sitting on my desk where I'd left it when I'd taken it out of my purse the morning after Collette was murdered.

You don't need Detective Guillotte specifically. Just call 911.

I put my hand on my phone and wondered if maybe I was just overreacting a bit. Understandable because of the break-in.

Calm down, Valerie.

I took a deep breath and acclimated myself—I was close to what she called a "conversation space," where a couple of chairs and a love seat were grouped around a small table. The dining room table was on the other side of the house.

Lorna was still banging around in the kitchen, completely oblivious to the fact that someone was (maybe) on the gallery or that the power had been cut on purpose. Her words were coming faster and faster, which meant she was working herself into a state where gin would be the only thing that could soothe her.

There—was that a creaking board out on the gallery? Scooter's caterwauling was so loud I couldn't be sure. "Lorna," I said in my normal tone, "will you stop making such a racket? It's hard enough to hear over Scooter. There's someone on the gallery."

The light I could see from my kitchen through the shutter went dark for a second before coming back.

My heart started pounding. There *was* someone out there.

And if my suspicions were correct, I knew who it was, too— and we were in deep trouble. He'd already killed once, and his being here could only mean one thing.

Both our lives were in danger.

Clearly, Lorna hadn't heard me, since she was still banging around in the kitchen area. "LORNA." I raised my voice, and the noise in the kitchen stopped.

"What?" she replied crossly.

"There's someone on the gallery!"

In the silence that followed, I heard a board groan in the gallery floor on the other side of the window from me. He was heading for the side door we'd just come through. I couldn't remember if Lorna had locked it behind us or if the lights had gone out before she had a chance. I stepped back over to the door and flipped the deadbolt closed. I felt along the doorframe for the chain and, hands shaking, managed to attach it. The door was mostly glass, though—and so many windows! Rows of eight-foot windows ran along the front and two sides of the house. If he wanted in, the deadbolt and the chain weren't going to stop him.

I stepped back away from the door with my heart pounding. I could feel adrenaline rushing through my veins, and my palms were sweating as I backed away from the door. I pulled my phone out of my bag and touched the screen to wake it up. I kept backing away from the door while I dialed 911.

"Nine-one-one, what's your emergency?"

"My friend and I are inside her house at"—I gave her the address—"and the power's been cut. My house was broken into earlier today—Detective Guillotte is in charge. Please, can you let him know there's someone out on the gallery? I think it's the same man who broke into my house and attacked a neighbor. Please get a car here as soon as possible." My voice sounded remarkably calm. "Please hurry," I pleaded.

"A squad car is on its way," she replied. "Please stay on—" I disconnected the call. I knew she was going to ask me to stay on the line; sure enough, my phone started ringing immediately. I sent the call to voice mail and tapped the screen to bring up my apps. I touched the flashlight app and turned it on, pointing it in the general direction of the kitchen, where Lorna was still opening drawers, but more quietly.

"Use your phone," I whispered, and turned my phone back to the side door. Someone was rattling the knob.

She nodded and reached for her purse on the counter.

There was a loud crash. The side door flew open and slammed against the wall, glass shattering and scattering across the floor. Lorna let out a quiet scream and ducked down behind the kitchen island. I turned and pointed the flashlight at the figure now standing in the doorway.

He blinked as the light blinded him momentarily.

It was Bamm-Bamm.

The resemblance to Tony was uncanny.

And he was holding a gun.

I turned off the flashlight and ducked down, trying to remember how Lorna's furniture was spaced out in the enormous open space. I got on my hands and knees and started crawling toward the front of the house. Maybe if I could get to the front door—

"There's no point in hiding," he called out softly. "I know you're both in here, so why not stop wasting time and come out? You're not going to get away."

I crawled a few more steps to put a wingback chair between him and me. "I've called the cops. They're on their way," I called out, starting to crawl again. Since Lorna was in the kitchen, she could get out the back door. He couldn't shoot us both at the same time. If I could get to the front door before he caught either of us . . .

"I'm not kidding," he yelled, and fired the gun. I winced, and glass shattered on the other side of the house. Every instinct in my body told me to stand up and put my hands in the air, but even as I started to move, I knew it was a bad idea. I stayed put.

"Come on out, Valerie," he called again in a loud whisper. "If you come out, I might even let your friend live."

"Do you really think we're that stupid?" Lorna shouted. I couldn't swear to it, but it sounded like she'd moved out of the kitchen. Maybe she had the same idea I did, about getting to the front door?

My heart sank as I realized the front door wasn't an option, after all. The minute we opened the door we'd be targets. The streetlight was right in front of her house. We'd be outlined in the doorframe like one of those targets they use for practice at firing ranges.

We'd be sitting ducks no matter how fast we went out the door.

But we had to keep moving. We'd be easier to find if we stayed in one place.

If only we had more light! Even with the side door open, the glow from my kitchen windows was too faint. My eyes had adjusted somewhat to the dark, but I couldn't see everything.

And Lorna's cats had toys everywhere.

"Why'd you kill her?" I shouted, waiting to move until I saw him turn in the direction my voice had come from. I scooted across the floor to the next wingback chair. I was maybe twenty yards from the front door? *Just keep him talking while you keep moving.*

"She was my mother!" I could hear the anguish of a child in his voice. "She promised she was going to make everything up to me!"

Out of the corner of my eye, I saw movement to my left, on the opposite side of the big room. It had to be Lorna, and yes, she was also making a break for the front door.

"Tony was your father, wasn't he?" I called out before moving to the next table. I was still trying to imagine the layout of the big room. There was another couch around here somewhere, I was sure of it, and that might give me enough cover to crawl for the front door.

He laughed nastily. "Oh, finally she gets a clue. Brava, Valerie. You're a lot smarter than Collette ever gave you credit for! Yes, she got pregnant all those years ago. And when he left her for *you*, she went away to have the baby and gave it up. That was Liam's condition for taking her back, you know."

Keep him talking keep him talking kept running through my brain as I moved through the dark.

"Why didn't she tell Tony?" I shouted, then moved as he turned toward the sound of where my voice had come from.

"She did tell Tony," he sneered. "He didn't believe her, told her she was a liar and crazy and to stay away from him. *Arthur*

270

did that. He hated her, but he promised her if she went away and stayed away from Tony, he would leave everything to her. And me. But he was a liar!"

"Why did you break into her house?" Lorna asked. She sounded much closer to the front door than me. "Why did you hurt Michael?"

"You two really aren't that smart." He laughed again. "We both were looking for Valerie's will. Good old Mom stopped by a couple of times to try to find it."

"It doesn't matter what I do with my will," I shouted, and moved again. "You and Collette never bothered to check out inheritance law, did you?"

He didn't answer at first, then screamed, "Uncle Arthur screwed us over, but Collette was smart enough to figure out a few things. You didn't read dear old Uncle Arthur's will, did you, Valerie?"

"He left everything to the heirs of Tony Cooper," Lorna shouted. "If you're his son, you're entitled to a piece of the estate. *Arthur was just cutting out Collette. She was playing you!*"

He was entitled to a share of the trust . . . but not Rare Things.

Rare Things had been left to me independently of the trust and the rest of the estate. It was mine, but if I died intestate . . .

If I died without signing my will . . .

Everything would go into a living trust, and he could make a claim on Rare Things too.

Or could he? Stupid inheritance law!

Violence is an exception to forced heirship. If he kills me, he'll get nothing.

Could I convince him?

Keep him talking.

"How did you get the alarm code?" I'd reached the couch. I glanced back at the side door. It was still open and I could make out some of the furniture around it in the glow from the lights in my kitchen.

I didn't see Bamm-Bamm.

I peeked my head up from behind the couch and peered through the gloom. I didn't see either him or Lorna, but then there was a loud crash from my right and the sounds of a struggle. Lorna started swearing again, and between the curse words, she was shouting, "Let go of me!"

I stood up, turned on the flashlight app of my phone, and pointed it in the general direction of the noise I was hearing.

They were both facing the light. He was standing behind Lorna, with one arm around her throat and the gun nozzle against her temple. He was smirking at me. Water drops glistened in Bamm-Bamm's bluish-black curls. I could also see Collette in his face—that was her smirk if I'd ever seen it—and, despite the circumstances, I couldn't help but feel sorry for him.

The accident of his birth wasn't his fault.

"I'll let her go if you leave with me," he said, the smirk still in place.

"I can see your father in you," I said softly, moving around the end of the couch, keeping the light trained on them. Lorna was standing still and doing something with her eyes—no doubt trying to signal me, but I had no idea what she meant.

"*They both abandoned me!*" he shouted, and Lorna winced. "No one ever told me the truth! When that awful woman who raised me gave me my birth certificate and everything was there—my parents' names, right there in black and white, and the official state seal of Louisiana. Collette Monaghan, Anthony Cooper. Two years ago."

"Did you come to New Orleans to confront her?" The young man Jill thought she was having an affair with was her son.

He gave a nasty laugh. "Yes, I made an appointment with her at New Orleans Lifestyles, told her I'd come into some money and was looking for a house. The first house she showed me, I pulled out that little birth certificate and demanded some answers." He tilted his head to one side. "And some money."

She'd needed money. That was why she embezzled from her business.

"You were blackmailing your own mother?" Lorna said, still moving her eyes rapidly. "No wonder she gave you up, you nasty little thing."

"Shut up!" He tightened his hold around her neck and her eyes bulged a bit. "Are you coming over here, or do I have to kill her?"

"I'm coming, I'm coming!" I kept my flashlight beam focused on them as I picked my way around the furniture.

"He's going to have to kill us both anyway," Lorna said, "so stop! Don't make it easy on the little . . ." She swore again.

He clubbed her with the handle of the revolver, and she went down to the floor with a crash. He pointed the gun at me and gestured with his other hand for me to come closer.

I was maybe five yards away from him when I bumped into one of Lorna's little end tables. A gaudy, hideous ceramic ashtray in the shape of a mermaid that she'd gotten at Weeki Wachee in Florida rested on the top. I grabbed it with my free hand and shone the light directly into his eyes. He flinched, and I threw the ashtray at him as hard as I could while diving over the back of the couch. The gun went off again and there was another crash as the ashtray broke. I bounced off the couch and hit the floor hard, knocking out my breath for a moment.

"Where are you?" he called out in a singsong voice. "Come out, come out, wherever you are!"

I heard Lorna moan and relief rushed through me—she was alive—and now I just had to make it to the front door—

I cried out as my head was yanked back by the hair.

"Not quite fast enough, Valerie," he said, pulling me up to my feet by the hair. I felt the cold metal of the gun pressed against the side of my head.

"Lorna's right, you're never going to get away with this," I said, my heart pounding so loud I barely could hear the words I was saying. "Your best hope is to give yourself up." I stopped myself from calling him Bamm-Bamm. "What is your name, anyway?"

"Hunter." He pushed the gun harder against my head. "Kind of appropriate, don't you think?" He laughed. "You really thought I was named King Creole, didn't you?"

Over the pounding of my heart, I could hear sirens approaching. "The police are coming, Hunter. Don't you think you'd be better off running? You're not going to get the inheritance now. It's the law—one of the exceptions to forced heirship is criminal activity, Hunter. Killing Collette . . . killing *me* . . . won't get you anything."

"I know." His voice choked off in a sob. "She really screwed me over, dear old Mommy did. This was all her fault."

"Tell me," I said, stalling for time and for the police to arrive.

"She got me money at first," he said, "and set me up in a real nice apartment. She kept telling me that we had this inheritance coming, that my dad's great-uncle had always promised to take care of us if . . . if we didn't cause any trouble for my dad."

So Arthur had known. Arthur had bribed Collette to leave us alone.

Of course she had gone to Tony's wealthy uncle when she found out she was pregnant. Arthur, wanting her out of Tony's life, had taken care of her and her unborn child. He was friends with Randall—already knew what a nightmare Collette was, had bailed him out when she'd sucked him dry before—and then changed his will before he died to ensure Collette wouldn't benefit but the child would still have a claim.

Arthur didn't know he was setting me up to be murdered.

The twins wouldn't have cared about Rare Things or the property and easily could have been talked into selling it all back to Randall.

Or to Collette.

Collette *had* wanted to kill me.

My mouth was dry and my palms were sweaty. The sirens were getting louder, and I heard Lorna moan from somewhere below.

"Why did you kill her?" I asked. *Keep him talking just keep him talking until the police get here.*

"She changed her mind." He pressed the gun tighter against my skull. I was going to have a bruise there, if he didn't shoot me. "It was all so simple, you know. It was her plan. She got into your house and looked for the will—"

"How did she know my alarm code?"

275

He laughed nastily. "You can think your stupid British friend for that. When Collette came by here to drop off the ball invitations, that was really cover for scoping out your place. And your friend has your alarm code written on her whiteboard next to your name." He recited the code out loud, and I swore at Lorna under my breath.

But in fairness to her, why would she ever have thought someone in her house would see it and use it for nefarious purposes?

I felt pressure on my left ankle. I glanced down—not easy, when you can't move your head—and saw that Lorna was moving quietly. I was blocking her face from his view, and she was gesturing slightly with her head.

She was planning something.

The sirens were so loud now they had to be almost here.

The living room filled with flashing red lights as brakes shrieked out in front of Lorna's house. I heard car doors slamming and voices out in front of the house.

I realized, my heart sinking, that it was too late for him to try to get away.

And we were now hostages.

"Headbutt," Lorna said clearly.

I knew immediately what she meant and slammed my head backward into his face as hard as I could without stopping to think. I felt his nose shatter under my skull, and he screamed, letting me go and dropping the gun at the same time. There was another loud crack and thud. Breathing hard and dizzy from the close call, my head hurting a bit from slamming into Hunter's face, I turned on the flashlight and spun around.

Hunter, his face completely bloodied, his eyes closed, was lying on the floor. Lorna was busy tying his wrists together with a bungee cord, and she blinked in the light.

"Well done on the headbutt," she said with a satisfied nod. The gun was resting in her lap.

I exhaled. "Let me go let the cops in."

Chapter
Twenty-One

Randall came by to see me three days later.

The poor man looked like he hadn't slept in days and had aged twenty years since the last time I'd seen him. He was unshaven, his eyes bloodshot, and smelled slightly of stale alcohol. As always, he was impeccably dressed in a three-piece suit and a tie, but little things gave away his mental distraction. A button had been missed, the knot in his tie wasn't pushed all the way up the collar, and his shoes were dirty. "May I come in?" he asked in a low, broken voice. His head was bowed, and my heart went out to him.

I didn't even think twice, reaching up to give him a tight hug. The poor man had lost his only daughter.

His body went rigid at first, but I kept holding on to him until he finally relaxed and put his arms back around me. He leaned his head against the top of mine. His body shook for a moment before he pulled himself together. He let go of me and smiled sadly at me. "I'm glad you're okay, Valerie. You must believe me—I had no idea what Collette was up to. She didn't confide in me." He shook his head, his eyes getting wet again. "I still can't wrap my mind around it."

I said, "Come on, let's go into the kitchen and have some coffee and talk about it. I've been worried about you."

"I don't deserve your worry," he said, following me into the kitchen. "Secrets are poison, and this one—I never dreamed it would ever turn out this way."

I made two cups and set them down on the kitchen table. "It's okay, Randall. I don't blame you for anything. How could you have known?"

He stared down into his mug. "I'm sorry, Valerie. I'm sorry about everything." He shook his head, unable to look me in the eye. "I should have told you the truth from the very beginning. I just—I just didn't know how, or what to say. It wasn't my secret to keep, you know, or at least that's how I justified it to myself. But you could have been killed . . ." He shivered again.

"Well, to be fair, Randall," I said, wondering if I should offer him some food—he looked like he hadn't been eating. "I'm not exactly sure how one would work *My daughter and your husband had a child together over twenty years ago* into a casual workday conversation."

He barked out a bitter laugh. "Collette certainly made a mess of her life," he said, sipping his coffee. "I spoiled her, I suppose. Her mother thought so, and Arthur"—he winced as he said the words—"told me that all the time." He rubbed his eyes. "That last time I saw him before he died, he was so angry with me, with Collette. He never liked her."

"Collette made her own choices, Randall," I replied, reaching over and resting my hand on top of his. "She was an adult, and at some point we really have to start taking responsibility for ourselves and stop blaming our parents for our bad decisions and the things that go wrong in our lives."

"How could I have been such a horrible father that she grew up to be such a broken adult?" His eyes filled with tears again, which he wiped away angrily. "And poor Hunter. I failed him the most of all. I should have put my foot down all those years ago. I never should have allowed any of that to happen."

Hunter.

Tony's son.

The Coopers had been stunned when I told them. I believed they didn't know, which made it a lot easier to believe that Tony hadn't known either.

It was hard for me to accept that Tony had turned his back on his own son.

Not the Tony I loved, married, remembered.

How would I have reacted had he told me?

I didn't know. Maybe I would have broken up with him. I was only nineteen or twenty when he'd swept me off my feet. And since he died . . . well, hadn't I kind of idealized him? Turned him into the perfect husband and father? He hadn't been perfect.

No one was.

I handed him a box of tissues. "He won't see me, you know," I said, while he wiped his eyes and blew his nose. I'd tried twice to get in to see Hunter. Both times he'd refused to see me. The boys had come down from Baton Rouge after that horrible night at Lorna's. They'd also tried to see their half brother. He'd also refused to see them. I'd asked Stacia to find him a good defense attorney—I'd find the money to pay for it.

I took a deep breath and asked the question I wasn't sure I wanted to know the answer to. "Tell me the truth, Randall. Why did Tony turn his back on her? Hunter said Collette told him she was pregnant, and he didn't believe her."

"He didn't." Randall shook his head. "You have to understand something, Val." He hesitated. "Tony didn't know Collette was married when they got involved."

"What?" That was one thing I hadn't understood about any of this. Tony had been adamant about cheating, always. How could that man have had an affair with a married woman? "He didn't know?"

Randall shook his head. "They'd been seeing each other for a few months before Arthur found out. He told Tony, and of course, Tony broke it off with her immediately."

"I—" I closed my eyes. "I don't think I understand the timeline, Randall. Were Liam and Collette separated?"

"Liam had run for mayor and lost," Randall said. "Their marriage was never the best, but Liam wanted to make it work. He didn't think he could ever get elected if he were divorced." Louisiana was a conservative state, but I wasn't sure that was true. "She met Tony at Rare Things. She'd come by to talk to me about leaving Liam, but . . ." He hesitated. "There was a prenup, you see. When Collette got pregnant in college, Liam's father insisted on it. If she ever left Liam, she'd get nothing."

"Why would she sign that?"

"She was pregnant when she married Liam, and she was desperate. She thought she was in love with him, thought one day she'd be First Lady of Louisiana." He laughed hollowly. "She couldn't have known about all the elections he would end up losing." He cleared his throat. "Funny how differently her life would have turned out if she'd used birth control. Anyway, she met Tony and fell for him. I didn't know what was going on—she kept it from me. Arthur was the one who told me. He was furious. He blamed her for my financial problems." He glanced at me. "Everyone thinks Collette . . . yes, I spoiled her, but I made some bad investments. That's why I went broke, needed Arthur to bail me and the store out. Sure, I gave her and Liam money for his campaigns, and helped them out now and then—Liam didn't want anyone to know that the Monaghan fortune was also long gone, you see. And Liam kept her on a tight leash. Arthur, after he found out about Tony and Collette, did everything he could to break them up and get Tony away from her. Including breaking the news she was married. That was a dealbreaker for Tony."

"I can't . . ." I stopped myself.

"Things had already started going bad between them, you see. She was willing to throw it all away, leave Liam, even give up custody of her other children, but Tony wouldn't do that. He couldn't trust her. She'd lied about being married, lied about having kids already, and she . . . didn't take it well. She started showing up at his fire station, started you know, calling him at all hours, showing up at his apartment unannounced . . . threatened to kill herself. When she told me she was pregnant and it was Tony's, I told Arthur." His voice shook. "Arthur warned Tony, told him that I had said she was going to pretend to be pregnant with his child to trap him. So when she did tell him, he didn't believe her. She'd already told him so many lies . . . so she decided to go back to Liam."

I felt sick to my stomach. "That must have been horrible for her."

"Liam agreed to take her back, but he . . . he refused to raise the child, wanted nothing to do with it. He was willing to get a divorce if it came to it, scandal be damned. That was when

Arthur stepped in. He paid for her to go away and have the baby in Redemption Parish; Arthur had found a childless couple who desperately wanted a baby, and he handled all the arrangements. He also . . . he also promised Collette he would leave his entire estate to her and the child in his will."

"So, basically, she sold her child." He looked stricken, and I apologized immediately. "I'm sorry, Randall, I shouldn't judge her. I don't know what she was going through."

"It broke her." He exhaled. "She was never the same after she gave up that baby and came back to New Orleans."

"Arthur again." I shook my head. "I'm thinking I should be glad I never met the man. Was this why he didn't reach out after Tony died?"

Randall shook his head. "Maybe. I don't know. But it would have been hard to explain—"

"It would have been easier to hear all this from Arthur."

Someday, I was going to get very angry about all this. But for now, all I could think about was how lives had been broken and ruined to keep a secret—one that never really needed to be kept. I wouldn't have been happy that Tony had a child with another woman, but would I have left him over it? There was too much hindsight involved and too much time had passed. Would nineteen-year-old me have accepted that reality, been able to live with it, been able to continue seeing Tony knowing he had a child with someone else? We'd been so happy together before he died, and the twins—I wouldn't trade the twins for anything.

But I couldn't say for a fact I would have gotten over it. Maybe I would have broken up with him, sent him back to Collette, told him to do the right thing by his child.

I'd only been nineteen. I doubt I would have been as mature about it as I wanted to believe.

"Hunter said—" I winced, remembering the circumstances. I'd had some trouble sleeping that first night after it all happened, so Lorna had slipped me a few of her sleeping pills and they'd knocked me out the next few nights. I'd slept without dreams and was worried I'd have nightmares if I didn't take a sleeping pill. It was a trauma, but I'd dealt with trauma before. Losing Tony had been a trauma. Hurricane Katrina had been a trauma. You don't give up on life just because you've experienced trauma.

You learn how to live with it.

There wasn't another option.

"The night it all happened, Hunter said he'd found his birth certificate, and that was when he went looking for Collette?"

"He was eighteen when he found out the truth," Randall said in a monotone.

I took his mug and brewed another cup for him. "I gather he wasn't thrilled."

He exhaled as I placed the fresh cup down for him. "I don't know if Hunter . . ." He rubbed his eyes. "He wasn't happy his father was dead. He wasn't happy to know he'd been the product of an affair and abandoned because his parents—his *mother*— couldn't deal with the fallout of his existence in her perfect world. And of course, Collette—you knew her. Being a mother was everything to her; she loved her kids and lived for them, and this? Abandoning a child because he was inconvenient? It damaged her, changed her. She was always unhappy, and giving up that child . . ."

"Of course you loved her and wanted her to be happy."

"But the unhappiness got so much worse after she gave away Hunter. The guilt ate at her, changed her in ways I didn't see or could understand. She *hated* you." He reached over and took one of my hands. "You can imagine my shock the day you showed up at Rare Things, wanting to help out and be a part of the business. I'd been hearing for years about what a monster you were, how Tony didn't deserve you, how you'd ruined her life, and then when Arthur changed his will . . ."

"When did you find out about that?"

Randall looked down at his hands. "I never told Collette that Arthur had changed his will." He hesitated. "She found out because she tried to get a bank loan, using the inheritance as collateral. Lucas Abbott had to tell the bank she wasn't . . . that I wasn't . . . and the date of the will . . ." He hesitated. "Hunter wanted money. He always wanted money, and of course she didn't have any. I didn't. So she went to Arthur. He owed her, she figured, and the new will was drawn up around the same time he gave her money for Hunter. They'd argued—she told me about it later once she knew about the will—and he told her she wasn't getting another cent from him."

"She didn't think he meant the will," I replied, thinking. "But Arthur set up the trust for *the heirs of Anthony Cooper*," I said slowly. "Which meant if Hunter could prove he was Tony's son, he'd be entitled to a share of that trust. He cut Collette out, but he kept his promise about her child. But I still don't understand why they wanted to kill *me*."

"I didn't know they intended to kill you. You have to believe me, Valerie." Randall's voice shook with emotion. "If I'd known that, I would have gone to the police, I would have done *something*. I don't know what, but something. I wouldn't have let that happen."

I patted his hand. "I believe you, Randall."

"One more thing," he said as he stood up awkwardly. "Another reason Collette was so desperate was that Liam had asked for a divorce at long last. She'd been stalling, playing for time until Arthur's will was probated . . . and then . . ."

"Arthur screwed her over yet again." I shook my own head. Poor Collette. Her whole world had come crashing down around her.

"I've taken up enough of your time. I need to finalize the arrangements for her service. It's going to just be for family—" He cut me off when I started to say something. "Please don't be offended. Just a small, intimate quiet service."

I walked him to the front door. He paused with his hand on the doorknob. "As for Rare Things . . ."

I took a deep breath. "Randall, I've enjoyed working there since I started. I'd like to go on working there, learning the business and getting a handle on it all. I know you've always intended to buy the business back from Arthur, and if that's what you still want, we can work out something. But I don't think I want to be bought out completely." I gave him a tentative smile. "I can see why you wouldn't want me to be around— I'd be a constant reminder—but I hope you'll take some time and think about it."

He looked at me for a few moments before replying, "I'm going to go away for a while. I need some time. But Dee will be opening the shop tomorrow."

"I'll be there at ten."

I closed the door behind him and walked back to the television room. I sat down with my coffee and relaxed in my easy chair.

Maybe it *would* be too weird to go on working at Rare Things. Maybe it would be awkward. But I liked Randall and I liked Dee. I liked feeling useful, and I liked learning on the job. I would never have Randall or Dee's expertise, of course, but I could certainly learn enough to cover for them when they took time off. It had been years since my teenage days working retail, but being polite and helpful to people wanting to spend money was something I did have some experience with. Maybe Rare Things wouldn't work out for me, maybe it would, but it was worth giving it a try. I had to do something with the rest of my life.

I couldn't help but feel sorry for Collette. How must it have felt when Tony didn't believe her? Arthur must have really done a number on him. And then to change his will, cut Collette out entirely?

God, how she must have hated me.

Tony had been eager for kids. He'd worshiped the twins from the moment I told him I was pregnant. He'd wanted five or six total but hadn't argued when I told him I didn't want more than the two. (He did continue hinting, though, right up until he died.) The twins were more than enough for me to handle, and much as I loved them, I was also kind of glad they were almost completely out of my hair.

I was still young enough to make a new life for myself.

Maybe someday I'd be willing to sell the house. But not now. I loved my neighborhood. I'd never find neighbors like Lorna,

John, Michael, and Mrs. Domanico anywhere else. My lawyer Stacia lived down the block. I knew almost everyone on both sides of the street, and we all watched out for one another. I might not get that again if I sold the house and moved.

"Never say never, though," I said out loud.

I was doing the dishes and working on cleaning fingerprint dust powder out of places the cleaning service I'd hired had missed when my doorbell rang again. As I walked through the living room to the front door, I could see the shadow of a man standing on my front gallery. I saw myself in the mirror by the front door and recoiled inwardly. No makeup, my hair pulled back in a greasy-looking ponytail, a shapeless baggy paint-spattered sweatshirt, and a pair of yoga pants with the inner seam on the left thigh starting to open.

"Detective Guillotte!" I said, opening the front door with a smile. "You have an uncanny knack of turning up when I look terrible." I stepped aside and gestured for him to come in.

He looked rumpled, as always, but smiled at me warmly. "I just wanted to come by and let you know that Hunter Dennison has entered a plea agreement with the district attorney. He's pleading guilty to second-degree manslaughter and looking at serving about ten years, depending. His story is he didn't intend to kill Collette, but when she refused to continue helping him get his share of Arthur's inheritance, he lost his temper, grabbed the dagger from her scabbard, and stabbed her in the heat of the moment, and he's sorry."

"So, no trial?" I swallowed. That was a relief. I didn't want all this dirty laundry aired in public. It was going to be bad enough as it was.

"No trial."

"Come into the kitchen and let me get you some coffee." I was already heavily overcaffeinated. He followed me into the kitchen and sat on one of the island stools. I made him a cup of dark roast, remembered that he liked cream and sweetener, and placed the mug in front of him.

"How are you doing, Ms. Cooper?" he asked. "You've been through quite a bit these past few weeks."

"All things considered, things could be a lot worse." I sat down on a stool facing him across the island. "I'm sure one morning I'll wake up and have a nervous breakdown, but for now I'm doing okay." I thought for a moment. "The twins are handling it all well, but they're teenagers and things still just roll off their backs." I shook my head. "Knowing their dad had another son didn't diminish Tony in their eyes—Tay actually said, 'So Dad was a stud?'" I rolled my eyes. "And of course, they've very curious about Hunter, but he won't see any of us." I exhaled. "I'll write to him in prison, and maybe someday, I don't know, we can come to some sort of understanding?"

"You're very forgiving."

"I feel *sorry* for him. I know that sounds crazy, but I do." I frowned. "I've reached out to his adoptive parents, too, but they haven't responded to me either."

"He tried to kill you, Mrs.—Valerie."

I took a deep breath. "Has he said why?" This was something I was having trouble wrapping my mind around. Lucas Abbott had called just the afternoon before to let me know he was notifying the probate court about Hunter's criminal activity. *The heirs of Anthony Cooper.* Louisiana law disallowed anyone from profiting from their crimes. He'd disqualified himself from Tony's estate—the living trust for the twins—by trying to kill me. As I'd been named a trustee of Arthur's estate, Lucas was moving to have the same rule applied there.

I wasn't sure how I felt about that, to be honest.

"I don't know." I didn't, really. "I just feel bad that . . ." I sighed. "If Collette would have just come to me and told me about Hunter. If Randall would have said something. If Arthur would have reached out after Tony died . . . all of this was preventable. Collette didn't have to die. I would have been happy to share everything with Hunter—it would have been a shock, sure, but he was Tony's child. And Collette—"

"—couldn't see past her hatred of you to see you as an actual human being who might be reasonable?"

"Well, yes." I smiled back at him. "I guess Collette couldn't—well, Collette couldn't imagine anyone reacting to the news differently than she would have in my place, and that was her real failure, wasn't it? She was so determined to hate me and blame me for everything that had gone wrong in her life, she couldn't see anything else." I shivered. "I do feel sorry for her, the poor thing. All those years, married to Liam, miserable. I guess she thought she couldn't leave him without money? I don't know, will probably never know. I've tried imagining how her mind must have worked, how she viewed things, but it's a dark place and I don't like going there, frankly. But all those years, fantasizing about a life she might have had with Tony had he never met me . . . it must have festered and unhinged her a little." I smiled. "And having had the good luck to have been married to him myself, I *can* imagine how that would make her bitter."

"You might not feel so sorry for Collette after I tell you this." He flipped through his notepad. "Arthur died in a fall down the stairs. It was ruled an accident at the time."

"And it wasn't?"

He shook his head. "According to Hunter, Collette went to see him again to get money. Hunter saw her later that same night. Apparently, she and Arthur had argued, and he grabbed her and she pulled away from him . . . he lost his balance and went head-first down the stairs. He was dead when she got to him."

"And she just left him there?"

He nodded. "It was right around this time that she stole from her business."

I blew out some air. "I guess we'll never know why Arthur did things the way he did, or why he stayed away from us, or why he wouldn't let Tony let us know about him. Gah!" I slammed my fist down on the island hard enough to hurt. "Ouch." I said, shaking my hand. "All of this could have been prevented if people hadn't been so determined to keep secrets." I laughed. "I'm not sure when my life became a storyline on *The Young and the Restless*, but they need to write me out of the show." I snapped my fingers. "Oh! Collette's dying words. Was she really trying to tell me something, or was that just nothing?"

"She never called him Hunter, you know." He snapped his notepad closed. "She'd wanted to name him, ironically, *Archer*. She met your husband at, of all things, a costume party, and he'd gone as Robin Hood. When she gave the baby up, she told the adoptive family she'd named him Archer; they changed it to Hunter. So—"

"She was trying to tell me *Archer* had killed her." I shivered.

"Collette also had told Hunter you hadn't signed your will," he said as Scooter started running against his legs. He reached down and idly scratched Scooter's head.

"So that was what she was doing when she stopped by," I replied, remembering walking into the kitchen and finding her there getting a drink of water.

"When he broke in and attacked your neighbor, he was coming for the will."

"I'd noticed it was gone," I replied. I had since signed another copy in front of a notary, with Lorna and Michael as witnesses. I shivered. *The heirs of Anthony Cooper.* Arthur had really screwed me over with that sentence. Stacia had explained that since Arthur's will hadn't finished going through probate, my death without a will would have created another forced heirship, and the probate court would have probably added everything from Arthur's estate into the living trust.

Only I would no longer be living. Hunter and the twins would have shared everything.

I was sorry Arthur was dead. I had a lot of questions for him.

"Thank you for everything, Detective."

He stood up. "Well, I think that's everything I wanted to tell you."

"I think I'll miss you, Detective Guillotte," I said as I walked him to the front door.

He paused on the threshold. "Now that the case is over . . ." He hesitated.

"Yes?"

"I was wondering if maybe . . . maybe sometime you'd like to have a drink with me? Coffee? Dinner?"

I felt my skin turning red. I knew I was smiling and couldn't stop. "Are you asking me out on a *date*, Detective?"

"Ed," he replied, giving me a big smile in return. "Call me Ed. And are you saying yes?"

"Yes." I smiled. "Call me?"

"I will do that."

I watched him walk down the front steps and out the gate. He saluted me with a smile as he got into his car.

I watched him drive away. Lorna wasn't going to believe this.

Michael was futzing with the cone in the pothole again, wrapping orange and black beads tightly around the neck. He waved at me, and I waved back.

Halloween was still two days away, and I hadn't decorated the house at all. I didn't have candy for trick-or-treaters. The boys planned on coming down for the weekend—who doesn't want to spend Halloween weekend in New Orleans?—and now, as I looked up and down the block at all the decorations, the pumpkins and jack-o'-lanterns, the cobwebbing, the witches and ghosts and demons and devils and ghosts adorning houses and porches and balconies and front yards, the house felt practically naked.

The widow Cooper.

It had been a terrible thing to say to me, but Collette had been right. It was time to move on with my life.

I closed the front door and walked back to my desk to make a to-do list.

Acknowledgments

Like every author, I could be here for the rest of my life thanking people for their friendship, support, and generosity. This is by no means an exhaustive list, but I'll give it the old college try.

Everyone at my day job, Crescent Care Health, makes going into the office every day a pleasant experience, and your dedication to your jobs and your clients is inspiring. First off, those who have left us for greener pastures since I started writing this book: Jean Redmann, department head and a close friend for years; Joey Olsen and Allison Dejan, my last two supervisors; and coworkers like Chris Daunis, Ashton George III, Cullen Hunter, James Husband, and Beau Braddock—I will always miss you guys. My current coworkers are the best, and I'm proud to work with you: Narquis Barak, Blayke d'Ambrosio, Naomi Langlois, Jordan Probst, Leon Harrison, LaToya Galle, Fernando Cruz, Foster Noone, Jeremy Schroeder, Kyle Mills, Bryson Richard, Katie Connor, LaKarla Williams, Jasmin Davis, Ellis Lee, Corinna Goldblatt, Conchita Iglesias-McElewee, and Celeste Onujiogu. I love you all.

Acknowledgments

Terri Bischoff has been a dear friend for any number of years and was an amazing editor to work with. Everyone at Crooked Lane has been a pleasure to work with—thank you all for not minding my amateurish questions and inability to get anything done on time. I really appreciate you all. This whole experience has been wonderful, and I'll always be grateful to the Crooked Lane team for making this happen.

And of course, so many friends. I owe Paul a debt of gratitude for always believing in my dreamsnd pushing me to do better. Thanks also to Pat Brady, Susan Larson, Michael Ledet, Jesse and Laura Ledet, Tracy Cunningham, Michael Thomas Ford, Wendy Corsi Staub, Elizabeth Little, Nadine Nettman, Susanna Calkins, Jess Lourey, Erica Ruth Neubauer, Chris and Katrina Niidas Holm, Bill Loefhelm and AC Lambeth, Julia Dahl, Kellye Garrett, Alex Segura, Laurie R. King, Toni L. P. Kelner, Dana Cameron, Leslie Budewitz, Sara J. Henry, Catriona McPherson, Margaret Fenton, Tammy Lynn, Beth Terrell, Carolyn Haines, Dean James, Dawn Lobaugh, Karen Bengtsen, Valerie Fehr Ruelas, Mike Smid, Twist Phelan, Jessie Chandler, Vince Liaguno, Rena Mason, Wanda Morris, John Copenhaver, Marco Carocari, Darren Brewer, Carsen Taite, Rachel Spangler, Nell Stark, Trinity Tam, Lynda Sandoval, Anne Laughlin, Lisa Girolami, Lisa Lutz, Dan Stashower, Larry Light, Alafair Burke, Jeff Abbott, Meg Gardiner, Donna Andrews . . . and anyone I've forgotten. Well, I'm old. Sorry.

And of course, the FLs. Perhaps I will see you all soon at Bluestone Manor? I miss you all so much!